Following Destiny

Endorsements

Derinda Babcock did it again! *Following Destiny* is an emotionally charged finale to the Destiny Trilogy. The historical research in the three books is impeccable and skillfully woven into Lexie Logan's stories. Lexie's dip into genealogy and family history is poignant and motivating to find one's own decades old pictures and letters. Her soul-pressing sense of urgency to discover her ancestry before something happened to her Gran accelerates Lexie's search for God's destiny for her life. A glimpse into life and language on the foreign mission field in Guatemala is a masterful touch to show God's leadership and care. Derinda made me care so much about Lexie Logan in Dodging Destiny I feared the slip-time adventure ended when Lexie returned from 1857 to the twenty-first century. In *In Search of Destiny*, Lexie's influence reached further and had more impact on the families she met in 1857 Kansas than she dreamed possible. It's a reminder that our actions and conversations can have a powerful influence where we least expect it. While these books can stand-alone, reading them in sequence is rewarding.

—**Linda Farmer Harris**, Author of *Treasure Among the Ruins (Voices in the Desert Book 1)* and "The Lywater Bride" from The California Gold Rush Romance Collection: *9 Stories of Finding Treasures Worth More Than Gold.*

Following Destiny

Derinda Babcock

Elk Lake
PUBLISHING, INC.
Plymouth, Massachusetts

Cover Design: Derinda Babcock
Interior Design: Cheryl L. Childers
Editor: Deb Haggerty
Published in Association with Hartline Literary Agency

PUBLISHED BY: Elk Lake Publishing, Inc., 35 Dogwood Dr., Plymouth, MA 02360

Library Cataloging Data
Names: Babcock, Derinda (Derinda Babcock)
Following Destiny/ Derinda Babcock
298 p. 23cm × 15cm (9in × 6 in.)
Description: Elk Lake Publishing, Inc. digital eBook edition | Elk Lake Publishing, Inc. POD paperback edition | Elk Lake Publishing, Inc. 2016.
Identifiers: ISBN-13: 978-1-946638-08-3 (e-bk) | 978-1-946638-09-0 (POD) | 978-1-946638-32-8 (Trade)
Key Words: Time Travel, Missionary, Ancestry, God's benevolence, Christian, Romance, Relationships
LCCN 2017948784 Fiction

DEDICATED TO ...

FRANCES AND NATHAN ROSS, AND TO OTHERS LIKE THEM, WHO MAY HAVE GIVEN UP COMFORT, SECURITY, AND YEARS OF THEIR LIFE TO FOLLOW THE LORD'S CALL TO THE MISSION FIELD.

How beautiful are the feet of them that preach the gospel of peace, and bring glad tiding of good things!
Romans 10:15b, KJV

ACKNOWLEDGMENTS

THANK YOU...

Deb Haggerty for polishing and fine-tuning the manuscript,

Paul Dutcher for sharing your knowledge about jet fuel, flying times, and FBOs,

Dale West for insights into the workings of law enforcement,

Beta-readers for making time in your busy schedules to read Lexie's story and offer comments,

Seydie Coronado and Xinia Quesada Arias for your help with the culture and customs in Costa Rica, and

Marco Nij for helping me to understand what problems Lexie might face in Guatemala, and for bringing me newspapers from the country. *¡Gracias por todo!*

PART ONE

ONE

Lexie Logan stared at her reflection in the mirror of the luxurious hotel bedroom. Her appearance hadn't changed. The red-gold highlights in her light brown hair captured and held the sunlight from the window. The dark brown eyes, straight white teeth, athletic build, form-fitting, blue jeans, and purple tee were the same she'd seen many times before.

Only moments before, she'd been staring at the reflection of Mary Bell Johnson. Mary wore the same maroon-colored dress she'd seen her mother, Edna, pull from the trunk when Lexie'd stayed with the Bells for three months—in 1857, almost two hundred years in the past. Mary's long black hair had been pinned at the sides, but the rest flowed down her back in a different style. Maturity now graced her friend's face.

When Lexie had placed her right palm on the mirror, Mary had raised her left to touch the same spot, fingers spread. They smiled at each other, and Lexie asked about her family and the Johnsons, but couldn't seem to make herself understood. Finally, she'd lifted her eyebrows in question and mimed holding out a necklace.

Mary nodded and pulled the chain with the diamond heart from its resting place under the bodice of her dress. Lexie smiled to see the gift she'd given to Mary on her seventeenth birthday, three months before the girl's wedding to Jesse Johnson.

Lexie touched the mirror again, wishing she could call Mary forward in time to chat with her about those she'd left in the nineteenth century.

"Lord, how much historical time has passed from the moment you snatched me off the piano bench in 1857 and returned me to the twenty-first century? Mary looks much older. Surely her appearance reflects more than a two weeks' separation." She leaned her forehead against the cool glass. "I ask your blessings on them."

"Lexie, hon, are you ready?"

She jumped at the knock and looked toward the door then back at the mirror. She rubbed the red scar which traveled from the outside of her left elbow to the inside of her forearm as she opened the door to her fiancé, Lance Garrett.

Seeing his face after months when she'd given up hope of ever being able to do so again always brought moisture to her eyes. She flung herself into his arms and hugged him like she'd never let him go. His strong arms encircled her.

"Are you all right?"

She nodded but didn't lift her cheek from the place where his neck joined his shoulder.

"Lexie, look at me."

She lifted her face and looked in his concerned brown eyes.

"Something hasn't been right since you came back from Manhattan a couple of weeks ago. Are you sure nothing happened to you while you waited for the advisor at K-State?"

She hesitated. "Something did happen to me, Lance, but I can't tell you yet."

"Why can't you?"

Tears choked her voice, "Because if I did, you'd think I was crazy, and you'd probably ask for your ring back."

"Never. I love you. Until death do us part—remember, Lexie?" He lifted her left hand and kissed the finger where his gold and diamond engagement ring again rested.

He didn't let her hand go, but turned her arm to trace the scar with his finger. "Does what you can't tell me relate to this and to the fact that when you decided to ask for my ring back, you wanted to meet at the Kansas Historical Museum?"

"Yes."

He waited, but she said nothing.

"Hmm. I'll wait as long as I need to, sweetheart, but I wish you'd trust me."

"I do, Lance. I'm not sure I trust me. I just need a little more time."

He stroked her hair. "Well, you won't have much time during the next couple of days. Too many people at your family reunion want to talk. They've never had one of theirs decide to join her life to a missionary who wants to serve God by working with orphans in Guatemala. You're unique, you know?"

She twined her arms around his neck and drew his lips to hers for a quick kiss, then pulled away. "I'm ready." Linking hands, they walked together toward the luncheon tables set up on the manicured lawn near the pool.

"Over here, Lexie. Lance."

Her dad stood and waved them toward a long, linen-covered table. Lance seated her next to her mom, then greeted both of his soon-to-be-in-laws before he sat next to Lexie. "David. Olivia."

Olivia tipped her perfectly coiffed head toward Lance, but Lexie noted her forced smile. Her mom and dad liked Lance a lot and had even agreed to their marriage, but they'd agreed before they found out God was leading him to the mission field. Several times over the past two weeks, they'd told her they struggled with the idea of her giving up her dreams of a master's program and the chance to play violin with the Topeka Symphony Orchestra to follow him to Guatemala as a missionary's wife. Lexie admitted to herself she'd had a hard time too.

She looked up at the sky and whispered, "But I surrendered those dreams to you, Lord. I learned my lessons. Please don't send me through time again. I'll trust you have better dreams for me, even though I don't know what they are."

"Mom, where's Steven?" She looked around the crowd for her brother.

"He and the boy cousins his age went to shoot some hoops, but they should be here soon."

The waiters rolled out silver-covered carts and began to serve the people who sat at the tables when her brother arrived.

"Umm. I'm starving. I could eat a mule."

"You mean a horse," David teased.

An image of the Bell's mules standing hitched and ready to pull the large Conestoga wagon to the homestead on the Kansas prairie flashed through Lexie's mind, and she blinked. "I think you'll much prefer the steak, lobster, or grilled chicken they're serving, and the fresh steamed asparagus or other fresh veggies, Stevie." Olivia smiled.

When the white-clad waiters and waitresses began to serve relatives at their table, Lance reached for Lexie's hand and then waited for David, Olivia, and Steven to clasp hands. They bowed and Lance asked God to bless the food.

"Avocados, Miss? They're perfectly ripened." The server waited for Lexie who, at the mention of avocados, had again flashed back to the time when she lived on near-starvation rations and longed for a loaded avocado sandwich with no hope of ever tasting such a treat again.

"Lexie?" Lance touched her hand and frowned.

She refocused and smiled at the waiter., "Yes, thank you."

Lexie wondered if, or when, these sudden flashbacks would stop. From the time she'd returned to the twenty-first century, she'd looked at her life with new eyes. She'd caught herself standing in front of their infrared convection oven and running her fingers over the buttons, or turning on the faucets and letting the warm water run over her hands as the bathtub filled. When she bought yogurt at her favorite shop, she'd sit and look at the texture and color before eating with slow bites. On two occasions, Mom had found her standing in front of the refrigerator, doors open, looking at the colorful, well-stocked shelves, and just last week, her mother had asked her why she was watching the clothes spin in the front-loading washing machine.

"What's wrong, babe?" Lance spoke low enough her parents couldn't overhear. "Do you realize you've been fading in and out of conversations lately?"

Lexie massaged the scar without thinking.

He stopped her hand and caressed the scar. "Where do you go when you're not here?"

She didn't answer.

"Everything is related, right? Everything goes back to what happened at K-State?"

She touched his cheek. "I promise I'll tell you soon, Lance. I don't know what you'll say or think, but I will tell you. Then you'll have to decide if you still want to marry me."

Distinct alarm widened his eyes, but he patted her hand. "I'll always want to marry you, Lexie, because you're my soulmate. Whatever the problem is, we can get through this together."

He hesitated and whispered near her ear, "Were you raped?"

Her eyes widened, and she shook her head. His sigh sounded relieved.

"No. God broke me and poured me out in a way I'll never forget. This scar is a daily reminder of the lessons he insisted I learn."

Lance stared at her, a thousand questions firing from his eyes.

She shook her head. "Not now, but soon, love."

They looked away from each other when Olivia's maternal aunt Jennifer leaned forward and spoke around Steven.

"David, so glad you made the reunion," she said. Her smile took in all of them. Steven moved his chair back so his spritely, gray-haired aunt had no trouble seeing their faces. She patted his shoulder.

"Thanks, Jenny. I didn't think I'd have the opportunity to come because our firm won the bid for the new office complex just outside of Topeka. Construction will start soon, and I won't be able to go anywhere then."

"Olivia said the project is something special. Why? I mean, an office complex is just another office complex, right?"

David shook his head. "The building will be the first of its kind in this area to be fueled primarily by wind and solar energy, and the design also incorporates some straw-bale construction."

"Someone told me you'd developed a passion for renewable energy and green technology. The topic sure is big these days."

He nodded and spoke more about the project.

"Where's Grandma Audrey, Aunt Jen?" Lexie asked looking around when her father paused.

"My sister's getting everyone lined up for pictures," Jennifer answered. She caught Steven's and David's eye rolls. "You're not to disappear, the either of you. Getting everyone together to preserve family memories is important to her."

"Here she comes." Jennifer grinned at Steven. "I have to admire my sister—she sure can marshal the troops. Our mother is just like her, at least she was in her younger days."

"How's great-grandmother Rebecca, Aunt Jen? Does she do well with the other old folks in the home?" Steven asked.

"She's in her right mind and sharp as a tack, but she has her good days and bad, just like any other eighty-five-year-old. She's had more down days since your great-aunt Ruth died last year." She looked at Steven and Lexie. "A visit from her great-grandchildren is sure to perk her up."

"You're right, Gram. I'll visit her when we return."

"Here you are." Audrey signaled to them. "The photographer is ready for us. We're getting pictures of the individual families, and then we'll take a group shot. The photographer said she'd have proofs ready for us tomorrow. We can purchase what we want. I'm going to buy them all and make them into a book. Imagine, we can do this online, and the book looks professional."

Lexie grabbed the leather bag-the same bag that had traveled with her to the past-and followed the others to the photo shoot.

The photographer finished with some of her dark-haired, blue-eyed cousins. Her attention sharpened. Did her eyes deceive her? One of the women and one of the younger boys were dead ringers for Mary and Matthew Bell, her family from the past. Even their expressions and body movements were similar. She grabbed her phone out of the bag and snapped their pictures with the phone camera. She couldn't help but stare.

"We're next," Steven said. Lexie handed her bag to Lance and stepped into place.

After the family shots, Audrey wanted one more of all the women cousins. Lexie stood in the group and smiled at Lance. He stared at them, his expression intrigued.

"Did you know several of you have a strong family resemblance?" he asked when she returned to him. "I never really paid much attention until I saw you, your mom, aunts, and some of your cousins together. Whoever your ancestor was sure left a mark on you all."

"Hmmm," Lexie responded, her attention elsewhere. She tried to see where the Bell look-a-likes had gone. She turned to him. "Do you want to go for a walk, Lance? I need to develop some photos, and I saw a place where we can do so about three blocks from here. There's a walking path we can take for most of the way."

"Sure."

"I'll let Mom know we'll be gone for a couple of hours, but that we'll be back in time for the festivities tonight."

She returned quickly, and he held out his hand. "No. Let's jog for a bit. I need some exercise."

His smile grew, and he fell into a comfortable stride beside her. They soon increased their pace to a run but slowed as they neared their destination.

Lexie uploaded selected photos from her phone to the store's computer and placed her order.

"Hey, hon. There's a sidewalk café next door. Do you want to get something to drink while we wait?"

"I'd love a cold glass of water with lemon slices if they have them." Lexie walked toward an empty table and waited. Lance returned with two huge glasses of ice water and a small bowl of lemon slices.

"Do you want me to make you my brand of lemonade?"

At his nod, Lexie squeezed the lemons and added stevia powder she now carried in her bag. She'd learned her lesson. The bag now contained her "survival gear" and went with her everywhere.

"Umm. Good." He relaxed into the cushions.

"I craved this when I was—" She felt the blood draining from her face when she realized what she was about to say.

Lance waited. "When you were ...?"

She swallowed. Why couldn't she open her mouth and let the words flow? Why did they always get stuck when she tried to admit the truth?

"When-when I was away for three months."

He sat up and leaned forward. "When did you go away for three months?"

"Lance, I—I—" Her heart pounded and blood rushed to her head. She massaged her left temple and tried to stop the tears. A few escaped, which made her more upset.

He frowned and scooted closer. "Tell me, Lexie. Just open your mouth and force the words out."

She looked in his eyes and took a deep breath. "On June 10, 2014, I went to sleep in the library of Kansas State University and woke up on June 10, 1857, in the back of a Conestoga wagon belonging to Jim and Edna Bell. They were headed to their homestead on the Kansas prairie. I stayed with them and their family through September, before God answered my prayers and brought me home. He returned me to June 10, 2014."

Lance's mouth dropped, and he stared at her. She waited for the disbelief to cross his face and the thought she was crazy to enter his eyes. When he didn't react, she spoke.

"So the only sane thoughts you can be thinking right now, love, are either I'm lying or I'm crazy."

"Lexie, I don't know what to say. I don't think either. Could your travel have been a dream?"

"No, because I left things in the past and brought things with me into the future. God made sure I remembered my lessons."

They sat in silence for several minutes until Lance reached over and caressed the scar. "Tell me about this. You didn't have the injury on June 9 when we broke up, but you had the scar on the tenth when you took my ring back. These types of wounds take time to heal, Lexie, and this isn't fresh."

She told him about saving Mattie during the buffalo stampede and then about Mikák'ehinga making a poultice for the long cut.

"Who?" Lance's concentration intensified. She knew he tried not to drown in her story.

"Mikák'ehinga was a Kansa brave. He and his sons, Allegawaho and Washunga, stopped by to trade and to play music with us."

Lance closed his eyes and pinched the bridge of his nose. When he opened them, Lexie waited for his response.

"You said God did this to teach you lessons. What did you have to learn, hon?"

She grimaced. "The afternoon we broke up, Stevie tried to relieve my grief by getting me to exercise. I'd already done so for hours before, but I didn't tell him that. While we were shooting hoops, he asked me what was so bad about going with you to Guatemala. I gave him four reasons I'll remember until I die."

"Why?"

"I'll remember them because I didn't put the pieces together as to why the Lord sent me to the nineteenth century until September of 1857. I was like Jonah. God commanded him to do something, and he ran the other way." She lowered her head. "After I'd given the reasons why I couldn't go with you to Guatemala, Stevie asked me what God wanted. I had to admit I hadn't asked."

"Why, Lexie. Why didn't you ask?" Lance reached for her hand, and she grasped his fingers.

"Because I was afraid he would tell me to do something I didn't want to do."

"Did he?"

"Yes, he told me to marry you and head to Guatemala."

Lance's eyes lit with love. "What's so bad about that?"

"I didn't resist the *marrying you* part, but the going to *Guatemala* part made me rebel."

"What were the four reasons you gave as to why you couldn't do this?"

"The first was I had my own dreams. I wanted to continue my degree program and play with the Topeka Symphony Orchestra. You know what his answer was to me on this one?"

Lance shook his head and listened with his whole body.

"He said: *Not thy will, Lexie, but Mine be done.*"

She continued at his nod, "Then I said, even though I have a real aptitude for all things musical, I didn't for languages. I barely passed my French class with a grade of C. I didn't know how well I'd be able to communicate even after language school, and I was afraid, Lance."

"I understand. I have some of the same fears, sweetheart. What lesson did you learn?"

"I was able to communicate with the Kansas through music, sign language and by being unafraid, though they were startling-looking people when I first saw them. They wore scarlet or blue breechcloths, leggings, and moccasins of deerskin. Beaded tin and porcelain trinkets hung from slashes in the outer cartilage of their ears, and you should have seen their tattoos, Lance. They covered large portions of their bodies, but what I noticed most was the hair had been plucked from their arms, chins, eyebrows, and scalps. Only a narrow strip of vermilion-colored hair covered the top and back portions of their heads."

She opened her bag and took out the necklace she'd brought back. "I traded a protein bar for this."

He held the necklace. Several moments passed as he seemed to process what she'd described. He handed it back to her.

"What was the third thing you told Steven?"

"I said Guatemala is a third-world country, and if I got sick, I'd probably die. After the Lord told me to give all my Tylenol to Fergus and the Clarks—I'll tell you about them later—I learned he could care for me, regardless of my circumstances."

"And the last?"

She reached for his other hand. "I said I didn't think I was a good enough Christian to be your wife."

"What? I don't want you ever to think such a thing. Ever, Lexie. How did the Lord respond to that one?"

She closed her eyes and quoted, "*He said: There is none righteous, no, not one. For all have sinned and come short of the glory of God, Lexie, but you are justified freely by His grace through the redemption that is in Christ Jesus. I have made you a new creation, old things have passed away, and all things have become new.*"

"Wow." Lance brushed moisture from his eyes and moved his stool close before caressing her face. "He gave a much better answer than I would've."

"The last thing the Lord said to me in September was: *One month for one day, Lexie. For each day my servant, Jonah, spent in the belly of the great sea creature I prepared to receive him, and for every day My Son endured rejection and the coldness of the grave for your sake, you have spent one month as a prisoner of time. My Son died to set the captives free and then rose to sit at My right hand of power. Behold, it is better to obey than to sacrifice, child. Will you obey My voice?*"

She kissed his palm. "I decided to obey, and here I am."

"Here you are." He hugged her. "Do you think God would have left you in the nineteenth century had you not chosen to obey?"

Lexie shrugged and leaned back in his embrace. "I'd already

given up hope of being returned, Lance, so I'd mentally prepared myself to do everything I could to fight against slavery. I taught Peter, a slave, to read and write, even though I knew doing so was against the law. I stirred up a lot of trouble, though I didn't mean to. I wish you could've met Peter and his parents, Mammy Sue and Big Tom. I thought maybe God put me there to make a difference—maybe he wanted me to sacrifice everything I cared about to make life better for the slaves.

"Then," she hesitated, "three men wanted to marry me. I didn't know if I'd have to marry one of them if I stayed. Life back then was so very hard on women, Lance, especially one without a man."

"Marry you!" Lance stiffened. "Did you have a preference?"

"No, the only man I ever wanted was you. To think you might have gone on in my absence, assuming I was dead, and married another about killed me."

He relaxed at her words and then pulled her to her feet. "Let's see if the pictures are ready. I have to move, or I'll explode."

"Let's go to my hotel room, Lance. I want to show you something."

"We'd better get cleaned up first. There's not a lot of time between now and all the action tonight. Your folks won't be happy if we're late."

She slung the strap over her shoulder and pressed the bag close to her body. "You're right. I'll get ready and then meet you in an hour. Come on, let's run."

When Lexie opened the door to him, he'd showered and dressed in dark blue slacks, black shoes, and a silky, white-fitted cotton shirt. The shirt, unbuttoned at the neck, tapered from his broad shoulders to his trim waist, and though the material hugged the muscles of his arms, the fabric was still loose enough for him to move comfortably. He pulled a dark blue tie from his pocket.

"I brought this thing, just in case, but I'm not wearing a tie unless the other men have theirs on." He whistled. "Wow, you're beautiful. I always liked that dress on you."

"You said I looked like cotton candy, remember?"

"Well, that or something sweet and good to eat." He studied the bright pink sleeveless dress with the fitted and sequined bodice, round neck and loose, flowing skirt. She wore matching heels and a strand of pearls. "Come here and let me taste."

Lexie went into his arms, and he kissed her well. She finally pulled away. "Stop now, Lance, or you'll make me forget what I want to show you. Sit here."

He sat in the leather chair at the desk.

"Look at the pictures in front of you."

"Are these the ones we developed today?" He picked up the first photo and studied the historic-looking family.

"Yes. I had them enlarged. Tell me what you see," she said, and stood next to him.

"I see three very large, muscular men standing in front of an adobe wall. They're at least six-ten or taller."

"I guessed six-three, but I knew I was wrong after I remembered you're six-three and the new kid at church, Mike, is exactly seven feet. They're closer to his height. What else do you see?"

"The one on the left is an older looking man whose hands and posture make me think he has arthritis. He probably doesn't have the strength of the other two."

"Yes. Go on."

"The two men next to him look like hard-core bodybuilders. I'd say they're the old man's sons because there's a strong family resemblance. They have black hair, though the old man's is graying. I can't really tell the color of their eyes, but I'm guessing blue. The women standing in front of them are much smaller, though this impression may be wrong since they're standing so close to the large men. The women look like mother and daughter. The boy must be the son. He has the same black hair. He's thin for his age, though I think he's about seven. They're dressed in period costumes of the nineteenth century."

Lance looked up. "Are these the Bells? You lived with them?"

"Yes. The older man is Fergus, father to Dwight and Jim Bell who are standing next to him. They're blacksmiths. The older woman is Edna, the younger is her daughter, Mary, and the boy is Matthew. We called him Mattie. Do you see the necklace Mary's wearing?"

Lance drew the picture closer to his face and turned toward the light.

"It looks like—is that your diamond heart necklace, Lexie? The one your parents gave you for your twenty-second birthday a few months ago?"

"Yes, I gave the necklace to her for a birthday and wedding gift. She and Jesse Johnson planned to marry in December. I didn't have anything else of value."

She pointed to the next photo. "Describe this one."

"I see three African Americans at rest. They're all dressed in old-fashioned clothing and are talking to each other. They don't seem to be aware you're taking their pictures. I'd say they are father, mother, and son. The son is about sixteen or seventeen, and if he ever grows into the shoulders of his father, he'll be an impressively strong man. Who are they?"

"They're Peter, Mammy Sue, and Big Tom. Nathan Johnson's slaves."

"Slaves?" He studied the three people. She could tell he couldn't grasp such a foreign concept.

"Now this one."

"I think the three men who are lifting the heavy bags into the wagon are related because of their size and facial features. Most likely the father and two sons. They're also strong, but my guess is they couldn't match the blacksmiths for sheer power." He tipped his head and looked at the men. "I've seen that look of raw, hungry, barely restrained power before, but not often. They'd be fierce competitors. That fourth man doesn't seem to fit, though. He's muscular, but not as big. He's too—I don't know, sophisticated, I guess. He looks like a lawyer, teacher, or businessman even dressed the way he is. The expression on his face makes me think he doesn't like one of the sons very much." He studied her face. "They didn't know you took their pictures, did they, Lexie?"

"No," she said and pointed, "that's Nathan Johnson, his two sons Jonathan and Jesse, and Sean West, a neighbor."

He gazed at all of the pictures for several minutes. Finally, he looked up. "Are any of these men the three who wanted to marry you?"

"Yes. Dwight Bell, Jonathan Johnson, and Sean West."

He stiffened, and his lips tightened. "All strong, competitive, handsome men. And you lived in the same house with Dwight Bell. Are you the reason West was looking at Jonathan Johnson like he wanted to punch him?"

She squeezed his shoulder. "Probably. But I chose you, Lance. I chose us. They all knew about you because I told them."

"What did you tell them?"

"I said you were the most amazing man on the planet."

"I'm humbled, Lexie. Truly humbled." He kissed her hand and whispered, "I love you so much."

"I love you, too. If I'd stayed and had to marry one of them, my choice would've been second best. You're the one the Lord has chosen for me, not them. I want to show you another thing, and then we'll go. I hope my proof substantiates my words of time travel."

She pulled out her phone and chose a video file, "These are the Bells telling about themselves. When they finally believed I came from the twenty-first century, they let me record. They wanted to hear and see themselves, so I told them to say their names, when and where they were born, and to tell what the hardest things were they had to endure when they traveled the trail to Kansas territory. I've got another file of just Fergus telling me stories of his life, but we don't have time for that. I also recorded the Johnsons and Sean West when they didn't know."

Fascinated, Lance listened to their stories. He stared at the images of the Bells when they talked, his eyes and thoughts focused on Dwight Bell. Though the man had died more than a hundred and fifty years ago, he still lived in Lexie's recent memory. His fists clenched and an unfamiliar urge to fight rushed through his system. Yet how could he battle a dead man? He looked at the other photos. Make that dead men.

"Come on. Time to go," Lexie picked up the violin case and held out her hand. He kissed her fingers and put his arm around her waist.

"I feel like I've lived a lifetime in these last few hours, babe, so I hope you don't expect me to stay up much after midnight."

"I know. Since I've returned, there are days when I feel like I have jet lag. Today started out as one of them."

TWO

When Lexie and Lance entered the hotel's ballroom, Audrey met them at the door. She, like everyone else, wore party clothes. She smiled, kissed them both, told them how beautiful they looked together and handed Lexie a tagboard sign with her name and picture.

"Hang your picture on the branches of the family tree below those of your parents and beside Steven's. The images help everyone understand how we're related. Here are name tags for both of you. You'll need to wear them until we finish some of the mix-and-mingle activities. The photographer will be taking candid shots and will let us choose what we want tomorrow before we leave."

Lexie studied the wall where names and pictures of relatives hung on the branches of the life-like cardboard tree.

"Did you do all of this, Grammy? You're amazing." Lexie admired such attention to detail.

"Some, but not all. I had help. Your aunt, mother, a few of your cousins and I got together and formed committees. You were still in school, or we would've asked you. With computers, the internet, and an office supply place close by, our jobs were relatively easy. The money everyone gave paid for everything."

"How many of the cousins showed up to this reunion?" Lance studied the people who milled around the base of the cardboard tree. They often pointed to pictures as they chatted.

"We invited a hundred, but eighty showed." Audrey patted Lexie's arm. "Notice the images on your name tags? At each round table, you'll find one of the same pictures. We're going to work this like a progressive dinner. You'll sit with family members with the same first image for appetizers, and then when we signal, you'll move to the table with the picture of the second image matching yours for your salad and conversation with different family members, the third for your entree, the fourth for dessert, and so on. Each table seats eight. Lance, I figured you'd be more comfortable staying with Lexie, so your images are in the same order."

"Thanks, Grandma Audrey. I can now breathe."

She chuckled and pointed them toward the tree.

Lexie hung her name and stepped back.

"Hey, cousin."

She turned.

Sandy, the cousin nearest her in age, gave them both a smile and hugs. "I'm so glad you could come, Lexie. Mom told me you both just arrived, so I thought I'd find you."

Lexie's eyes traveled around the room. "Quite a crowd. I don't know some of my cousins."

Sandy agreed. "We're going to have such fun tonight getting to know them better. I'm especially looking forward to the after-dinner activities and music. I'm glad you brought your violin.

Others brought their instruments, and Aunt Audrey made sure a baby grand piano was available for our little family concert tonight. I hope you're prepared to play both the violin and piano?"

Lexie nodded, but at the mention of playing, her thoughts returned to the Edwards' living room as she sat at their piano and poured her grief and sorrow out to God. At that moment, she understood the lessons he wanted her to learn. The moment she'd surrendered, he'd placed her back into the twenty-first century. Her skin burned at the memory, and she rubbed her bare arms.

Lance's hand on her elbow refocused her attention.

"Are you okay, Lexie?" Sandy tilted her head. "For a moment there, you zoned out."

"I'm all right."

Sandy looked beyond the pair. "Uh-oh. Mom's waving to me. Wonder what she wants? Better go. See you soon." After Sandy walked away, Lance spoke, "Where did you just go?"

"I was seated at the Edwards' piano pounding out my anger and fear. I wanted to drown out the sound of angry words and the look of shock and upset on the faces of the others. Mary, Edna, and Mattie were in the room, but I couldn't see them in the dim light. I saw my stubbornness and pride instead. The pain I'd caused myself by running was unendurable, Lance. I thought I'd lost you forever.

"The moment I repented and asked for forgiveness, the room darkened and the thunder intensified. The rain pounded the windows, and the space around me seemed to shrink and move. Lance, I imagined I was in the belly of the great fish with Jonah being burned with stomach acid."

Lance put his arms around her and looked in her face. "But what happened before to upset you all so? Why were the men angry? Why were the slaves hiding in the shed?"

She hesitated. "Frank Edwards intended to beat Peter with a hoe handle for stealing the orange Bible I'd given him. Do you remember the New Testament we got from the Gideons when we were at the community event in the park?"

"Yes."

"Well, Edwards caught him reading the Bible and assumed he'd stolen it. I stepped in front of Peter before that man could hit him. I was so angry, Lance. I was trying to figure out how I could move quickly enough in the long, bulky dress I wore to yank the handle out of his hand and beat him instead. Not very Christian of me, I know. My instinctive reactions make me wonder if I'm good enough to be a missionary's wife. I fail so often and so miserably."

Lance shook his head and caressed the scar on her arm with the pad of his thumb.

"Everyone deals with these emotions, Lexie. Go on."

"That's when Nate Johnson stepped up and accused me of teaching his slave to read. The situation got ugly then. I told Nate to name Peter's price and I would pay, no matter the cost. He asked me if I had any money, and I said, no. That's when he said-he said-"

She closed her eyes but opened them when he led her toward a sofa near the large fireplace. Drawing her down onto the sofa, he asked, "Then what happened?"

"You're not going to like what I'll say, Lance."

"I already figured that out, sweetheart, so just tell me."

"Nate demanded I marry his son, Jonathan, the same day."

"What!" Lance tensed.

"Shh. Keep your voice down."

"I bet Jonathan liked the price," he growled. "Where were your other two suitors? What did they have to say about this?"

"Jonathan didn't like what Nate had done. He told me he wanted us to marry, but he didn't want me to be forced to do so. Dwight and Sean stood next to each other ready to fight."

"I wasn't there, but I'm mad enough to fight right now."

Looking in his angry brown eyes, she murmured, "Don't be, Lance. I left them in the past. I'm home with you." She stood and pulled him to his feet. "Come on, Mom is signaling us to gather for the blessing. I hope you won't be too bored being with a bunch of people you don't know."

"I won't. I like watching all of you." Lance took a few deep breaths as if to settle his anger.

During the first rotation of appetizers, when Lexie sat next to a second cousin, she heard about great-aunt Ruth's mother, Alexandria.

"You knew your great-grandmother Rebecca and your great-aunt Ruth were identical twin sisters, didn't you?"

When she nodded at his question, he continued, "Seems twins run in this family, though they jump to every third or fourth generation."

An older female cousin chimed in, "Yes, Alexandria was born at the end of the Roaring Twenties. Imagine, she was alive when the Wright brothers made their first flight and when World War I ended. Heard she was quite a woman. Rebecca has a bunch of old photos of her. I wonder where they are now that she's in a home? My dad saw several of them and wanted to archive and compile them, but then he died before he could. Too bad. They would've been great to show at the reunion."

During the second rotation, she ate with a great-uncle who admitted he'd seen the photos but didn't know where they were.

"There were letters and diaries, too. The last time I saw them, they were stored in old trunks. I was young and didn't appreciate all the history, though I do remember I was fascinated with Alexandria's mother, Olivia Anne. She was born to one of two identical twin sisters. I think their names were Rachel and Sarah. If you're interested in that kind of thing, you might be able to find out their ancestry.

There's so many of those kinds of sites on the internet these days. I just remember she was alive when Nellie Bly made her successful trip around the world and beat the time given in Jules Verne's story, Around the World in Eighty Days. I always enjoyed that story when I was a boy."

He chuckled. "I discovered she was also alive when the Lakota Sioux chief, Sitting Bull, was killed. At the time, I was more interested in finding newspaper clippings about Eastman making roll film for cameras. I thought I wanted to be a photographer."

Lexie listened with as much interest and attention as she had when she'd sat with Fergus and Meriwether "Christmas" Jackson at the box supper and listened to their stories. Christmas had fought in the War of 1812, and shrunken, skinny Ray Roberts, the octogenarian who'd bought her box, had been born in 1777, a year after the signing of the Declaration of Independence. She wished she could have recorded more of their stories, just as she wished she could record the stories her relatives now told. Lexie reached toward her phone.

During the third rotation, Lexie sat directly across from the Mary and Mattie look-a-likes. She tried not to stare.

"Lance," she whispered behind her napkin. "That woman could be Mary Bell Johnson."

He glanced at the black-haired, blue-eyed woman and nodded. "This is starting to freak me out."

"So, you believe me?"

"Yes."

Everyone at the table introduced themselves and followed the directions to tell one or two things important to them. Lexie smiled at her family members and said, "I'm Lexie Logan, and this is my fiancé, Lance Garrett. We'll be married in September, then head to language school in Costa Rica at the first of the year on our way to the mission field in Guatemala. We'll be working at an orphanage."

Mary's double introduced herself as Kimberly Bell and her brother as Weston Bell. Kimberly said she'd recently graduated from college with a library science degree and would start working in a university library when she returned to Oregon. Her brother, an older version of Mattie, said he'd just graduated high school and would take a year or two off before deciding what he wanted to do. He grinned and said he planned to hunt and fish in the mountains of southern Colorado in the fall.

Lexie felt the color leave her face and her eyes widen. She massaged the scar until Lance held her hand under the table.

"Oregon?" Olivia spoke from Lexie's right. She smiled and looked at Kimberly. "You and my daughter have a lot in common then. When she has any extra time, she's either on the internet or in the library reading. You'd think four years of study would make her want a break."

Kimberly tilted her head. "What do you study?"

"I've developed a fascination for travel on the Oregon Trail and the Civil War."

"Wow! The mid-to-late nineteenth century is also my favorite era." Kimberly's eyes widened in interest, and she started to ask more questions, but her brother cut in.

"No more books for me. I've had all I want for a while." Weston grinned. "If I could spend my days fishing, hunting, or windsurfing on the Columbia and make money doing so, I would."

When Lance commented about hunting and fishing in Colorado and spending summers there as an intern park ranger a few years before, the teen sat up and leaned forward. They were soon deep in conversation about the great outdoors.

Lexie smiled. Mattie had shown the same enthusiasm for windsurfing when she'd told him about the activity, though the sport wouldn't be popular for almost two hundred years. He'd spoken with similar starry-eyed excitement.

"I'd like to chat with you more and get to know you better, Lexie. Are you interested in exchanging email addresses and phone numbers?"

"I'd love to." Lexie hesitated. "Do you know how we meet on the family tree?"

She shook her head, and Lexie turned to Olivia. "Do you know, Mom?"

"I'm not sure, but I know we crossed several generations back. Too bad your great-grandmother couldn't be here. She'd know."

They exchanged emails and phone numbers just before the signal to move to the next table was given.

"Before you go, may I take a photo of you two?" Lexie looked from Kimberly to Weston and back.

"Sure," the young man said, and moved next to his sister.

"Let me take yours and Lance's." Lance embraced Lexie, and Kimberly snapped their picture.

Olivia touched Lexie's arm. "Your grandmother is signaling for you to get your violin."

They parted and went to the next tables to participate in quick activities, while Lexie got her violin case.

Grandma Audrey stepped to the microphone. "I'm so glad you all got to come to the cousins' reunion. Before we get started with our family music and talent hour, I want to thank the hotel staff for their excellent service and the delicious food. Please show your appreciation."

After the clapping stopped, everyone waited for Audrey to continue. "Did you like visiting with your family and new cousins?"

The crowd clapped, whistled, and said, "Yes!"

She smiled and recognized the reunion's organizers. Then she held up a piece of paper.

"This list shows the order of the performances. You have one at each table. If you'd check the order, make your way to the back just before your turn, and then slip up the side aisles toward the front, we'll keep the entertainment moving. To start tonight's program, I've asked my granddaughter, Lexie Logan, and my nephew, Daniel Gray, to play "Dueling Banjos"—one of my favorites, though you can see we have a violin and guitar. Enjoy, everyone."

Lexie and Daniel moved to the front. They'd practiced earlier that morning and were ready. Lexie raised the violin to her chin and poised the bow above the strings. She looked at Lance, who smiled his encouragement, then nodded to Daniel. He grinned and began. Not too long into the music, the family members were on their feet and clapping. Several of the younger children danced jigs next to their tables. Lexie smiled when she remembered how Fergus had been inspired by the toe-tapping fun of the music to dance with Mary. Unfortunately, he'd stepped on Mary's foot, tripped himself, and bonked his head on the ground. His concussion wasn't severe, but he'd given the Bells and her a scare.

When they finished, they bowed to enthusiastic whistles and clapping and made room for the next cousins.

"Great job, babe," Lance said, and held her hand when she sat down.

Other family vocalists and instrumentalists followed, though a ventriloquist, a cowboy poet, a comedienne, and a group sing-along were placed in between some of the music sets. The short break in the middle of the program allowed everyone to stand up and move around. When the cousins returned to their seats, the music resumed, but Lexie's mind had wandered back to the nineteenth century.

"You're up next, hon. You're last," Lance whispered. She nodded and stood.

As soon as Lexie sat on the bench, all the lights except the one over the piano dimmed. The cooled air brushed her skin and raised goosebumps. The room was so quiet she could hear the rapidly falling raindrops as they flicked themselves against the windows. A summer storm had arrived without notice, and she closed her eyes when she heard the distant thunder.

She placed her fingers on the keys and the memories of the last day she spent in 1857 returned. The anguish and sorrow overwhelmed her, and she again let the heartache flow from her fingers to the keys.

Remember what you have learned, Lexie. Remember what I have done for you.

"I praise you, Father," she whispered.

The intensity of the music shocked the listeners, and from the corner of her eyes, she noticed they sat up and leaned forward. Judging by the emotions flitting across their faces, they appeared to be immediately engaged. When she lightened the tone to a more jubilant sound, they sat back and sighed. When she finished, they rose to their feet and clapped and whistled. A few had tears in their eyes.

Lexie acknowledged her appreciative audience with a head bow, but she was so spent she could barely smile. She walked toward her seat on rubbery legs. Lance opened his arms and she went into them.

"You were there again, weren't you?" He whispered next to her ear, and she nodded.

"I'm so tired, Lance. I've got that jet lag feeling again." She didn't lift her cheek from his neck.

"Here comes your mom and dad."

Lexie forced her head up and turned in his arms.

"That was amazing, honey. I wish we'd recorded you."

Lexie recognized the pride in her dad's voice and eyes.

Olivia kissed her cheek. "You made me cry. I've never heard the arrangement, but it was beautiful."

The love she felt for her parents softened her voice, "Thanks, Mom. Dad. I'm going to head up to my room now. I'm exhausted. Will you ask the others to please excuse me from the games and after-concert activities?"

"Sure. We won't be much longer. We'll see you in the morning." Olivia turned to Lance. "Are you staying?"

"No. I'm tired too, Olivia. I'll see Lexie to her room, and then I'm going to crash. What time is breakfast tomorrow morning?"

"The buffet lasts from eight to ten o'clock. The photographer will be there with the proofs, so you can order what you want."

"Thanks, Mom." He kissed Olivia's cheek and shook David's hand. "I'll see you tomorrow."

"Night, Mom. Dad. I love you." Lexie kissed them both and walked away, her fingers linked in Lance's.

They took the elevator to the seventh floor and walked the length of the corridor to Lexie's room. Her parents and Steven were across the hall, but Lance was next door.

She unlocked the door and turned to him for his kiss. "Good night, love. I'll see you in the morning."

He kissed her again and sighed. "Three more months, Lexie, and these walls won't separate us."

She traced his firm jawline and smiled. "Three more months and I'll be married to the most amazing man on the planet."

He chuckled and turned to leave. "And I'll be married to the only woman time-traveler I know."

Before visiting the buffet the next morning, Lexie and Lance walked toward the photographer's table. The woman greeted them and pointed at the proofs spread across the surfaces of three long tables.

"Here's a paper and pencil for you. I've numbered each photo, so write your contact information and which pictures you want, and I'll get them to you within the next week. I take major credit cards, and you can order now or online."

They nodded and started down the line of tables.

"Look at this."

Lexie moved to Lance's side and looked at the picture he held.

"This is the shot of all the female relatives. Do you see?"

She studied the faces. "You're right. I didn't realize how strong the resemblance was until we stood together."

They slowly made their way down the tables adding numbers to their papers.

"I want these." Lance held up three more proofs.

Lexie frowned. "She took our pictures when we were sitting on the couch talking. Look how serious we are. This one is too private for others to see."

Lance pointed to the other proof. "She also took your picture when you played the violin and piano. Got you from several different angles."

When Lexie picked up one of the proofs of her playing the piano and saw the raw look on her face as she spilled out her emotions on the keyboard, she cringed and signaled to the photographer.

"May I help you?"

"He and I want these pictures, but we don't want these two available to others. Can you do that?"

The woman looked at the proofs and made notes on her tablet. "Just these, or all of the ones you're in? It would be a shame if your other relatives didn't have anything to remember you or last night's stunning performance."

"No, just these two."

"Yes, I can do that."

"Would you be willing to print a couple of others in sepia tones?" Lexie pointed to the Bell cousins' photos and the female cousins' photos.

"Sure."

"I'd like to purchase the digital files and copyrights for these."

"All right. I'll give you a signed release form."

Their transactions complete, they turned toward the buffet.

"What are you planning to do with sepia-toned photos?" He handed her a plate, and they started down the buffet line.

When he seated her, she said, "I want to collect these and the ones I took in the past into an album or something. I'm not sure yet of the exact form. Ideas are buzzing around in my head."

She rubbed the scar, and her words slowed as she revisited her last moments in 1857. "I've got to remember."

They ate in silence. As Lexie thought of her rapidly approaching future as a missionary's wife in a foreign country, her hunger disappeared. She rubbed her arm faster and harder to dispel the chills of apprehension and uncertainty.

Lance stilled her hand. "What's wrong? Your breathing is too fast and your pupils are dilated."

She swallowed hard. "I'm scared, Lance."

"Of what?" He leaned toward her to hear the whispered words.

"Of ... of everything. I'm afraid I'll fail ..." She made a movement with her right hand. "What if I fail you, me, and God?"

Lance considered her words. "Do you remember when the Lord took the Last Supper with his apostles?"

Lexie nodded.

""After the Master told the men one of them would betray him, do you remember what the Lord said to Peter after he said he would never forsake him?"

She nodded again. "He told Peter that before the rooster crowed, he would deny him three times."

"Did he?"

"Yes."

"Was his denial the end of their relationship?"

Lexie stared into Lance's face for several moments. "No. After the resurrection, Jesus said to go and tell his disciples and Peter that he would meet them in Galilee."

"What did the Lord say to Peter when he saw him?"

Suddenly, Lexie's thoughts returned to the Bells' soddy when God spoke to her through Scripture. "He asked if Peter loved him, and then told the apostle to feed his lambs and sheep."

"So, he wasn't finished with Peter even after his friend had failed?" Lexie shook her head, dropped her eyes and massaged the scar.

"Honey, look at me."

She did.

"We're both going to fail. I'll fail more than I want and so will you. We're humans. The apostle Paul recognized his carnality and wrote that he didn't do the good he wanted to do, but instead the evil he didn't want to do because his inner being-the spiritual part that wants to delight God-was at war with the desires of his humanness. He said the only way we'll be delivered from this struggle and the law of our sinful nature is through Jesus Christ."

Lexie chewed on her bottom lip as she considered his words. "I don't like to fail, Lance. I don't like to let people down."

"I don't either, babe, but we're going to have to reconcile ourselves to the fact we will fail. The question is going to be how we'll respond when we recognize our failures."

Lexie sighed. "Let's go home, love. I can't seem to shake this mental fatigue. I need to be alone to think and pray before all of the busyness of our wedding arrangements rush back to claim my attention."

He stood and kissed her then led her toward the door.

Audrey saw them and waved. "Are you headed out?"

"Yes. I'm going to tell Mom and Dad we're leaving."

Audrey hugged them. "Don't become strangers, you two."

Lexie stooped and gave her grandmother a kiss. "We won't, Grammy."

"Don't forget you said you'd go and see Mama soon, okay?"

"I won't forget. I'll make plans to see her the day after tomorrow."

"Take Steven with you."

Lexie smiled but didn't nod. She had questions only her great-grandmother could answer, and she wanted the woman to be able to focus without the added distraction of her brother's presence. Steven could see her at a different time. An urgency in her spirit told her time was of the essence, and she must discover the location of the letters, photos, and diaries before her great-grandmother passed out of this life. She didn't know why these documents were relevant, but her sixth sense told her they were, and whatever she discovered would impact her future.

THREE

Lexie knocked on the half-opened door and waited for someone to admit her. Clothing rustled, and a nurse in her thirties opened the door wider and smiled.

"Hello. Are you here to see Rebecca?"

"Yes. Is she able to have visitors now? I'm her great-granddaughter."

"Sure. Might perk her up a bit to see family." The nurse lowered her voice and tilted her head toward the room's occupant, "I think she got up on the wrong side of the bed this morning. Don't let her crankiness get to you. She's usually not so pessimistic."

"Who's there, Amanda?" Her great-grandmother's querulous tones stopped her for a moment.

"It's me, Granny Becky. Lexie."

"Come in, child. Come in and sit in the chair by the window so I can see you." The old woman struggled to sit up higher in the bed then looked at the nurse. "Close the door after you, Amanda. I won't need anything for a while."

The nurse grinned and left.

Lexie bent over Rebecca and kissed her wrinkled cheek. She straightened the coverlet and smiled. "How are you, Gran?"

"Getting older by the second, child. My memory and health are failing, though not as bad as some of the inmates here. Doctor says I have congestive heart failure." She sighed. "I'm ready to go home anytime the Lord sees fit to take me."

Lexie patted her grandmother's hand and looked around the room. She tried to find words that would move Rebecca's thoughts to a more positive place.

"Your room is lovely."

Rebecca looked at the flowers and the family pictures on the dresser and nodded. "It's empty, though, except for me, and I'm just a shell. The last roommate I had died a week ago. What's the month? July? The one before her died in May." She shook her head and grimaced. "She sure was a strange woman. Had the crazy idea the nurses or other patients were stealing her things. The old girl told me she intended to put pins and needles in the toes of her house shoes so they stuck out far enough from the end that she could kick the thieves with them."

Lexie chuckled, and Rebecca's face relaxed. Her eyes began to twinkle. "I have to warn you, Granddaughter. The janitors clean every day, but it doesn't seem to help. The place still stinks, though I don't notice the odor much anymore. You've got to watch out too, because this whole place is filled with nothing but old people who use canes, walkers, or wheelchairs, excepting the doctors, nurses, and secretaries, of course. Best stay out of their way if you see any coming. Pedestrians don't have the right-of-way around here."

Lexie thought of the box supper she attended on July 4, 1857. She thought of Fergus Bell, Christmas Jackson, and little Ray

Roberts. "Old people often have fascinating stories to tell, Gran. I bet you have a lot."

"Filled more than eighty-five years with them, though a few are getting gray and foggy around the edges."

"Grammy said you weren't feeling well enough to come to the family reunion we had a few days ago. I wish you had been, Gran, because you could have cleared up how some of us crossed on the family tree."

"Tell me about the reunion." Rebecca folded her hands and waited.

Lexie watched her grandmother relax as she listened.

"Wish I could've heard you play. Bring your violin the next time you come." Rebecca closed her eyes. "Sing to me now, Granddaughter."

"What do you want me to sing, Gran?"

"Sing about heaven, Lexie. Sing about the Lord."

Lexie thought for a moment then began to sing the first stanza of "Heaven Is a Wonderful Place." She didn't make it to the repeat before she heard Rebecca's soft snore.

For several moments, she watched the rise and fall of her grandmother's chest then bent over, tucked the covers around her and kissed her cheek. She studied the lines and planes of the old woman's face and realized in another sixty-five years, she would look very much like her great-grandmother. Lexie shivered. She wondered how God would fill her life between now and then. What heartaches and triumphs would come her way? Would she, like Rebecca, be ready for heaven when the time came, or would she be living with regrets for what could or should have been?

She stroked Rebecca's hand and turned toward the door. Lexie stopped in front of the framed photographs which stood in the place of honor on the dresser. She recognized Audrey and Jennifer, though the shots had been taken when they were teenagers in the late 1960s. Several other group pictures of uncles, aunts, and cousins were clustered together by families. Lexie smiled to see a photo of Olivia, Grammy Audrey, and Grandpa Stephen when Olivia was Lexie's age. Had her mother been wearing a ponytail and blue jeans instead of a dress and hairstyle from the 1990s, the image could have been hers.

The last black-and-white photograph caught and held Lexie's attention. She reached for it and turned toward the light. Two identical twin sisters stood next to each other dressed in the hats, fitted bodices, and the full, below-the-knees dresses of the 1950s. They stood on a lawn and smiled for the camera. One of the twins held a newborn toward the lens. Lexie turned the frame over and gently removed the back to look at the inscription on the photo.

Ruth, Rebecca, and baby Audrey, June 7, 1950, Topeka, Kansas

Lexie studied the photograph for several more moments before putting it back in the frame and placing the photo in its spot on the dresser. The sense of urgency returned, and she dialed her grandmother's number as she walked out of the nursing home.

She was relieved when Audrey answered on the second ring.

"Hi, Lexie. I sure like this new phone with caller ID."

"Hi, Grammy. I'm just leaving the nursing home and wondered if I could stop by your house for a visit, if you don't have other plans?"

"Please do. You'll be just in time to try the new protein bar recipe I'm making. I don't have to bake anything."

Lexie made a face into the phone. Audrey's last efforts had been less than successful.

"Okay. I'm on my way."

Lexie sat across from Audrey at the kitchen table and hesitated before taking the small square bar her grandmother offered.

"I used almonds, unsweetened shredded coconut, coconut oil, flax, vanilla, and a scoop of my green powder among other things. The bars are sweetened with stevia, so you don't have to worry about processed sugar. They have to be refrigerated, though, because they'll melt if the temperature gets into the seventies."

Lexie eyed the light brownish-greenish bar then took a tiny bite.

"What do you think?"

"It tastes better than it looks, Grammy."

She finished the bar and watched Audrey sample hers.

"How was Mama today?"

"The nurse said she got up on the wrong side of the bed. She wasn't grumpy with me, though. I told her about the reunion and sang to her. She was asleep when I left."

Audrey nodded, and her mouth drooped with sadness. "Her heart's giving out."

"She had a picture of you as a baby. Gran held you, and great-aunt Ruth stood next to Gran."

"Yes, Daddy took the picture on the day I was born. He was so proud of that camera. I've got boxes of his photos."

"When I was at the reunion, some of the relatives said Gran had trunks full of old photos, letters, and diaries. Do you know where they are? I'd like to see them."

"Hmm. You know, that's a good question. I have a lot of old photographs, but the trunks you're talking about contained family history from back before Alexandria's time. I wonder what happened to them?"

"You didn't see the trunks when you moved Gran into the nursing home?"

"No. One of your great-uncles took them. If I remember correctly, he wanted to use some of the information in a paper he was writing. That was several years ago. I'm trying to remember who took them."

"Do you think it was anyone at the reunion?"

Audrey appeared to press her mental review button and search through all the cousins who attended. "No, he wasn't there. He was one of the twenty who couldn't come."

"Do you still have the list of people you invited? Maybe looking at it will refresh your memory."

"Good idea. I've got the list in my desk drawer. I'll get it. Have another protein bar if you'd like."

Lexie nibbled on one more of the rich almond-coconut bars, then washed the crumbs down with cold water.

"Here's the list." She pulled her chair next to Lexie's, and they both bent over the piece of paper. "Of the twenty who didn't show, we can eliminate half the people on this list because they're women. I can mark off seven more of the men because none of them are professors, and I know the uncle who borrowed the trunks was a professor."

"So that leaves three men who could have them. Do you have their phone numbers? Where do they live?"

Audrey ran her finger down the names. "William Moore was Alexandria's nephew on her husband's side. The address I have for him is Denver, Colorado. No phone. Samuel Garth is Mama's youngest brother. I have a phone number for him. He lives on a ranch outside of Amarillo, Texas. The only other possibility is A.P. Harper. He lives in Albuquerque, New Mexico. I have two numbers for him."

"What does A.P. stand for?"

"I don't know. He's always used his initials."

"Is there a chance you'd be willing to call them and ask about the trunks, Grammy?"

"Sure. I'd like to get them back. With all the new technology, maybe we can get the letters, photos, and diaries archived so more of the family can appreciate our history."

"We?"

Audrey grinned and tilted her head. "Well, I can't very well do the task by myself. I'm not getting any younger, and I'm not as technologically literate as my nieces, nephews, and grandchildren, you know."

"I'll help all I can in between planning a wedding and researching everything I can about Guatemala," Lexie's throat tightened on the last word.

Audrey said nothing for a few moments.

"You're nervous, aren't you, sweetie?"

Lexie rubbed the scar on her arm with the thumb of her right hand. "More like overwhelmed, uncertain and downright scared, Grammy."

Audrey's brows furrowed in concern when she saw the angry-looking scar.

"What happened to your arm?"

Lexie looked down and realized what she'd been doing. She dropped her hand and stood. "Long story."

She bent and kissed Audrey. "I need to go, Grammy. I'm meeting Lance after he gets off work today."

"Does he still like his job?" Audrey walked her to the door and out to her car.

"Yes. He says the life of a civil engineer is exciting, even if he's only been one officially for a year while he waited for me to graduate.

You should see his eyes glow every time he talks about some of the projects, Grammy. When we were younger, his family lived down the street from us, so we went to the same schools. From the time we were in elementary school, he's been interested in building bridges, roads, dams, and buildings. I think he likes this type of work because he gets to be outside sometimes.

"Did you know Lance has been surrounded by engineers of one type or another from the time he was born? His dad's a chemical engineer, his mother's a mechanical engineer, his older sister's a computer programmer for an aeronautics organization, and his older brother is a commercial airline mechanic."

Audrey chuckled and watched Lexie slide behind the wheel. "I can just imagine their dinner-time conversations."

Lexie laughed. "Listening to them is like being with someone from another planet. They try to stay grounded when I'm around, but they invariably bounce into the stratosphere every now and again during the conversation. I try to follow the best I can."

As Lexie backed out of the driveway, she murmured to herself, "Though I sometimes don't understand the Garretts, I never feel as strange with them as I did with the Bells. I remember how much of an alien I felt in 1857. I didn't know what a lot of objects were, and if I did, they were so primitive I didn't know how to use them." She thought of the wood-burning stove and made a face.

"I was uncomfortable and ungraceful wearing those long full skirts when I had to put them on, but most of all, I felt disoriented and other-worldly when I listened to the Bells' conversations about slavery, living in a sod house, and allowing a seventeen-year-old girl to marry."

Lexie missed them. She wanted to hear their voices. She wished she could hug them and see their faces. While she waited at a red light, she reached for her phone and scrolled down to one of the audio files she'd recorded of Fergus. As soon as she pushed play and heard his scratchy voice, tears filled her eyes. She played the recording to the end.

"How are you, Fergus? Did you all get to Oregon? I know you've been dead a long time, but you're still alive to me. I wish I could talk to you."

More tears tracked down her cheeks, and she brushed them away. "What happened to you all? How's Peter?"

The urgency returned, and Lexie glanced at the sky. "Do you want me to find out what happened to them, Lord? How do I do that? They've been gone for so long."

Kimberly Bell's face popped onto her mental screen. "Okay, Lord. I'll start with Kimberly."

Lexie listened to more of the audio files while she waited for Lance, and by the time he tossed his workout bag into the trunk and greeted her with a kiss, she'd made some tentative plans to begin her search.

"You smell good." Lance caressed her cheek. "I've been looking forward to our class all day, hon. Are you ready?"

Lexie laughed as she pulled away. "You just like to show me up, don't you?"

"No way. I like getting out of these white-collar clothes and into something more comfortable. Most of all, I like how I feel after I've exercised."

Lexie laughed again and drove toward the gym where they were taking another karate class. They'd been inspired to take martial arts classes after watching the several years ago. "Your enthusiasm for moving and doing reminds me of Jesse Johnson. His energy seemed boundless."

"Tell me more about him." Lance listened and asked a few thoughtful questions. "He would've been of prime age for fighting in the Civil War. Would he have enlisted with the North or the South?"

Lexie saddened. "My guess would be for the South because his family members were slave owners, though I don't know how much influence Mary had on him."

"I wonder if these people survived the war?"

"Every day I wonder the same thing, Lance. I intend to search for more information. The Bells planned to travel to Oregon in the spring, so they probably escaped. If I'm effective with my searches, maybe I can discover something about the Johnsons. I don't know about the West brothers, either. They were against slavery, so if they fought, it would've been for the North. I wonder if my heart can take the knowing."

Because her thoughts remained with the Bells, Johnsons, and Wests, Lexie couldn't concentrate as well as she needed to during class. As a result, she found herself pinned on her back more often than usual.

Lance helped her up. "What's wrong, Lexie? You know how to counter that move. We've practiced a hundred times."

"I can't focus very well right now, Lance. I've got too much on my mind."

He smiled. "Just the kind of victim an aggressor likes."

Lexie chuckled and forced herself to attend the rest of the lesson.

That evening after dinner, Lexie called Kimberly Bell.

"Hey, Kimberly. It's me, Lexie Logan."

They chatted for several minutes before Lexie finally got to the point of her call. She told her cousin what she wanted to find.

"Do you have access to historical documents that might give me a starting point?"

"Yes," Kimberly replied, "Names and date would help. When I have a little downtime, I could check for you."

Lexie provided her with the names and dates the Bells had given her when she recorded them.

"I sure appreciate this."

"You're welcome. I wonder if these Bells are related to me? I'll have to ask Dad if he has any information. What you're doing sounds challenging and fun. I'll let you know if I find anything."

The next morning Audrey called. "I didn't have any luck contacting William and A.P., Lexie, but I left a message at the two numbers A. P. gave, so hopefully he'll respond. I guess we'll have to write a letter to William. Come by tomorrow, and we'll write it. I did reach Samuel Garth, Mama's brother. He said he didn't remember borrowing any trunks, but since he's eighty-two, he thought there's always a good chance his memory is failing."

Audrey chuckled. "He sounded like the same old Samuel I knew from the past—full of sauce. He said there are some trunks in his attic, but he insists he's too old to climb the stairs to look."

She could hear the laughter in her grandmother's voice, "Sam invited you to come out and look for yourself if you want to."

Lexie gasped. "Go to Texas?"

"Yes. He said he's got a room for you and anybody else who wants to come. You know what I think? I think he's lonely. Since his wife died a few years ago, he doesn't do much but read books, work his cattle and fiddle with things on the ranch. The only other people he sees unless he drives to Amarillo to church on Sundays are a couple of hands who are almost as old as he is."

"He works on a ranch, yet he's too old to climb the stairs?"

"Now you know why I think he's lonely."

Lexie thought of all the things she still had to do. "I guess I can spare a weekend, Grammy. Will you come with me?"

"No, honey, I don't feel right about being away from Mama now. You know what you should do?"

"What?"

"Ask Lance to go with you. Maybe he could fly you down in his dad's fancy plane."

"Maybe. I'll see. What's Uncle Samuel's number?"

Audrey gave her the number, and Lexie saved the information to her phone. "Thanks. I'll call him to see if next weekend might be good for me to come and visit."

Lexie reviewed her mental list of things to do for the wedding: order wedding favors, shop for and reserve the men's formalwear, finalize the guest list, get everyone's mailing addresses, order the invitations and thank you cards, and choose her dress. She also needed to remind Lance to renew his passport. Fortunately, Mom was going to see to the menu and catering, and the rental of table linens. She would touch base with the vendors to confirm dates, and would also deal with deposits and other details, which allowed Lexie some breathing room.

After she said goodbye to Audrey, she looked at her watch, then dialed Lance.

"Good timing, hon. I just got out of a meeting."

"Do you have plans for next weekend, Lance?"

"Not really, unless you're tired of all the wedding arrangements and want to elope. Why?"

"You're funny. Can you fly me to Texas for a few days?"

"Texas? What's in Texas?"

"An elderly uncle who may have the missing trunks stored in his attic."

"Sounds fun. I'll check with Dad and Greg to make sure they don't have any plans for the Cessna. If not, I'll make certain the plane is serviced and ready to fly. I'll let you know."

"Great."

"Hey, why don't you come over for dinner tonight? Mom said

it's okay. Greg and Patty will be there. Patty said her husband and kids are visiting his mom, so things won't be so noisy."

"I'd love to. I'll let my folks know. Bye, Lance."

The Garretts lived in a comfortable three-thousand-square-foot home across town. Though the rooms were spacious and pretty, the house didn't match the income of the people who lived there. Lexie knew they could afford a million-dollar house on acreage if they wanted, but they chose to live more simply in the suburbs and to invest in things of greater value to them than big houses, expensive cars, and a houseful of servants. Because of all the traveling Lance's parents and brother did with their jobs or for other projects, they considered the Cessna a necessity rather than a luxury.

Nothing in the décor or furnishings of the house was ostentatious, and Lexie always felt at home when she entered.

Lance opened the door at her ring, but Lexie read the words on the new doormat before stepping inside to receive his kiss.

I had rather be a doorkeeper in the house of my God,
than to dwell in the tents of the wicked. Psalm 84:10

"Come on in, Lexie," Amy Garrett, Lance's mother, called from the kitchen, "Dinner's almost ready."

Patty Jackson, her soon-to-be sister-in-law, walked from the kitchen to the dining room, her hands loaded with a couple of platters of food. She grinned when she saw the couple and tipped her head toward the kitchen.

"Lexie, there are a couple more platters if you want to grab them. Lance, "Baby Bro," Mom says to go out to the garage and tell Dad and Greg to come and eat."

"Yes, ma'am." He saluted and left.

Setting the platters down, Patty laughed and tucked a tendril of long, reddish-brown hair behind her ear. Hugging Lexie, she said, "I'm glad you decided to come. How are the wedding plans going?"

"Thanks. I'm making progress toward checking things off the to-do list, though I couldn't get as much done without Mom's help. She's so organized."

Lance returned with his dad, George, and his brother, Greg. All three had the same look of intent interest on their faces as they chatted about low-wing cantilever monoplanes, T-tails, tricycle retractable landing gear, three spar wings, turbofan engines, and aluminum alloy construction.

Lexie assumed they were talking about the plane, though Lance told her the Cessna wasn't just a plane. The bird was a Citation Mustang, Model 510, very light jet, or VLJ. George, Lance, and Greg had gone in together and purchased the plane, used, from a wealthy businessman who wanted to upgrade as his global business expanded. They bought the Cessna for a little more than half the $3.2 million new-plane price tag. Lexie grinned. A real steal. Not available on Craig's List.

Suddenly, her thoughts returned to 1857 when, in a state of grief, she'd remained curled in a fetal position in the back of the Bell's Conestoga wagon and refused food and drink for more than a day. Fergus had sat outside the wagon and had tried to convince her to come out. When she'd finally emerged, he'd encouraged her to talk about her life in the twenty-first century.

She mentioned being able to fly from one place to another in a short amount of time. Fergus thought of the amount of time he'd spent on the trail to Kansas and had responded with, "Wish I could'a done that a-comin' out here, Lexie. My old bones ain't what they used to be and all those weeks of bumpin' around in the wagon made 'em ache somethin' fierce."

Lexie wished Fergus could see the Garretts' little jet.

"Have you found a wedding dress yet, Lexie?" Amy asked after they'd all sat down to a tasty dinner.

Lexie refocused. "Not yet. Finding one is on my to-do list."

"What are you looking for?" Patty asked between bites of baked sweet potato. "Anything special?"

"Oh, I don't know, but I'll know the dress when I see it."

They discussed all the things still to do before September, and Lexie began to massage her scar. Lance reached under the table and stopped the movement.

Greg rolled his eyes and mentioned his fiancée, "I'm glad Lisa doesn't want me to do much except show up, look good in a tux, pay for some things and stay out of her way." He sighed with pleasure. "Just the way I like it."

"I hope that's not how you'll spend the rest of your lives together," Patty teased.

The sparkle of love in his eyes and the grin stretching Greg's mouth told everyone at the table he had no concerns Lisa would turn into a termagant. "No fears. She knows me, and I know her. She doesn't cross the line."

"What did you decide about your condo? Will you move into her place or will she move into yours?"

"Well, I've been talking to the three L's, and—"

"Who?" Amy raised her brows as she cut her meat into small pieces.

"You know—Lance, Lexie, and Lisa—and we've come up with a plan." He looked at his brother. "You want to tell them, Lance?"

"Sure. After the wedding in September, Lexie and I'll move into Greg's condo. Mom and Dad said Greg could stay here with them for three months. When we leave in January for Costa Rica," Lance held Lexie's hand before she could reach for the scar. "Greg's going to let Lisa remodel his kitchen, repaint the rooms and replace most of the carpet with hardwood floors before their wedding in the spring. Then she'll move in with him."

"Tidy," Patty said, "Very tidy."

"We thought so," Amy agreed.

The conversation veered to the use of the Cessna for Lance and Lexie's jaunt to Texas, and Lexie gave them the abbreviated version of why she needed to go. Only Lance knew there was more to the trip than she'd told them.

"What did he say when you talked to him, Lexie?" Lance asked, "Is he okay with us showing up at his place next weekend?"

"Yes." She chuckled. "Uncle Sam sounded a lot spryer than I thought he'd be, and he seemed to want us to come. He said he wants us to fly in on Thursday evening if you can get off because he has a real treat in store for us on Friday."

"I'll check with the boss. I've been saving most of my vacation days for the wedding and honeymoon."

"Are the honeymoon plans still secret, Lexie?" George passed Lance the cherry pie after he slid a piece of the dessert onto his plate.

"Yes, even from me. Lance is making those arrangements. All I know right now is I need my passport, suntan lotion, and a bathing suit."

They looked at Lance, and he grinned. "The plans are still in the works, Dad. Just a few more tweaks and everything'll be ready."

Lexie slipped her right hand up under her hair and pressed the skin just below her right ear. Her pulse throbbed against her fingertips, and her heart pumped joy, excitement, and fear through her body. George had told her the maximum speed their Cessna could reach was Mach 0.63, with Mach 1 being the speed of sound, but the future rushed at her like an oncoming projectile traveling at Mach 3. She hoped she could avoid a collision.

FOUR

The next day, Lexie wrote to William Moore and mailed the letter on her way to visit Rebecca. Audrey sat in the passenger seat and related some of the stories her mom had told her about her grandmother, Alexandria Garth.

"Mama said Grandmama Alexandria was twenty years old when Mickey Mouse first made his debut as Steamboat Willie on the big screen in 1928. Her first husband, Mama's dad, took her to see the short film. Can you imagine? Mickey and Minnie Mouse seem to have been around forever but, in reality, they've only been around a little more than eighty years."

Audrey continued, "A year earlier, she saw the Babe hit his sixtieth home run in Yankee Stadium."

"The Babe? Babe Ruth?" Lexie frowned as she tried to put historical events in order on her mental timeline. She glanced at the recording device to make certain the red record button was still on.

She'd have to write everything down when she got home.

"Yes, from all I've heard, she was quite adventurous. For a while, she wanted to be like Amelia Earhart and fly solo across the Atlantic Ocean."

"So, she was born in 1908? Alexandria was six when World War I began?"

"Yes," Audrey sighed. "Poor thing. Wall Street crashed in September of 1929, three months before Mama and Aunt Ruth were born. Alexandria's husband died in a car accident the month before that. I can't imagine how hard raising two babies during the Great Depression was for her, though I think she got help from her parents. No one blamed her for remarrying Louis Garth two years after Granddaddy died."

"Hold on, Grammy." Lexie slotted her car into the parking space at the nursing home. "You're telling me that Uncle Sam is half-brother to Gran and Aunt Ruth?"

"Yes."

Lexie shut off the recorder as they walked to Rebecca's room, but made a mental note to turn the device on again when her great-grandmother started talking.

"Hmm. Mama's not in her room. I wonder if she's feeling well enough to sit outside in the sunshine?"

They made their way through the lounge area to the covered patio. Rebecca sat in a padded chair, her cane close at hand. Soft snores escaped her open mouth.

"Mama?" Audrey touched Rebecca's cheek, and the old woman opened her eyes.

Audrey smiled. "Mama, Lexie and I have come to see you. How are you?"

She struggled to sit up, so Audrey and Lexie helped her. "Better, now that you two are here."

Rebecca indicated Lexie should place some chairs on each side of hers so she and Audrey could sit.

"Your mother and brother came by earlier this morning. Steven looks like David."

"I know. He even has some of the same mannerisms, Gran."

"Yes, and you and Olivia are cut from the same cloth."

"We look like you, Granny Becky."

She glanced at Audrey, then took Rebecca's thin, blue-veined hand. The skin felt as fragile as parchment.

"Grammy was telling me stories you'd told her about your mother, Alexandria. Will you tell me some more?"

Rebecca nodded. Lexie smiled and caressed the old woman's hand. "I just found out Uncle Samuel is your half-brother. Lance and I are flying out to see him soon."

"Good old Sammy. He's almost as old as I am. Let's see. Mama had him in 1932, and the way I remember, he was always such a curious boy. Into everything. Didn't he become a teacher in Texas, Audrey?"

Audrey nodded.

"Why are you going to see him?"

"I want to retrieve the pictures and diaries he has in some old trunks in his attic."

"Ah, yes. Our family treasures. Someone borrowed them to do something with." She frowned. "I don't remember who I loaned them to, though, or why."

She remained quiet for several moments while she tried to remember. Finally, she shook her head and wiped away a tear. "My memory's fading. I just can't remember."

Seeing her mother's distress, Audrey patted her hand. "Don't worry, Mom. Lexie and I will find the trunks. Tell us more about your mother."

Lexie started the recorder.

"My mama had the heart of a lion. Nothing seemed to stop her, not even the hand-to-mouth days of the Great Depression or the loss of Daddy. She survived two World Wars and everything that came between. She cheered when the end came for the murderers, Bonnie Parker and Clyde Barrow, and she mourned when the country buried FDR. I think she inherited a lot of the old pioneering spirit because she always wanted adventure and to see and learn new things. Life with her was never boring, even when we didn't know where our next meal would come from."

"Did she have family members to help during the hard times?" Lexie couldn't imagine what hardships her great-great-grandmother had faced, and she gave thanks for the comfortable life she'd had so far, though she wondered what kind of changes would come to her in Guatemala. Would some of them be as hard as Alexandria had faced? Her throat tightened. Would people say she had the heart of a lion? Or that nothing seemed to stop her?

"Oh, yes. For a few years, we lived with Grandma and Grandpa West on their farm. We didn't have money, but we did have food and a roof over our heads."

West?

Chill bumps raised on Lexie's arm, and she sat up straighter.

"Gran, what was Alexandria's name before she married Louis Garth?"

"She was Alexandria West Bell. Albert Bell was my daddy, but she was born to Olivia Anne Johnson and Franklin West."

"Do you know who his father was?" Lexie's whole body tensed as she waited for Rebecca to answer. The old woman closed her eyes, and her face puckered.. Finally, she answered, though she continued to frown.

"Some days I can remember things, and some days I can't,

Granddaughter, but I think we called him Pappy Corbin."

Johnson? Bell? West? Could it be? Did the blood of the people she loved from the nineteenth century run through her veins? How could that be? If this were true, from which Johnson, Bell, and West men had she descended? The faces of Jonathan, Jesse, Sean, Ben, Dwight, and Mattie were as clear in her mind as if she'd seen them only yesterday, and she had difficulty visualizing any of them as her ancestor.

Disoriented and light-headed, Lexie stood. "I'm going to run to the restroom for a minute. I'll be right back." She handed the recorder to Audrey.

Lexie splashed cold water on her face and stared into the mirror. Though her eyes were open, she looked at her life as it had been in 1857.

"Can this be true, Lord?" she whispered. The tight, pressing feeling returned along with a sense of urgency.

When Lexie returned several minutes later, Audrey was helping Rebecca to her room. She handed Lexie the recorder. "Mama's tired, so I'll help her get back in bed."

"Wait." Rebecca held up a trembling hand and looked at Lexie. "Did you bring the violin?"

"Yes, it's in the car. Do you want me to play for you now, Gran?"

"Yes."

By the time Lexie returned, violin case in hand, Audrey had covered Rebecca with a quilt. The air conditioner made a soft purring sound.

"Is there anything special you want me to play, Granny Becky?"

"Play songs about heaven and Jesus."

Lexie progressed through only one verse of "My Jesus, I Love Thee" before Rebecca slept soundly. Audrey bent and kissed her mother, and then tiptoed out of the room with Lexie.

"Mama gets a lot of pleasure out of hearing you play. Perhaps you could make a recording of songs so she can listen anytime she wants. She has a CD player on her nightstand. With all this technology, making a CD should be easy, right?"

She nodded and thought of the pleasure on Fergus' face as he listened to the music on her iPod. "Yes, I can make a CD."

After Lexie dropped Audrey by her house, she phoned Olivia.

"Hey, Mom. Are you busy this afternoon?"

"What's up, sweetheart?"

"I want to get as much of the wedding shopping done as I can before I leave for Texas. Do you want to come with me?"

"I'd love to. Where are you now?"

"Just dropped Grammy off."

"Okay. Swing by, and I'll be ready. See you soon."

In a matter of hours, Lexie breathed a sigh of relief at the number of things she and her mother had accomplished. She felt lighter.

"The most pressing thing you need to do now is to choose your wedding gown and what you want the others in your wedding party to wear." Olivia checked off entries in her planner and turned toward Lexie as they drove home. "I know you've been looking on-line and in stores for the right dress. Haven't you found anything yet?"

"Not yet, though there are a couple of dresses I might consider. Once I get back from Texas, I'll decide on something."

Olivia nodded.

"Anna and Sharon from the church said they'd make your bridesmaids' dresses as part of their gift to you and Lance. I expect the sooner we can get the patterns, materials, and notions to them, the sooner they can start. They did a lovely job with Natalie's bridesmaids' dresses, didn't they?"

"Yes, they were beautiful. When I get back, we can look for patterns."

"Mom, I also want to invite Kimberly and Weston Bell to the wedding. Maybe Kim would like to be a bridesmaid."

"You don't know her very well, do you?"

"I haven't known her long, but I feel I know her fairly well." Lexie thought of the Mary-look-alike and smiled. "We've talked a lot on the phone. She's helping me with some research."

"What about the numbers of bridesmaids and groomsmen? Won't they be uneven?"

"Lance and I'll figure that out. Who knows? Maybe Weston can be convinced to make up one of the party."

"All right. We ordered extra invitations just in case." She heard the shrug in her mom's voice.

Lexie called Kimberly that evening and smiled at her cousin's excited acceptance. She heard Weston in the background telling his sister to relay some information to Lance, but Lexie gave Lance's number to her instead and told Weston to call Lance himself.

"I'll buy both your tickets, Kim. You'll fly out of Portland, right? Do you think you'll be able to come out a couple of days early? You and Weston are welcome to stay here with us."

"I think so. Your wedding is Friday, September 19, right? Well, classes don't start until the 29, so that'll work. What about the bridesmaid's dress?"

"I'll get back to you on that within the next couple of weeks."

"I talked to Dad about the Bell family history, Lexie, and he gave me some names. I'll send what I have to your email."

"What did you find out?"

"Daddy is Nathan Bell. His dad is Randall Bell, and Randall's dad was Aaron. Aaron's sister was Katheryn. I'm still searching online archives for the names you gave me."

"Did your dad know Aaron's father's name?"

"He said he'd heard, but didn't remember. He'll let me know if anything comes to him."

"Thanks for checking, Kim. I appreciate your help so much. I'm looking forward to seeing you again."

They chatted for a while, then Lexie closed the conversation. "Send your size and measurements to me when you get a chance."

Lexie sat at her desk, a large, flat-screen iMac in front of her, and listened to Rebecca's audio file. She stared at the Bell family photo while she listened to her great-grandmother's voice. All the photos she'd shown Lance earlier, plus the ones she'd bought from the photographer, were spread around her work area. She was so focused, she didn't hear Lance enter.

"Lexie?"

She startled and turned. "Hi, you."

"Hi, yourself. What are you doing?" He stepped next to her and kissed the top of her head.

"Pull up that stool, and I'll show you." Lexie made space for him and pointed to the spreadsheet she'd created to keep her information organized. "I've started to work backward from the twenty-first century to the nineteenth. See? The columns represent spans of years in decades, and just below the header information, I've put any important events Gran, Grammy, or any other relatives associated with my ancestors. Below this, I've put the names of family members in their decades. What do you think?"

Lance studied the information she'd entered. "I'm impressed. I heard Rebecca talking about Alexandria when I came in. She must've been something."

"Yes. Did you pay attention to who she said Alexandria's parents were? Their last names were West, Lance. West and Johnson, with a Bell thrown in."

"Do you think their names could be a coincidence?" Lance sorted through the historical photos and stopped on the one of Nate

Johnson, Jesse Johnson, Jonathan Johnson, and Sean West. He laid the Bell family photo next to the images.

"Do you?"

He studied the photos for a few more moments. "No."

Lance stared at the image of Sean West. "So you think Sean is an ancestor?"

"Well, either he or his brother, Ben, would be the most likely candidates given their association with the Bells and the Johnsons. I think it's reasonable to assume that if they stayed near each other after they all married, their children would have grown up together."

"Tell me about Ben."

She did, and when she finished, she studied the photos again.

"I feel like I'm a puzzle piece, Lance. I don't know where I fit. The Bells, Johnsons, Wests and all the relatives in between are also pieces. I don't know where the edges are, or what the whole picture looks like. I don't understand why the Lord wants me to figure this out, but there's an urging in my spirit to do so."

"Then you'd better find out. I don't want you to be sent back to the nineteenth century to learn more lessons."

Lexie eyed her leather bag and ran her fingers over the scar. "Don't even think that."

She collected the photos into a stack and saved the spreadsheet.

"Hey, do you have to go right away, or can you stay and help me make a music CD for Gran? You can monitor the settings in Garage Band while I play the violin. I'll switch to the keyboard for the last songs."

"Sure."

Lexie caught the pleasant aroma coming from the kitchen. "Do you want to stay for dinner?"

At his nod, she said, "I'll let Mom know."

When she returned, they began the recording session and only paused long enough to eat dinner. The CD was finished by nine that evening.

"I made Grammy a CD, too. I'll drop them by tomorrow." Lexie held up the copies for her mom to see, then laid them on the counter as she walked Lance to the door.

Lexie and Lance left for the airport as soon as he got off work on Thursday. Lexie climbed into the co-pilot's seat and strapped herself in while Lance talked to the tower and went through the pre-flight routine. She looked around the cabin and noted the four passenger seats in the aft cabin and the small toilet. She hoped she wouldn't need to use the tiny facilities during their forty-five-minute flight, though she didn't have any confidence she wouldn't suffer from motion sickness if they hit a pocket of turbulence. To spare her stomach, she'd not eaten anything that afternoon, but she'd drunk a glass of stevia-sweetened ice water with ginger.

Lance handled the controls with ease, and once they reached their cruising altitude, he lowered the microphone of his headset and smiled. "I wonder what 'treat' your great-uncle has in store for us tomorrow? I'm curious to see what an octogenarian considers fun."

Lexie laughed. "Well, we probably won't hike the Palo Duro Canyon. But Uncle Samuel does work cattle. The treat might involve an adventure from the back of a horse."

"Hmm. Sounds like a good way to return home—stiff from saddle sores."

In a seemingly short amount of time, they landed in Amarillo, and Lance taxied to the General Aviation area.

"How will we get to Uncle Sam's?" Lexie hoped Lance had

thought about this little detail.

"TAC Air has arranged everything. They're the FBO here in Amarillo."

"What's an FBO?"

"Fixed Base Operator. They'll bring an SUV plane-side after we park. I thought we'd grab a bite before heading to the ranch."

"Great idea. I'm starving."

Two hours later, they sat on Samuel Garth's sofa and listened to the remarkably agile old man tell about his experiences as a history professor at West Texas A&M. From there, he told Lexie and Lance how he'd found and bought the ranch, and then began asking them questions about Rebecca.

"Gran said you were a very curious little boy and got into everything."

Sam chuckled. "She would know. Mama always told Becky and Ruth to keep an eye on me while she worked, but I think doing so was a difficult job. When I was six, I slipped away from my sisters and hid in Grandpa West's silo. They looked everywhere for me. Ruth found my cap near the pond, and they thought I'd drowned. Eventually, they found me asleep on the grain in the silo. I explained to them I didn't mean to fall asleep-that I was only teasing them. I used my best innocent-little-boy look, but Becky boxed my ears anyway and told me if I ever did such a thing again, she'd make me sorry."

Lexie tried to picture a nine-year-old Rebecca, but couldn't. Gran had always seemed old to her.

She checked the recorder to make sure the device was still on. "What do you remember about your mother's folks?"

"We lived with them during the Great Depression. They had a farm in Kansas. My daddy, Louis, had to find work wherever he could, so he traveled a lot. We stayed with Grandma Olivia Anne and Grandpa Frank. They raised their food and animals, so even though we didn't have money, we had food in our bellies. Many didn't. The farm was a great place for a little boy like me."

"When you think of Olivia Anne and Franklin, how would you describe them?"

"Well, physically, you look a lot like Grandma Olivia—same height, same coloring, similar features. She wasn't as strong as you look to be and her teeth weren't as straight. We didn't have braces back in those days. Grandpa had light-brown hair and gray eyes. He was a little under six feet tall and carried himself well. Most people thought he was a doctor or teacher instead of a missionary-turned-farmer."

Lance straightened. "A missionary? Where?"

"He and Grandma Olivia worked with the Cherokee in Oklahoma. In 1838, the Cherokee were forcibly removed from their homes in the Southeastern United States and relocated to Oklahoma, which back then was called Indian Territory."

Samuel tilted his head. "You ever heard of the Trail of Tears?"

Both Lexie and Lance nodded.

"Well, in 1907, Grandma and Grandpa moved to Oklahoma right after they were married. Olivia was twenty, and Frank was twenty-three. They stayed there for many years and served the Cherokees. Mama was born in Oklahoma and grew up with the Cherokee children. They sure loved those people. Talked about them all the time."

"Olivia Anne and Frank moved to Oklahoma from where, Uncle Sam?"

"Oregon," he said, "Or maybe Boston. I don't remember for sure, but I do remember Grandma Olivia Anne talking about relatives in Oregon and Boston. I didn't know where either place was at the time."

Lexie's eyes widened, and she tensed. The fingers of her right hand began to caress the scar.

"Gran said Alexandria was married to a Bell before she married your dad—Ruth and Rebecca's father. Do you know much about him?"

"Not much. His name was Albert, and he was the son of Robert Bell and Martha Johnson. The only reason I know this is because I played with Albert's daughter, Katheryn, and his son Aaron, and they talked about them."

Aaron and Katheryn. Kimberly's ancestors.

Samuel must have seen the confusion on her face when she asked, "Albert was married before? He had a son and daughter, who would've been your step-sister and step-brother?"

"Yes, he was a widower before he married Mama. His children lived with other relatives instead of us, though they sometimes came to visit."

The old man made no other comment about his step-siblings, and she wondered why Gran hadn't mentioned them.

"What happened to Aaron and Katheryn, Uncle Sam?"

"Aaron died when his B-17 was shot down by the Germans in 1944. Katheryn married a man named A.P. Harper, but died of cancer in the seventies."

A.P. Harper. The man in Albuquerque who might have the trunks.

The grandfather clock chimed, and Samuel stood. "Well, it's eleven o'clock. We'd better hit the hay because I want to take you to a special place tomorrow. Follow me, and I'll show you to your rooms."

Lexie noted the ease with which her great-uncle climbed the stairs and grinned at Lance.

He whispered, "What are the chances this place is only accessible by horseback?"

"Pretty good, I'd imagine," she whispered back.

In her room, Lexie looked at the clock, calculated the time in Oregon, and dialed Kimberly.

"Hey, it's me. Guess what? I know how we're related. Wait until you hear what I've learned."

They finished the conversation twenty minutes later, and Lexie turned out the light and got into bed. She now knew how she was related to Kimberly, but she still sensed there was more she needed to find out.

"What do you want me to learn, Lord?" she whispered and snuggled under the covers. Her eyes drooped. "Please help me be quicker at figuring things out than I was when You sent me back in time."

FIVE

Lance was obviously relieved when, instead of piling onto the back of a horse, they piled into the air-conditioned SUV.

"Better to take your rig," Samuel commented as he pointed to his dented and paint-peeling truck. The vehicle looked as old as he was. "Not enough room to ride three comfortably. Besides, the engine's started to make noise."

Lance followed Sam's directions, and they pulled up in front of a huge building on the West Texas A&M campus in Canyon, Texas.

"This is the Panhandle-Plains Historic Museum—the largest in the state of Texas. Had to come on Friday because they're not open on Saturdays."

For the next four hours, they admired the exhibits. Lance enjoyed the huge antique oil rig exhibit, the antique cars, and the extensive weapons collection the most. Lexie was particularly interested in the Civil War display and studied the pictures carefully to see if she recognized any of the dead. The life-sized pioneer town set up in the basement also fascinated her. She looked at the log cabin and explained to Lance how the Bell's soddy had been arranged.

"Thanks, Sam," Lance said as he drove them to a nearby restaurant for lunch, "That was a treat. I'd like to come back sometime and bring my dad. He'd enjoy seeing this."

Back at the ranch, Sam told Lexie she could spend the rest of the day in the attic going through the trunks if she wanted, though he thought this activity sounded like a boring way to spend the afternoon.

"I want to show Lance the place and introduce him to a few people. You okay with this? We'll be back for supper."

She nodded. Lexie could tell Lance was hoping the tour would be done from a vehicle and not from a saddle.

"Let's take the SUV, Sam, since your truck needs repair. I'll be happy to drive."

I bet you will. Lexie grinned, and Lance smiled in recognition of her thoughts.

"There're all kinds of food in the kitchen if you get hungry, Lexie, and Jenny will be in around five to cook our supper."

"Thanks. I appreciate you letting me do this. Preserving family history is important to Audrey and me. We're hoping to save everything digitally so the other family members can enjoy learning about our ancestors."

"Well, whatever is up there is yours. Someone'll have to do something with all the stuff after I die, so better to deal with the junk now rather than later. I don't have any kids or grandkids to give anything to."

"I hope you won't die for a long time, Uncle Sam."

Samuel smiled and patted her cheek. "Everybody's got to go sooner or later, niece."

When Lexie climbed the stairs to the attic and opened the door, she gasped in dismay. She'd need hours to look through everything. She surveyed the room from wall to wall. She'd have to try and bring order out of chaos and make space. With decisive movements, she began to reorganize the attic. After one hour, she'd moved all the furniture pieces to one side of the room, placed the boxes side-by-side on the other wall, and pushed the two large trunks to the middle of the floor. After two hours, she'd opened the boxes and scanned the contents of each, and after three, she'd opened the lid of the first trunk and read several of the letters. There were no diaries, and most of the papers were letters, newspaper clippings, tax records, and memorabilia Harriet, Samuel's dead wife, had collected.

At the end of four hours, Lexie opened the second trunk and reached for the large cardboard box resting on top of other boxes of various sizes. She removed the lid with care, and her breath caught when she realized what lay inside. With gentle fingers, she lifted the creamy lace wedding gown from the box and watched the fabric unfurl as she held the dress against her. Thirty-six satin-covered buttons stacked one above another, closed the front of the lace overdress. When closed, the buttons looked like a long straight strand of creamy pearls that reached from the neck to four inches below the tapered waist. The wide lace collar on each side of the buttons was scalloped around the edges, and the material matched the delicate lace on the dress. The collar was wider in front than in back and laid flat on the bodice and shoulders. Underneath the long-sleeved overdress was a thin-strapped silken gown of the same creamy white.

Lexie stepped toward the old cheval mirror. The material hung to her ankles in graceful folds, and the train of cream-colored netting pooled on the floor near her feet. She stared at her image. This was the dress. This would be the dress she'd wear at her wedding, assuming the size was right.

With extremely careful movements, Lexie unbuttoned several buttons on the overdress. She removed her clothes then slid the silky underdress over her head. The dress settled around her figure in a perfect fit. When she donned the overdress and buttoned the satin buttons, she could only stare at her reflection. With a different hairdo, she'd be looking at a woman from the early- to mid-nineteenth century.

After several moments in front of the mirror, Lexie removed the wedding dress and put on her clothes. She returned the dress to its box and reached for the lid. She examined the faded script near the top right-hand corner. "The dress my mama, Olivia Anne Johnson, wore on the day of her marriage to my father, Franklin Benjamin West. 1907."

Franklin Benjamin West?

Shoes, hats, and other clothing from the 1900s lay below the dress. Old photos rested at the bottom of the trunk, and Lexie's heart pounded in her throat. Uncle Sam said she could take what she wanted, and if he really meant what he said, she'd take the dress and the contents of this trunk.

Lexie could scarcely contain her excitement while she waited for the men. She took a three-mile round-trip run down the road and then returned to shower and help Jenny, Samuel's cook, prepare the meal.

"I can tell you've found something," Lance said as soon as he stepped into the living room with Sam. "Your rosy cheeks and sparkling eyes give you away."

Lexie nodded and spoke to her uncle, "I found Olivia Anne's wedding dress and some clothes from the nineteenth century. There are a few photographs. Are you sure I can take these, Uncle Sam?"

"Of course, Lexie. What would I do with Grandma's wedding

dress and a trunkful of old clothes? They would've stayed shut away in the attic or been given to a museum if I'd remembered they were there."

Lexie and Lance remained another day with Samuel and then returned home. They stored the large, heavy trunk between the four seats in the aft cabin.

"I sure wish Uncle Sam would've agreed to come to our wedding. He says he's too old to get on a plane, but I think he's scared to fly, Lance."

"That old man is Alexandria's son. I don't think he's scared of much, though if he is, maybe I can fly out and pick him up."

"Would you?"

"Sure."

Lexie reached for his hand and kissed his fingers. "I love you, Lance. I give thanks every day I'm back here with you."

He removed his sunglasses and headset and looked in her eyes. "You don't know how grateful I am the Lord allowed you to return to me. I thank Him every day we have a future together."

He caressed her cheek then put the sunglasses and headset back on.

She laid her head on the backrest and thought of the wedding dress and the plans she'd have to make when she got home.

"Lance?"

He turned toward her. She knew he could hear her without removing the headset.

"Would you have any objections to having a theme-based wedding?"

"What do you mean?"

"I intend to wear Olivia Anne's wedding dress, and the wedding party would look strange if they wore twenty-first-century garb while I wore nineteenth century. I'd like for the matron of honor, the three bridesmaids, you, and your groomsmen to wear period dress to match. I don't know if I can convince Dad, Mom, and your parents to join us, but I think we'd have fun if they would. The theme is really *family* with a historical twist."

He considered the idea as he looked at her. "What we wear isn't important to me, hon. That we become man and wife is, so do whatever you like. Let me know what I need to do and what I need to pay for."

Lexie tried to visualize how everyone would look—what they would wear and how they would stand or sit for the photographs, but the image was unbalanced. She remembered the unequal number of people in the bridal party.

"Lance, did Weston call you the other day?"

He grinned. "Yes, he's hoping we can get together before the wedding and play racquetball. The sport seems to be his new favorite."

Lexie laughed. "He reminds me so much of an older version of Mattie. What do you think of him standing up with you as a groomsman since Kim will make the numbers uneven."

"Do you think you can get him into any formal wear?"

"You have a point," she said. "If I can convince him, do you mind having him?"

"No." One side of Lance's mouth quirked up. "I should probably ask him instead of you, babe. Maybe he'll take the request better if the question comes from me."

Back in Topeka, Lance drove Lexie home, hauled the trunk to her room and said good-bye to the Logans.

Following Destiny

"What's in the trunk, Lexie?" Olivia asked. She, David, and Steven studied the markings on the sides. "Did you find the diaries and letters?"

"No, but I found my wedding dress, Mom. The dress belonged to great-great-great-grandmother Olivia Anne West. I'll show you as soon as I wash my hands."

When David and Steven found out the trunk contained only old clothes and photos, they headed downstairs to watch television.

"Oh, it's beautiful, honey," Olivia exclaimed when Lexie held up the dress for her inspection, "It's so feminine, and the lines are excellent. You'll look stunning."

She held up the matching slippers and frowned. "Do you intend to wear these?"

"No, they're too fragile. I'll get some low heels in the same color."

Olivia quoted, "Something old, something new, right?"

"What?"

"Haven't you heard the expression that brides should wear something old, something new, something borrowed, and something blue?"

"Not until now."

"Well, the dress is old, the shoes will be new, and we'll have to think about something borrowed and something blue if you want to stick to tradition. I wore a blue garter for my wedding. Your dad removed the thing at the reception and shot it into the crowd of single men like brides usually toss their bouquets to the group of unmarried females."

Lexie explained her ideas for the theme and held her breath to see what her mother would say.

Olivia stared at the wedding gown now hanging from the door of the closet. She finally nodded. "We should start looking for patterns and select materials this week. I'll check with the cleaners to see how the dress should be cleaned."

Audrey called on Monday.

"Lexie, do you think you can look on the internet and see if William Moore has a phone number? We should've heard something from him by now."

"He's in Denver, right?"

"Yes."

"Okay, Grammy. Mom and I are at the fabric store. I'll look when I get home."

"Oh, A.P. called and left a message while you were gone. He said he'd put some trunks in storage when he moved into a smaller place but didn't remember if the trunks belonged to his deceased wife, Katheryn, or to us. Guess what?" she said laughing. "He said you could come and look. He said any weekend is good for him. I texted you his number. Just call and let him know."

"Yikes! I wonder what Lance will say if I ask him to fly me to Albuquerque?"

"He's going to say he'll fly you to the moon or anyplace else you'd like to go. I've seen the way he looks at you."

Olivia's mouth tightened when Lexie told her she needed to fly out on Friday after Lance got off work to meet with A. P. Harper in Albuquerque, New Mexico.

"Do you think finding all this family memorabilia is as important as preparing for your wedding?"

Lexie could feel her mother's frustration. How could she explain?

"Yes, finding answers is important, Mom. I think the information I'll find will impact my future."

"How so?"

Lexie paused to frame her words, "I don't think I can tell you because I don't know. I feel I have to search."

Olivia considered Lexie's words and shrugged. Her mouth curled into a rueful smile. "I guess you've got to do what you've got to do."

Lexie hugged her. "Hopefully, William Moore won't tell me to come to Denver and look for myself."

"William Moore? You think Gran may have loaned the documents to him?" Olivia's eyebrows rose. "I don't see why she'd do that. He's only related by marriage. Grammy calls him uncle, though there's no blood connection."

"Is he a professor?"

"He was. I think he taught at Colorado State University."

"Grammy said the man who borrowed the trunks was a professor, and he wanted to use some of the information in a paper he was writing. Do you think William Moore could have asked to borrow the documents?"

"Oh, I guess her lending the trunks to him is possible, though I don't know what a professor of agriculture would want with them."

"Agriculture?"

"Yes, if I remember correctly, he was associated with that department or school, or whatever they called the place back then."

Suddenly, Olivia stopped in front of a bolt of lace in a creamy tan. "Lexie, look at this. The color would look fabulous next to your wedding dress."

Lexie held the fabric toward the light and turned the material in different directions. As always, Olivia's sense of color was perfect.

"Wow, this has an antique-modern look. The bridesmaid can wear this over a silk underdress in a similar tone. Since I'll wear long sleeves, I think I want the bridesmaids' and matron's dresses to be sleeveless with simple lines. I can picture a lace bodice connecting to a wide, neck-hugging, scalloped-edged collar."

"What about adding a wide satin waistband in a creamy white to match your dress? A simple, palm-sized decorative rose in the same color as the band would be beautiful to add to the center of the waistband."

Lexie visualized the dresses and nodded.

"It's a good thing Patty, Kimberly, and your friend, Sienna, all have toned figures. The style and color should look good on all of them."

Back in her room, Lexie sat down in front of the computer and typed William Moore, Denver, Colorado, into the search bar. She sighed when she saw the results. After studying the entries, she called Audrey.

"Hi, Grammy. There are more than sixty William Moores in Denver, Colorado. The list includes anyone named Will or Bill. Even if I eliminate all those under seventy, more than half the listings include men over seventy or those of unknown age."

"Well, we can't call all of them to see if they're the right person, so I guess we'll have to wait a bit longer to see if he'll respond. I hope he hasn't died."

"Mom said he's not a blood relative."

"She's right. He was an old family friend of ours, but we called him uncle out of respect."

"Grammy," Lexie hesitated. "Uncle Sam said Alexandria's first husband, Albert Bell, was a widower with two children."

"Yes. Katheryn and Aaron were his daughter and son. They were a few years older than Mama and Ruth. Both are dead now."

"Why do you suppose Gran didn't say a word about them when she told me stories? Uncle Sam said he played with Katheryn and Aaron when they came to visit."

"Mama doesn't say much about them, so I can't speculate. Ask A.P. when you see him. Katheryn was his wife. If he doesn't tell you much, maybe you should ask Gran the next time you visit. Oh, that reminds me. She said she loves the music CD you made for her and listens to the songs every day."

"I'm glad."

Lexie spent the rest of the afternoon in front of the computer screen looking for vintage patterns, searching through ancestry records, and reading about the history, politics, and geography of Guatemala. Two hours before Lance picked her up for Bible study at seven, she turned off the monitor, rubbed her eyes, went for a run and had a bite for dinner.

"I'm so glad to get away from the computer," she said as she slid into the passenger seat of Lance's car, stretched toward him for his kiss, and buckled in. "My brain is on overload."

"Did you find what you wanted?" He pulled away from the curb.

"I ordered patterns for both the bridesmaids' dresses and you and the groomsmen. Once they come in, we'll take them and the materials to the ladies who will sew the outfits."

"Will they be comfortable?"

Lexie laughed. "I hope so. I'll tell the ladies to sew in extra comfort."

"Any luck with the ancestry searches?"

"Not yet."

"Did you learn anything interesting about Guatemala?"

Could he see the trouble in her eyes at his question? "The country's had a violent and turbulent history, Lance. During the first ten years of their Civil War, which began in 1990, thousands of people were victims of state-sponsored terror. During the first part of the war, the targets were primarily students, workers, professionals, and opponents of the government, but then the fighting spread to combatants."

She shook her head and closed her eyes. "Did you know more than four hundred fifty Mayan villages were destroyed? The Mayans were the targets of government-sponsored genocide."

"Yes. During that time, more than two hundred thousand people died and more than a million people were displaced."

"Do you know what the most hurtful information I read was?"

"No, what?"

"Our government supported the dictators who ruled Guatemala. The CIA trained their paramilitary forces."

They remained silent for most of the drive to the church.

"Lance, the war ended in 1996. That's only eighteen years ago. How do you think the people will respond to us? Will we be hated? Will we be targets?"

"I don't know."

When they pulled into the church parking lot, Lance shut off the engine and turned toward her. He held out his hand to her. She smiled as she twined her fingers with his.

"Here's what I do know, Lexie. God has called us to go. He's asked for two years of our lives—one to be spent in Costa Rica, and one to be spent in service to him in Guatemala. He's sovereign, babe. He's omniscient. He's the Heart- Knower. There's nothing he doesn't know about the situation we're going into, but he's still calling to us."

She didn't reply because she thought of what she'd told the Bells about fighting the institution of slavery if God left her in the past. She'd told the family she would leave their home if this idea made them uncomfortable, and Fergus had asked where she'd go. She'd replied, "Away." The Lord had responded.

Even to Guatemala, Lexie? The people who sit in darkness need the Light.

"Turn to Second Corinthians, chapter eleven," Pastor Jeff said when all of the Bible study participants had seated themselves at the round table. "When we left off last week, Paul was deeply concerned about the church in Corinth. They'd begun to follow false teachers, and Paul felt forced to justify his apostolic credentials. In verses thirteen through fifteen, he no longer speaks with veiled irony, but comes right out and tells the church these false prophets are Satan's emissaries. Both they and their doctrine are false. Paul would not sacrifice truth for unity. Do you remember some of the Corinthians compared Paul unfavorably to the false apostles? And he decided to answer fools according to their folly?"

When everyone nodded, Pastor Jeff continued, "Let's pick up at verse sixteen."

Lexie tried hard to stay focused, but her thoughts dwelt on what she'd learned about Guatemala. She tried to squelch the fear wanting to surface.

> *"… in stripes above measure, in prisons more frequently, in deaths often."*

Lexie blinked and focused.

> *... five times I received forty stripes minus one. Three times I was beaten with rods; once I was stoned; three times I was shipwrecked; a night and a day I have been in the deep; in journeys often, in perils of water, in perils of robbers, in perils of my own countrymen, in perils of the Gentiles, in perils in the city, in perils in the wilderness, in perils in the sea, in perils among false brethren; in weariness and toil, in sleeplessness often, in hunger and thirst, in fastings often, in cold and nakedness ..."*

Lexie straightened. Paul had suffered all these dangers because he preached the gospel everywhere he went. She wouldn't experience even a tenth of what Paul went through while she and Lance were in Guatemala. Though almost two millennia separated her from Paul, he was a human just like she was. So how did he handle all his fears and trials? Did his success come from his mindset?

"Do you remember what Paul wrote in Acts, chapter twenty, when he said, 'I go bound in the spirit to Jerusalem, not knowing the things that will happen to me there, except that the Holy Spirit testifies in every city, saying chains and tribulations await me.'?"

The pulse in Lexie's throat pounded. She drew her Bible closer and turned to verse twenty-four in the twentieth chapter of Acts and read along.

"He wrote, 'But none of these things move me; nor do I count my life dear to myself, so that I may finish my race with joy, and the ministry which I received from the Lord Jesus, to testify to the gospel of the grace of God.'"

Pastor Jeff looked at each of his students. "Paul finished his race with joy. In the letter he wrote to Timothy just before he was beheaded, Paul told his friend, 'I have fought a good fight, I have finished my course, I have kept the faith: Henceforth there is laid up for me a crown of righteousness which the Lord, the righteous judge, shall give me at that day: and not to me only, but unto all them also that love his appearing.'"

Lexie remained silent as they drove home from the study.

Lance didn't speak until he'd pulled into the Logan's driveway.

"So, what are you thinking?"

"I was comparing Paul's tribulations to those I might experience in Guatemala and feeling ashamed of myself."

"I'm nervous too, sweetheart."

"Nothing much seems to bother you, Lance. You do all things well. You're smart, strong, sure of yourself, and-"

His eyes widened, and he laughed. "Are you kidding?"

She shook her head.

"Lexie, I'm giving up a job with benefits and a relatively secure future to take my soon-to-be bride into a foreign country to begin the first years of our lives together. There are a lot of unknowns. I don't know the language yet, and even after I finish school, I don't know how proficient I'll be in Spanish. I've never had to communicate in a language other than English, and I've never had to live without the comforts money provides. Oh, yes, I've spent weeks at a time camping in the woods, but I always returned to a comfortable home with a reliable source of clean, hot water, a well-stocked refrigerator, and a memory foam mattress. The Lord knows my fears and insecurities, but I've given them to him. Being moved so far out of my comfort zone forces me to rely on him, not on myself. Understand?"

"Yes. 1857 was the same for me."

She massaged the scar and sighed. "I just wish the lessons were easier to learn, and once I learned what I was supposed to, I could move on to another, but I seem to have to keep relearning the same lessons."

"Control is the issue, right?"

Not your will, but mine, Lexie.

"Yes."

"Well, I'm relying on the words of the Lord. He said we would have trouble in this world, but he would leave and give his peace to those of us who love him. The peace won't be what the world gives, hon, but he said not to let our hearts be troubled or afraid. We have to trust him with our lives and our futures. Are you willing to do that?"

"Yes."

"Even in Guatemala?"

"Yes."

He walked her to the door. "I'm glad you've decided to marry me. Lexie Olivia Logan Garrett has a nice ring, don't you think?"

She smiled and kissed him. "A lovely ring. Night, love."

SIX

Lexie grabbed her leather bag and opened the door of her hotel room to Lance. They'd shuttled from the Albuquerque International Sunport to a nearby hotel. A.P. Harper planned to pick them up and take them to dinner at a little Mexican restaurant not too far from the hotel.

"I should've insisted on driving," Lance murmured when he saw A.P.'s aged, stooped, and sparse frame unwind itself from the seat of his small, battered, four-door sedan.

"Pretend you're getting onto a crowded bus or into a taxi in Guatemala," Lexie whispered, "I've heard a person takes his life into his hands when he gets into a public conveyance in some of these countries. Maybe this is the first step in preparing us for a new experience."

"Very funny."

Lexie shook hands with A.P., then introduced Lance.

Lance opened the door for her, and then slid into his side of the backseat beside her and buckled in. Lexie smiled. She didn't have to be a mind reader to know what he was thinking. If he sat up front, he might be a distraction to A.P., and he wanted the man fully focused on his driving. Lance tensed as soon as A.P. put the car in gear and drew away from the curb, and when he glanced at her seatbelt, Lexie grinned.

He returned the grin and shrugged.

"Thank you for letting us come to search the trunks. The contents are very important to my grandmother and great-grandmother."

He nodded.

"What do your initials stand for, A.P.?"

"Alexander Phineas. Now you know why I use initials."

"Phineas is unusual. Does one of your ancestors have the same name?"

He didn't say anything until he'd crossed a busy intersection without mishap. His sigh of relief matched Lance's.

"My granddaddy, Justin Harper, was a son of Susana Bell and Lee Harper. Susana was related to a couple of women who had fathers who were twins. I was named for each of the twins, though Daddy never told me why. My guess is they were excellent businessmen because those are the skills my dad admired. When I was in elementary school, the kids used to make fun of my name, so I started using my initials."

Susana Bell?

"Do you know Susana's parents' names?"

"Sorry, no."

Lexie pulled out her phone and clicked on the calculator. Assuming each generation of parents began childbearing in their early twenties, Susana's parents would have lived in 1857. Chill bumps raised on her arms. Were his ancestors related to Mattie or Dwight?

Lexie doubted Edna had any more children. She touched the photo app and stared at the Bell family photo for several moments. Lexie looked up and saw Lance watching her.

A.P. slowed and tried to parallel park in front of a house in an older, residential-looking neighborhood. He was successful after two tries.

"I know the place doesn't look like much, and it's off the beaten path," A.P. said, "but they've got the best Mexican food around."

Lexie hoped so. She didn't want to be sick for the remainder of her stay.

After the waitress took their orders, Lexie looked at A.P.

"Grammy said you were a professor at the University of New Mexico. What did you teach?"

A.P.'s eyebrows rose and he chuckled. "Teach? I was never a professor at UNM. I completed my graduate work there, though."

Lexie's heart sank, and she glanced at Lance. Was Denver to be her next stop? She was running out of time.

She asked about Katheryn and Aaron. Nothing he said indicated the two had any hidden secrets or peccadilloes that might cause Gran to refuse to say anything about them. When she asked if he knew of anything that might have happened, he shook his head.

Lexie sighed. She'd have to ask Gran, though there were more important things to talk about in the limited time Rebecca had left.

The food was delicious, and A.P. insisted on paying.

"Only if you allow me to drive us all to the storage unit tomorrow, A.P. You've been very gracious, and I'd like to show my appreciation. We have a comfortable SUV, and I'd be honored to drive you."

A.P. finally agreed, and Lance asked for the address of the storage facility. He typed the text into his phone as A.P gave him the information. Lexie grinned again. She knew he'd use the GPS on his phone instead of totally relying on A.P.'s directions.

Lexie battled disappointment as they pulled up in front of the metal storage unit the next morning. No matter what the trunks contained, the contents were most likely not what she hoped to find. Gran said she lent the trunks to a professor. A.P. was not, so that left William Moore in Denver, and he hadn't contacted them. She smothered a sigh and followed A.P. and Lance into the unit.

"There they are." A.P. pointed to three old trunks shoved against the wall. A hill of boxes and other items were stacked on top, so Lance and Lexie helped A.P. remove them. Lance was finally able to slide the trunks toward the front.

"They're not locked." A.P. sat on one of the boxes to catch his breath.

Lance frowned. "Are you okay?"

"Yes, just getting old and worn out. Smoking for half my life didn't help, either."

Both men watched as Lexie lifted the lid of the first trunk. She picked up the first stack of documents and looked through them, then set them aside and reached for the next.

"I found a photo." She studied the woman in the picture to see if she saw any resemblance to Mattie or Dwight. The woman looked more like Mary. She turned the photo toward the men.

"That's Katheryn. We had many good years together."

"What color were her hair and eyes?"

"Her hair was midnight black and her eyes were clear blue. She was a real beauty in her younger days."

Lexie set the photograph aside and continued digging. When she dug to the bottom of the trunk, she held up a thick, spiral-bound manuscript. "UNM. This looks like yours, A.P."

He nodded and took the manuscript from her. "My dissertation."

"What was your dissertation about?" Lexie opened the lid of the second trunk.

"I researched the—"

Just then Lexie's phone rang. She looked at the caller ID and asked A.P. to excuse her while she took the call. She stood and walked toward the door.

"Hi, Grammy. What's up?"

"I just got a letter from William Moore. He said he doesn't know about any trunks and has never borrowed anything from us."

Lexie returned and stared at the contents of the trunk she had just opened. She was silent for several moments. "Could Gran have been mistaken about the uncle being a professor? Could he have been a doctoral student instead?"

"Very possible. Mama's memory is fading."

She looked at A.P. "Listen, Grammy. I'll call you back later on this afternoon, okay?"

When Audrey hung up, Lexie turned and looked fully at A.P. "I'm sorry for the interruption. You were saying your dissertation was about ...?"

A.P. continued, "Yes. I researched the overland journey of pioneers to California and Oregon. I was particularly interested in noting the differences in perspectives between men and women who traveled the trail."

Lexie said nothing but knelt beside the trunk. Carefully, she lifted an old diary and opened the cover.

Diary of Olivia Anne Johnson West. Missionary to the Cherokee Indians, Oklahoma Indian Territory, 1907

"I've found them." Lexie smiled at Lance and A.P. and held up the diary and read the inscription aloud. "Olivia Anne was Alexandria's mother."

A.P. nodded. "Then the other trunk is probably yours too."

Lexie opened the lid of the third trunk and lifted out another diary or journal that looked older than the first. She opened the cover.

Diary of Olivia Aubry Johnson, Oregon, 1858.

Several more of Olivia's diaries filled a section of the trunk and the last was dated 1866-1867.

Lance and A.P. waited for Lexie to say something. She nodded and returned the diary to the trunk and closed the lid.

"Yes, these are the ones. Thank you for letting me come and look, A.P.""

He offered the dissertation. "Perhaps you'd be interested to hear what I had to say?"

Lexie took the manuscript. "Yes, I would. Thanks. I'll return this as soon as I've finished."

"Keep it. I have another copy."

Lance slid the trunks out of the storage unit and into the back of the SUV before returning to help Lexie and A.P. reorganize the boxes and other items.

"Lunch is on us, A.P." Lance offered, but A.P. shook his head.

"Thank you, but I have other obligations. If you'd drop me off at the house, I'd be grateful."

Two hours later, Lexie and Lance were airborne, with the trunks stored securely in the Cessna.

"Wow, do I have a lot of reading to do."

Lance lowered the microphone on his headset. "Do you want some help? If you tell me what you're looking for, I can search."

"I could use the help, Lance, but I know how much you'd hate reading all the journals and letters. I appreciate the offer, though."

"No, really." His smile was wry. "If I don't help you get through this mountain of reading, I won't see you until our wedding day. I know you."

"Okay, then. Come over in the evenings after work when you can. I'll start organizing the materials by date. When I find relevant information, I'll add what I can to my spreadsheet."

"When do you plan to start?"

"As soon as I get home."

"I figured as much. After I drop you and the trunks off, I'll go to my house and change."

"Plan on eating with us, love. I'll let Mom know."

After dinner, Lance helped Lexie rearrange the furniture so the trunks were accessible. Olivia opened the lids and stared at the contents.

Lexie turned. "Okay, I'm ready. My bookcases are cleaned out. We'll look at the dates on the letters, diaries, journals, and boxes and stack them on the shelves in order of most recent to earliest. I've labeled the shelves to make organizing easier."

"Why from most recent to earliest?" Lance handed her a box. "Early 1900s."

Lexie shrugged and placed the box on the shelf. "Only because my spreadsheet is set up that way."

They went to work and had all of one trunk and part of another unloaded before they quit three hours later. "Look at this, Lexie," Olivia exclaimed and held up a faded image. "Here's a picture of Mom, Gran, and Alexandria. The script on the back is faded but legible."

Lexie studied the picture, then placed it in the pile of images to scan.

"And you're planning on scanning and archiving all of this?"

At Lexie's nod, Olivia raised her brows and looked at Lance. "Watch out. She may forget about the wedding."

"No chance. I wouldn't miss my wedding for the world. Don't worry, Mom. Grammy said she'd help."

Olivia shook her head and waved her hand toward all the documents. "When do you hope to be finished with all of this?"

"Before Lance and I leave for Costa Rica."

Just before Olivia left, Lexie observed a look in her mother's eyes that disturbed her. Was the look disapproval? Hurt? Fear?

Lance walked to the door. "I know you're going to read for the next several hours, so I'll leave you too. Bye, hon."

She walked him to his car. When he drove away, she sprinted up the stairs to her room and chose the first letter in the stack. She propped herself up in a pile of pillows on the bed and settled herself to read. Several times, she got up to enter information into her computer.

Lexie had just noted Olivia Anne was born in 1887 and was the daughter of Rachel Johnson and Charles West when her phone rang.

"Hi, Kim. How are you?"

"I'm fine. Listen, I found some information for you. I just sent links to your email, and I've filled in more of the spreadsheet."

"Hang on. I'm at the computer now." She clicked the keys. "Got them."

Lexie opened the documents and her eyes widened. "Where did you find all this, Kim?"

"In some old Oregon census and population records for starters. I sent you links to the sites. For some of the information I found on Jesse Johnson, I read through three years of Kansas newspapers during the Civil War period. Papers listed the wounded, dead, missing or captured. Jesse was listed as wounded in the battle of Petersburg in 1864. I sent you a link to the newspaper entry."

Lexie's throat tightened as she thought of fun-loving Jesse. Poor Mary. She blinked back tears. "Did you see notification of his death?"

"No, not yet. I'll keep looking."

"You're amazing, cousin."

"Well, at least I now know my ancestors, thanks to you. Do you see, I filled in some of the information in the spreadsheet you sent me? I included only the father from each generation unless there was a Bell, West, or Johnson wife mentioned."

Sliding her finger across the spreadsheet, Lexie followed Kimberly's ancestry trail: Kimberly Bell, Nathan Bell, Randall Bell, Aaron Bell, Albert Bell (Alexandria West), *here's where we meet on the tree, Lexie* Robert Bell (Martha Johnson), Matthew Bell (Betsy Taylor West), Jim Bell (Edna).

Lexie stared at the framed Bell family photograph. She smiled at Mattie's image and whispered, "I'm glad you lived on in the DNA of your descendants, Mattie-boy. Weston's your spitting image."

"Did you say something?"

Lexie refocused. "No, sorry. I was talking to myself."

"Are you getting nervous yet?"

"Nervous?" Lexie immediately pictured Guatemala.

"Yes, silly. Your wedding day is only three weeks away."

"Maybe a little. The seamstresses are working hard to make sure they finish all the outfits before the wedding. Everything else is ready to go."

The future again pressed in on Lexie and as soon as she hung up, she knelt beside her bed and bowed her head.

"Abba, Father, help! You know the fears so easily besetting me. I pray you'd always remind me of your greatness and power, and that I, like Paul, would be able to say the trials and tribulation of my life don't move me because you've assured my future. Help me to keep my eyes on the prize. Lord, may I rest in your promises, and always feel the sense of your presence."

She was still on her knees when Olivia peeked in. Lexie smiled and rose.

"Are you going to bed?"

"Yes, Dad and Stevie are still downstairs, but they'll be up soon."

"Are you okay?"

"What do you mean?"

"Well, you've been quiet lately." Lexie hesitated then went and grasped Olivia's hands. She kissed her cheek. "Sometimes, when you look at me, I wonder if I've done something to make you angry, or if I've hurt you. Are you mad at me, Mommy?"

Olivia's lips thinned and tears pooled in her eyes, but she shook her head and squeezed harder on Lexie's hand. "No, sweetheart. But your dad and I don't want you to make a big mistake. Are you sure Lance is the right man for you?"

Lexie's eyes widened, and she nodded. Mental images of Jonathan Johnson, Sean West, and Dwight Bell flashed across her thoughts. "Totally sure. Why?"

Olivia shrugged. "You're giving up so much to be with him."

Five heartbeats passed before Lexie answered, "I don't think so, Mom. I'm not surrendering my will to Lance's, but we're both surrendering ours to the Lord. He's made his will clear." She covered the scar with the palm of her right hand, "I've learned I'd rather live in obedience to His command-in Costa Rica and Guatemala-than in disobedience here in Topeka."

Olivia didn't look convinced, but kissed Lexie good-night and walked from the room.

Troubled, Lexie shut the door and returned to her kneeling position beside the bed. She stayed there for quite a while.

Lance came by early the next morning.

"Don't you have to work?"

He grinned as he said, "Today's Saturday, remember?"

"Oh."

"I didn't think I'd ever be able to get you away for a run unless I helped you. So, what's on the agenda for today?" He waved to David and Olivia as he followed Lexie to her room.

"I want to finish emptying and organizing the contents of the last trunk. Then we can get some exercise."

They knelt in front of the trunk and began to remove old letters, diaries, and journals.

Lexie almost missed the small box hiding at the bottom in a corner. When she held the box to the light, she noticed a single letter L written in flowing script on the lid. She lifted the cover and her breath caught.

"Lance!"

He looked up, and she held out her diamond heart necklace-the one she'd given to Mary in 1857. He turned the piece of jewelry over and saw Lexie's name engraved in tiny letters on the back. Lance stared at the diamond heart in silence.

"Do you remember when we were at the reunion and I told you I'd traveled through time?"

Lance nodded.

"Well, just before you knocked on my door that day, I'd looked in the cheval mirror in my room and seen Mary instead of my reflection. She wore this necklace."

Lance stared at her. "Do you often see them?"

"Just Mary or Mattie, and once I saw Peter. This was the first time I saw Mary in a mirror in broad daylight. Usually, I see her or the others in my dreams."

"What kind of dreams?"

"Oh, now and then I see images, feel movement or smell things. Once, I dreamed of the Bells on the Oregon Trail. The dream seemed so real, Lance. I sensed they were near water, and I could hear the creaks and groans of the wagons as they moved. Several people yelled and popped whips. I thought I heard Edna tell Mattie to sit still, and when she spoke, fear laced her voice."

Lexie massaged the scar. "Once, I seemed to be in a Civil War battle. I don't know which one, but I felt the earth tremble as cannonballs exploded nearby. The movement, smoke, and noise confused me."

She looked at him, "Do you remember the time we visited that big slaughterhouse a few years ago? We wanted to see what was involved in getting cattle on the hoof into nice packages and into the coolers in the supermarket. Do you remember the strong stench of blood, entrails, and raw meat?"

He nodded.

"Well, in this dream, I heard screaming and smelled guts, blood, and burning."

Lexie shivered and shook her head. "I'm glad I haven't had a repeat of that one."

"You've been reading and studying a lot about those time periods. Could the dreams have come because of all your research?"

"Maybe. I know I've been concerned about finding out what happened to my friends from 1857, so maybe the dreams are a compilation of everything."

They returned to the contents of the trunk. "But the dreams seem so real. Lance, do you think God could be sending these snippets?"

"He's used dreams and visions in Scripture, but weren't they given to reveal and to warn? What would be the purpose of sending these dreams to you?"

She shrugged. Her fingertips caressed the scar. "Maybe the Lord knows how much I care, or maybe he knows the dreams give me a vague sense of comfort. Maybe he's warning me to remember the lessons I learned."

"Do you know you always touch your wound every time you talk about your trip to the past, or when you get nervous?"

Lexie looked at her arm and grimaced. "The scar's not as red and inflamed-looking."

They spent another hour organizing the materials before they ran.

"I'll pick you up at six o'clock for our meeting with Pastor Jeff," Lance said. "We have only one more counseling session before the wedding."

"Okay. In the meantime, I'm going to visit Gran."

Rebecca clasped her hands and smiled when Lexie told her she'd found the trunks and they were now stored safely in her room where she could sort, organize, and begin scanning and archiving the information.

"Gran?" Lexie hesitated. "Uncle Samuel talked about playing with Katheryn and Aaron Bell, Albert Bell's children, but I'm curious why you haven't mentioned them."

"They weren't a big part of our lives. Their grandmother, Martha, didn't approve of Mama. Said she was too daring and involved herself with things she shouldn't. Somehow, she and her husband, Robert, convinced Daddy Albert to let them raise the children. Those were hard days, and Mama already had Ruth and me to feed, so he agreed."

Lexie looked at a copy of her spreadsheet. "Martha was a Johnson before she married Robert Bell, wasn't she?"

"Yes."

"Do you remember any of Martha's relatives?"

Rebecca closed her eyes and frowned. "Just a minute, granddaughter. I've got to push my thoughts way back in time."

"Take your time, Gran."

Several moments passed before Rebecca opened her eyes, a pleased expression on her face, "Martha's mother, Sarah, was a twin. I think her sister's name was Rachel. I remember Grandmother Olivia Anne and Mama talking about her."

"Do you know Martha's father's name?" Lexie held her breath. Whoever the father was would most likely be either Jesse's or Jonathan's son, because he would have lived during the correct generation.

Lexie penciled the information into her spreadsheet while she waited for Rebecca to answer.

"William Jesse. That was her daddy." Rebecca yawned. "I'm sorry. All this traveling back in time has made me tired, Lexie."

"Then sleep, Granny Becky. I'll see you in a day or two" She helped Rebecca to settle, stooped and kissed her cheek and then tiptoed out of the room.

William Jesse. Was William named after his father, Jesse, or had Jonathan given his son the middle name of Jesse to honor his brother? Had he done this because Jesse had died from his war injuries?

Lexie showed Olivia her spreadsheet when she got home. Her mother examined all the information and then looked at her.

"How far back do you intend to go with this research?"

"Right here. This is as far as I go," She touched the column labeled 1857-1877.

"Why? I don't understand why this is so important to you."

Lexie could tell by Olivia's expression and tone of voice her mother thought she was wasting valuable time and energy. She reached toward the scar but forced her hand to drop.

"I can't explain, but I have to know." Lexie hadn't told anyone except Lance about her time-travel experience, so any explanation would seem lame.

"What does Lance really think about all of this?" Olivia waved her hand toward the trunks.

"He knows, Mom. He knows why I have to do this and he's supportive."

Olivia sighed and shook her head as she walked out of the room.

Lexie looked toward the ceiling. "Lord, what's going on with Mom? I pray for her. Give me wisdom to know what to say when she asks these questions."

She opened her eyes when her phone signaled an incoming text message from Kimberly.

> Good news. Found Jesse and Mary Johnson's names listed in Oregon records, 1866. Also, Jesse's father, Nathan, and brother, Jonathan. Link sent to email.

Jonathan and Jesse had survived the War, praise be to God, and the family had made their way to Oregon. She could visualize the homecoming. Lexie wanted to celebrate. She spun around several times, her arms lifted.

"Even cantankerous old Nate got there, Lord. Praise Your name!"

> You made my day, cousin. Will give you a hug when I see you in a week-and-a-half.

Lexie put down the phone and snatched up her violin. She played the happiest songs she knew as she danced around the room. Then a thought hit her, and she lowered the violin and stilled. Fergus had not been listed in the Oregon records.

She closed her eyes and certainty came. Her friend had not survived the Trail. Her excitement turned to sadness, and the notes slipping from under her bow strings mourned his passing.

"I'll see you in Heaven, Fergus," she whispered, "Save me a spot next to you and Jesus."

SEVEN

"What are you doing, Lexie?" Lance squinted at the clock, blinked sleep from his eyes, and rubbed the stubble on his cheeks. "The sun isn't up yet, and today's Saturday."

She turned. "Oh, just looking through all the wedding and honeymoon pictures and reliving the best parts of the last three weeks I've spent as Mrs. Lance Garrett. We had quite a time in Antigua, didn't we? All the food we wanted at the resort. Massages. Tours. Being able to walk through the clean beach sand and play in the azure waters of the Caribbean."

She sighed. "I woke up early thinking about things and couldn't sleep. Sorry if I woke you, love."

"Come back to bed, Lexie. You can see the pictures better in the daylight than you can with a flashlight. Besides, the room's a little chilly, and I'm getting cold."

Lexie turned, stubbed her toe on the edge of one of the trunks and dropped the flashlight.

"Ouch."

Lance rolled up to his left elbow, "Are you all right, babe?"

"Yes." She knelt to retrieve the flashlight. "This condo is too small for your things, my things, our things, and Greg's things. We've got to make a serious effort to organize all this stuff."

"You're right. We'll have to have a yard sale or something because we can't take even half of these things to Costa Rica."

Lexie slid in next to him. She turned her face to his, and he drew the covers up.

"Your feet and hands are freezing."

She touched the skin on his side, and he flinched.

"I don't know how you can say you're cold, Lance. You're as warm as a heater."

He grasped her hand and tucked her fingers under his arm until they warmed. In the dim light from the clock on the nightstand, she watched him study the lines and curves of her face, neck, and shoulder. He reached to caress her cheek.

"You don't know how much joy I feel every morning when I can open my eyes and see your face, babe."

"Yes, I do know, because I feel the same joy when I see yours." She rubbed the back of her fingers on his stubbly cheek, and whispered, "I'm so glad the Lord gave me another chance to return to you."

"I am too," he yawned his words. "Tell me more about your time in the nineteenth century."

She talked until she heard his deep, regular breathing and felt the heaviness of sleep in the muscles of his arm. Lexie turned over on her side and within minutes, was asleep too.

The sun had been up for two hours when she finally awoke. She opened her eyes to see Lance's smile. He'd rolled up to his left elbow.

"You're very lazy today." He tickled her face with a lock of her hair.

"It's Saturday, remember." She yawned and stretched. "Other than start a massive reorganization job, go to the gym with you to work the weights, learn new moves in the karate class so you land on the mat more than I do and then come home and dig into the diaries, there's nothing I have to do or any place I have to go until later this afternoon."

Lance's stomach growled insistently. "How about food before such a workout?"

"I'm up for the challenge."

They dressed in comfortable sweats and headed to the kitchen to prepare breakfast. Lexie said, "We must bring order out of this chaos, Lance. No more procrastinating."

"Agreed. We'll start as soon as we finish eating."

Lance reached for her hands. Once she bowed her head, he prayed.

"The way you talk to the Lord reminds me of Jim Bell's prayers."

"How so?"

"When you both speak to Him, your words are always grateful, humble, and never mundane or routine."

"Okay, what's first?" Lance asked.

"We've got to have space to work. Let's move all the things off the counters and put them in groups on the dining room table based on what they are. Keep like objects together. If you'll start moving the clutter, I'll wipe down and disinfect the counters. Then, we'll clean out the cabinets, and I'll wash and clean them. Greg said to put all his things in those boxes since he has to start packing everything to store during the remodel. He told me he'd take them to your parents' storage unit." There're a stack of newspapers on the coffee table to wrap all the glassware, plates, and bowls. You don't need to wrap plastic."

"I love this," Lance stated.

Lexie turned her head to see the object to which he referred, but he was just looking at her.

"What?"

"All this." He waved his hand around the kitchen then pointed to her. "Though I'm not fond of packing or unpacking, I love being able to laugh, talk, plan, pray, and work with you, hon. Everything is much more interesting when you're here, and you've already made my life much richer and more complete."

She went into his arms. "What a lovely thing to say. I agree."

When Lexie stepped back, Lance looked around the space.

"Now what?"

"Well, I think we should decide how we're going to operate in the kitchen, and then figure out where things should go to be most convenient. We can start putting plates, bowls, and glasses in the cabinets when we know."

A momentary image of Edna pointing out where she wanted everything placed in the soddy flashed across Lexie's memory, and she smiled.

Lance looked at all the objects awaiting placement and shook his head. "I think we should save ourselves some effort later by deciding what we need to sell or give away now."

He picked up a toaster box. "There's a receipt attached."

"Yes, most of the givers included a gift receipt so we can return anything we need to."

Lance looked at the appliance again. "We seldom eat toast or bread, so how do you feel about returning what we don't or won't use?"

"Good idea. I think we should simplify as much as we can."

"We'll get on the website tonight after we get back from your folks' house and look at the Institute's suggestions for what to bring to Costa Rica."

Lexie swallowed her anxiety and nodded. "I'm glad a significant portion of our friends gave money or gift cards as wedding gifts. I think we're going to need to save as much as we can."

They worked efficiently and effectively until noon and then paused for lunch.

As Lance ate, he looked around at the progress they'd made in the kitchen, dining room, and living room. "Looks great."

"Yes, I can finally breathe."

"I'll have Greg come by tomorrow after church and help me move out the furniture we're not using. This'll free up the extra bedroom, and you'll have enough space to set up an office." He grinned. "I'll move the trunks so you won't trip over them in the dark."

"Good idea. My toe still hurts."

"Hey, why don't I see if he can come by now? He and I can move all the packed and labeled boxes and get the extra bedroom cleaned out. There's only a bed and dresser there."

"Now sounds like an appropriate time. We won't have to look at boxes, no matter how neatly they're stacked."

Lance pulled out his phone and called. Greg showed up twenty minutes later in his truck, and within another hour, they'd removed the boxes, bedroom set, and extra pieces of furniture.

Lexie planned her office as she vacuumed, so when Lance and Greg returned and carried in the metal and glass computer table, rolling chair, printer-scanner, and trunks to the empty room, all she had to do was point where she wanted them.

"If you'll move the coffee table in here from the living room, I can keep my documents organized since I don't have shelves anymore."

"Why don't you use the two bookcases in the living room instead? They'd be better. Won't take me but a few minutes to box up the books and pictures."

"Thanks, Greg."

"What do you plan to do with those old trunks after you've finished doing whatever you're doing with the contents?" Greg asked, "They take up a lot of room."

"They'll go to Grammy's house. They're pretty enough she may use them for decorative pieces. The documents won't go back in them, though."

"Where will you put all of this stuff?" Greg eyed the journals, diaries, letters, and photos in one of the trunks.

"Well, right now, I'm scanning each item into the computer. Then I slide the documents into a sheet protector, attach a unique identification number to the outside, cross-reference the item on a spreadsheet, and then place the information into one of the large three-ring binders labeled by decades. There are tab dividers for each person within the decades."

"Wow. Sounds like a lot of work. Your grandmother will finish what you don't?"

"Yes. I'm showing Gram how to use my iMac and scanner, so she'll continue archiving whatever I can't get done before we leave."

"Speaking of leaving, if we're going to make the gym, karate class, and your parents' house on time, we'd better get going, Lexie."

She agreed and went to the bedroom to change and grab her gym bag. Lance soon followed.

The next few hours sped by, and when the two returned to the condo, they didn't have much time to shower and dress before they had to leave for the Logan's.

"What's up with your mom, hon?" Lance asked as he backed out of the driveway, "The last several times I've been around her, she's been distant-almost unfriendly."

"I don't know, Lance. She's been that way with me too-distant, but not unfriendly. Lately, I've had to watch my words and keep my conversation general to keep her from leaving the room in tears. She won't tell me what's upsetting her."

"Have you asked David?"

Lexie sighed. "No. Dad's tired when he comes home in the evenings. He eats, hangs out with Mom and Stevie for a bit, and then goes to bed."

"Well, I'm glad they asked us to dinner. Maybe we'll have time to talk and clear the air."

The Logans had invited other guests, so there was no chance for a heart-to-heart that evening.

"Honey," Olivia smiled and kissed Lexie's cheek, and then held her own up for Lance to kiss. Her cheeks flushed with excitement as she turned and indicated a small, black-haired, brown-skinned couple in their late thirties who strolled in from the living room. "I'd like you and Lance to meet Rudy and Antonia Monterro. They're from Guatemala. Rudy works with your dad, and I met Antonia at my hairdresser's several weeks ago."

She turned to the smiling couple. "Rudy and Antonia, this is my daughter and son-in-law, Lexie and Lance Garrett."

Lexie looked at the two with interest and shook hands. "Nice to meet you."

David clasped Lance's shoulder and hugged Lexie.

"Where's Stevie, Dad?" She looked for her brother.

"He'll be down in a minute. Come on into the dining room.

Dinner's on the table."

Steven showed up at that moment and grinned at Lexie and Lance. "How's married life?"

They looked at each other and smiled. Almost in unison, they said, "Great."

Lance added, "Better than I could've ever imagined."

David chuckled and indicated they should all sit down. They sat, and David nodded toward Lance.

"Let's pray," Lance said, waited a moment, and bowed his head and asked God to bless the food, family, and friends.

"Rudy's one of the electricians on our job site," David spoke as he passed a large, colorful salad to Olivia, who sat on his left.

"Rudy? Is that your given name?" Lance handed the green beans to Lexie after he smiled at the guest across from him.

"No, it's short for Rudolfo."

Antonia giggled. "He doesn't use Rudolfo because too many of his friends tease him about being Rudolph the Red-nosed Reindeer."

The meal was pleasant and unrushed. As everyone finished and helped clear the table, Lexie caught the expectant look her mother and father gave each other. She wondered what was up.

"Tell us about your experiences in Guatemala," David opened the conversation as they all sat around the living room enjoying their coffee, tea, or chocolate.

"What would you like to know?" Rudy smiled.

"Is it a dangerous place to live?" Olivia asked, and slanted her eyes toward Lexie as if making sure she was paying attention.

Both Rudy and Antonia nodded, though Rudy answered, "Very. The US government's advisory website lists Guatemala as the most dangerous, violent country in the entire Western Hemisphere."

"Is that why you came to the United States?" Steven asked.

"Yes, that's one reason. The other is to work."

"Our families in Guatemala live with fear continually." Antonia's expression saddened.

Lexie reached for Lance's hand to keep from touching the scar. "Of what are they afraid?"

The couple looked at each other before Rudy responded, "Robbery. Murder. Death. Kidnapping. Threats. Every day there is news of these. Gangs expect business owners like my family to pay them money every month. If they don't, they may be killed. Sometimes their families disappear and are never heard from again."

Olivia's eyes widened as she looked from the guests to her and Lance.

"Why doesn't the government or police do anything about this?" David asked, his brows furrowed in a deep frown.

Several moments passed before Antonia answered, her voice lowered as if someone else might be listening, "Most government officials, police, and the military are corrupt. They control the gangs and get them to do their dirty work."

Rudy nodded. "Last year, I was on a bus leaving Guatemala City. A couple of robbers got on at one of the stops and demanded the driver's money. He didn't move fast enough, and they shot him ten times. Three of the bullets hit the woman next to me. The men were known to be Guatemalan military. They do not value human life."

Lexie paled. She squeezed so hard on Lance's hand he removed his fingers, draped his arm around her shoulder, and drew her close to his body.

Steven stared at Rudy. "Why would they rob a bus driver?"

"Because their job is so risky and dangerous, the bus companies pay the drivers extremely well. These drivers are often targets of robbery. Many die."

Lexie looked at her mother and wondered if her face was as pale.

When Olivia spoke, her mother's voice trembled. She tried to lighten the heaviness in the room. "Tell us about these busses. Is this how most people get from place-to-place? Are they very crowded?"

Antonia nodded. "Yes. I think they seat forty-eight, but many more people get on and stand in the aisles."

"They stand in the aisles?" Steven laughed. "We'd never be allowed to do that. How do they keep from falling each time the bus starts or stops?"

"People grasp the rail on the ceiling."

"It's usually more crowded on market days," Rudy added, "Farmers put their grain and other bags on top of the bus and keep the chickens with them."

David's eyes widened. "Chickens on a crowded bus? Do they hold them in their laps?"

Rudy chuckled at their expressions. "Some do, but usually they tie their feet together and store them under the seats."

Lexie saw the look of horror on her mother's face, and wondered if hers mirrored the same. She could image all the germs.

"I bet the smell is something else." Steven looked at his mom and chuckled.

Both Rudy and Antonia agreed "Yes, the chickens smell. There is not much good water in Guatemala, so when the people come in from the country, they may have bathed only once or twice that month. Often there is a strong odor of unwashed bodies and urine."

"If there's not much good water, what did you drink?" Lance finally asked.

"We drank water first boiled on the wood-burning stove and then left to cool."

Lexie immediately thought of Edna's stove and of hauling bucketsful of water from the well to the kitchen. She remembered how strange the Bells thought her when she boiled all her drinking water, but Jim and Edna's two older children had died of cholera, and Lexie didn't want to chance getting the disease, or any other.

"No electric or gas stoves?" Olivia looked at Lexie with sad, pity-filled eyes.

Antonia answered, "Maybe in the cities, but I haven't seen any."

"What should my daughter and son-in-law know when they move to Guatemala? What would you advise?"

Rudy thought for a moment and then looked from Lexie to Lance. "Out of 365 days, you should expect rain for almost 300 of those days. You will be well-advised to prepare yourselves mentally and physically for the wet."

"How do you prepare mentally?" Lexie asked.

"You play games or read books. You try to find something interesting to do."

"What problems does all this rain cause?" Lance leaned forward with interest.

"In the country, the roads wash out every other day. In the city, there is flooding."

"Do the towns have heavy machinery available to fix the roads?"

David chuckled. "Ah, Lance. I can see your civil engineer's mind turning."

"Not usually." Rudy answered.

"Then how are the roads repaired?"

"By hand. The government hires crews to go out with shovels and fix them the best they can."

"How do the houses stand up to all this rain?" The look Lance gave Lexie said he figured they should get the worst out into the open.

Rudy shrugged. "The roofs are cement. Often the construction workers have not been too careful to make sure the cement dried level. Puddles from the roof leak into the houses. When you have so much rain, there is always mold."

"Mold?" Lexie massaged the scar. She looked at Olivia, who brushed tears from her eyes.

"Yes. Since the houses are less than a thousand square feet in size and have only one small window, there is not sufficient ventilation."

"Why only one window?" Steven asked.

"Robbers have a difficult time getting through a window so small. The more windows you have, the more of a target you become."

Lexie pictured the Bell's soddy. At least they had an extra window.

Olivia stood. "Can I get anyone anything else to drink?"

They said no, and she began to collect the cups. Lexie and Antonia rose to help.

Soon after, the Monterros said their good-byes. Lexie and Lance followed suit.

Lexie kissed her mom and dad and hugged Steven. "Thanks for dinner, Mom. The food was delicious as always."

Olivia nodded but pursed her mouth. Lexie knew she wanted to say something else, but had thought better of doing so.

"See you at church tomorrow?" Steven looked at his sister and Lance.

"Sure," Lance replied.

"Great. Hey, do you two want to shoot some hoops after lunch tomorrow?"

Lexie shook her head. "I'd like to, Stevie, but I need to get some more archiving done. Lance may want to meet you, though."

"Sure, Steven. I'll see you at the rec center at one-thirty. Will that work?"

"Yes. See you then." Steven waved and returned to the living room where he plopped down in front of the television.

In the car on the way home, Lexie said little. When they turned into their driveway, she looked at Lance.

"I'm shaking like Jell-o both inside and out, Lance. Just look at my hand!"

Lance shut off the ignition and turned toward her. "Did you get the feeling your mom and dad had ulterior motives for asking us over for dinner tonight?"

"I think so. They wanted us to hear what the Monterros had to say about Guatemala."

"For what purpose?"

Lexie chewed on her bottom lip. "I don't know. Maybe they wanted to provide us with primary sources of information so we'd go into our situation with eyes wide open."

"Do you think there could've been another reason?"

Lexie unbuckled her seatbelt and slid next to Lance. "I think Mom wanted to scare me."

"Why?"

"Because she's scared for me. Maybe she's trying to convince us not to go."

Lance unbuckled. "That's the feeling I got."

"You know what I think?"

"What?" Lance slid out and waited for her to do the same before he closed the car door.

"We haven't heard the worst about Guatemala."

"Then we'd best spend a lot of time on our knees talking to the Lord, babe, because He hasn't changed our directive."

Lexie was right. Over the next month, Olivia or David called, emailed, or texted tidbits of information they'd learned about Guatemala from either the Monterros or from the internet.

> Antonia told me there are a lot of venomous snakes near the area where you'll be. She said the tarantulas, scorpions, spiders, and cockroaches are huge all over the country, and the fleas are a real nuisance.

The results of these regular messages drove Lance and Lexie to their knees, into the Word of God, to the gym or to extra karate or jiu-jitsu classes to work off their apprehensions. Lexie started carrying around index cards with Bible verses printed on them, so whenever anxiety struck, she could be comforted.

> Fear not them which kill the body, but are not able to kill the soul: but rather fear him which is able to destroy both soul and body in hell. Matthew 10:28 KJV

Lexie repeated the Scripture over and over after she'd read the newspaper article Antonia sent her about a Guatemalan man who'd been tracked down and killed by gang members who'd got his cell phone number. They'd called him on a regular basis, followed him from place to place, and threatened him and his family. They demanded a large sum of money, and when he couldn't deliver the amount in the time they'd given him, the gang members executed him.

When she read about the lack of quality medical facilities outside of the cities, of the long lines of sick people waiting to see doctors, or of the poverty of the country, anxiety almost choked her.

What if I get sick? I'd probably die. She remembered expressing her fears to Steven when he'd asked her what was so bad about going to Guatemala.

Those were her words the day before God sent her to 1857 for three months. She studied the scar and realized she hadn't died.

The Spirit spoke to her heart and mind through the words of the Apostle Paul and John, the Beloved.

> *I have not given you the spirit of fear, Lexie, but of*

power, and of love, and of a sound mind. For you have not received the spirit of bondage again to fear, but you have received My Spirit—the Spirit of adoption—so that you can cry to Me and say, Abba, Father."

"Thank you, Lord, for reminding me. Help me to keep my heart focused on you."

My Spirit lives in you. I Am greater than the evil one. For the weapons of your warfare are not effective without Me, but are mighty through Me. I can tear down Satan's strongholds. I Am the Ancient of Days, the Judge of the universe. Nothing escapes My notice, and crimes will not go unpunished. I Am the heart-knower. I Am the only One seated on My throne, and I yield it to none. I have opened the book of records and appointed a day for each to stand before Me to give an account. Judgment is Mine, and I will repay. Do not fear.

"Keep reminding me, Abba."

Do not fear.

EIGHT

During the weekdays when Lance worked, Lexie spent hours reading the journals and diaries. Through them, she grew to love Alexandria, her lion-hearted ancestor who survived so many hardships. She laughed and wept with Alexandria's mother, Olivia Anne, as she and her husband, Frank, ministered to the Cherokees in Oklahoma territory, and Olivia Anne's diary yielded information for which she'd searched. Olivia Anne had been born to Rachel Johnson and Charles West. Charles was the son of Benjamin West and Laura Shoemaker of Boston, Massachusetts, and Rachel was one of the twin daughters born to Jonathan Johnson and Olivia Aubry of Oregon.

Lexie gasped and almost dropped the diary. *Jonathan* was her ancestor? The same Jonathan who wanted to marry her before Christmas? Who owned slaves, and who had a father who made her want to throw things when he was around?

She closed the diary and picked up the photo of Jonathan, Jesse, Nathan, and Sean. She went to the computer and brought up the audio files she'd transferred from her phone, and then clicked on Jonathan's recording.

Tears pooled at the corners of her eyes and ran down her cheeks as she listened to him talk to his father and brother. His face was still fresh in her mind.

"I have a hard time believing you're my ancestor, Jonathan. I remember how strong your arms were as you held me in the Clarks' cellar. I could hear your heartbeat next to my ear even though the tornado raged above us. I thought we'd surely die that day." She touched his image, "Knowing you've been in your grave for a hundred years or more makes me want to grieve as if you just died."

Lexie turned the picture face-down. "I hope your heart changed toward God before you met him, Jon." She shook her head. "You were so strong and sure of your own strength. You never gave the Lord a thought."

Lexie looked at the clock then reached for the diary of Olivia Aubry Johnson, Jonathan's wife, and her great-great-great-great grandmother.

When Lance came home later that afternoon, Lexie was sitting on the floor next to their bed, an old diary in her hands. Tears streamed down her cheeks. He hunkered down next to her, and she sensed his alarm.

"What's wrong, hon? Are you all right?"

She nodded and patted the floor beside her. When Lance sat, she handed him the diary and indicated a section. "Read."

Lexie wiped her tears and played with her diamond heart necklace as she watched the progression of expressions cross Lance's face as he read. His interest sharpened. Disbelief and shock soon followed.

He opened the cover of the diary and studied the date and inscription written on the first page, and then looked at her.

"If I ever had any doubts about your time-travel experience, which I didn't, this would have left none."

Lexie nodded, a deer-in-the-headlights look still remaining in her eyes. "I was only there three months, Lance. I could never have imagined-"

"That you'd influenced so many people in so short a time?"

She nodded again.

"Why don't we go into the kitchen and fix a bite to eat then, since you're not too far along in the diary, you can start over and read the entries to me."

"Okay. I've got jet-lag again, Lance. I feel like I'm living in two different centuries at the same time."

After they ate, Lexie placed the photos she'd taken in the nineteenth century and the ones from the family reunion on the coffee table in front of them, and then sat down on the sofa next to Lance and began to read.

> When I listen to Josie and Annie's tales of the Oregon Trail, I wonder if I've missed out on an exciting adventure. Father and I came to Oregon by ship, which was long, but unadventurous. The twins assure me I haven't missed anything but two thousand miles of dirt, mud, mosquitoes, Indians, cholera, graves, steep canyons, dangerous river crossings, bad water, little grass, little food, and miles of prairie. When I asked if there was anything that made the Trail endurable, both cousins immediately nodded, smiled, and said, "Dwight, Sean, and the others who traveled with us, of course."

Lexie looked at Sean's image then turned to Lance. "I'd never have thought Dwight and Sean would travel the Trail together. The tension between them because of me was noticeable. Maybe after I left they became friends."

"I've seen their pictures, but tell me more about these men."

"Dwight Bell is—was—amazingly strong. The first time we met, I could tell he was shocked to see my jeans and t-shirt, and he was suspicious of my presence in his home. He was a Christian but didn't allow the Word to influence him as much as Jim, and when he said things I didn't think were right, I'd challenge him. He wasn't used to women being so vocal."

Lance laughed. "I bet you were a real shock to him."

"I was a real shock to them all. When Dwight found out his family believed I was from the future, he thought they should say nothing to the neighbors. He knew Fergus, Jim, and Edna would never speak about me. Edna, poor woman, could barely call me by my first name at the beginning of my time there because she disliked me so much. Dwight made Mattie and Mary promise not to say anything—not even to the Johnsons who'd been there when the Bells found me on the prairie, and who'd seen me in my twenty-first-century clothing."

Lexie's jaw tightened in remembrance. "Then Dwight noticed Peter, who stood next to me, and his manner immediately changed, Lance. You know how some animals puff up to look more intimidating? That's what Dwight reminded me of at the time. He called Peter slave in a mean tone and started toward him. Everything about Dwight was threatening. I knew he intended harm or intimidation, so I stepped between Peter and him. I looked the stubborn blacksmith in the eyes and said if he ever spoke to Peter again in that tone, or ever lifted a hand against him, I would strike him as hard as I could with anything I could find that would hurt."

"I just bet you did, hon. What did he do?"

"Well, he didn't do what I expected. He smiled and said I was beautiful when angry, or something equally dumb. I made him give his word he'd never speak to Peter in such a way again or hit him. I told him he didn't have the right, regardless of what others of his time believed."

"Did he give his word?"

"Yes. After a while, Dwight began to see Peter's worth as a human, and not just a slave."

"What about Sean West?"

Lexie grinned. "Sean wasn't a believer, but he didn't support slavery, either. He was very educated and easy for me to talk to because we shared some of the same goals in life. He loaned me some Hebrew and Greek reference books to continue my Bible study about how God felt about war and slavery. I'll tell you about this another day."

She felt Lance's stillness at her words but continued speaking, "When someone did something or made comments Sean thought were silly, he could use logic, polite words, and a sarcastic tone to destroy their confidence. He'd use words with a bite to them, Lance, though he never spoke to me in such a manner. I suspect he knew I could and would take him on in a battle of words, so he kept his knife-words sheathed."

"Smart man. I wouldn't be brave enough to engage in such an argument with you."

Lexie shrugged and shook her head. "I don't like to argue, Lance, but if someone is trying to hurt others, or to tell me something is right when it's wrong, I have to stand up, even when I don't want to."

"Sounds like you and Alexandria have a lot in common. Maybe after your stay in the nineteenth century and your upcoming stay in Costa Rica and Guatemala, God will use your strengths and weaknesses to the point others will call you Lexie the Lionhearted."

Lance's words caught and held her attention. She heard the echo of Sean West's words the first time they'd met. "Ah. Lexie. The abbreviated form of the name Alexis and Alexandra; taken from the Greek meaning 'man's defender.'"

Could this be true? She'd have to think more about what he'd said.

"Sean regularly aggravated Jonathan, especially when I was around, though I didn't see him try his tricks with Dwight very often. They were just wary and tried to out-jockey each other. Wow, their game was exhausting. Most people didn't get close to Sean, because they were a little intimidated because of his education and monied background, though Dwight wasn't noticeably impressed."

Lance chuckled. "West knew if he provoked the big blacksmith too much, he might become a casualty of the man's huge fists."

"Probably."

"What else did Olivia write in her diary?"

Lexie continued.

> I've read their diaries and begged for their stories so many times they wonder why I want to hear them again. I wrote down everything they told me in another diary, so I can go back and relive their experiences with them. I've also been allowed to make copies of the letters sent between the Bells and Mary, and Peter and his folks. I have a hard time believing a freed slave like Peter can read, speak, and write as well as he does, but Sean told me he continues Lexie Logan's work with both Mattie and Peter, though many still frown on his actions of teaching a former slave to read. He doesn't care what they think. I

> have to smile, because sometimes Peter's phrasing could have come straight out of Sean's mouth.

"Well done, Lexie." Lance patted her thigh. "Your willingness to do what was right, no matter what others thought, changed Peter's life for the better."

"I hope so." The pulse in her neck beat with joy at the thought of Peter shaking his shackles, and Sean West helping him to do so.

> Lexie seems to be a paragon of virtues, from what Edna, Jim, Dwight, Mattie, and Sean tell me. All of them admire her musical ability, which must be great, because they tell me she can make the violin strings and piano keys sing with joy, sadness, fear, and anger like no one else. Her playing gave great joy and comfort to Fergus before he died, and touched even the hearts of a Kansa brave.

"I'm no paragon, Olivia," Lexie muttered and wiped away a tear. "If I were, I wouldn't feel so much fear and anxiety, and I wouldn't always be messing up."

Lance kissed her. "I think you're just about as perfect as they come, babe, even though you're human and make mistakes, just like everyone else."

"Thanks, love."

> Though none of them talk about Lexie very much, they do let a few things drop. Josie and Annie think they're all hiding something about her, and even though Josie set herself to find out what this was when she first heard about Lexie while they traveled the Trail, she hasn't been able to. Josie and Annie were immediately curious why

> everyone in the Bell family, Peter, and Sean were so stunned when they first saw them. They thought at first the strong reactions were due to the fact they're identical twins, but they all said, no, they reacted that way because they knew a woman who could be their triplet.

"Ah-hah." Lance picked up the photo of the women taken at the cousins family reunion. "Now we know what Josie and Annie looked like. Just look at yourselves."

> Josie's blacksmith husband is very tight-lipped when she gets too nosey, and tells her there a few things they can't talk about when speaking of this mysterious woman named Lexie. Annie can't get anything out of Sean, either. Jim and Edna tell her the same thing, and even Mattie doesn't spill the beans, which only makes Josie more determined.

Lexie laughed. "I like Josie. I know what they're keeping from her. How do you tell anyone Lexie Logan was a time-traveler from the twenty-first century who knew their history before it happened? No one would believe them, and everyone would think they were crazy or had an overactive imagination."

"Did you pay attention to the fact both Dwight and Sean each got two Lexie look-a-likes?"

Lexie nodded and continued reading.

> Sean talks about her education, Edna comments about her need to be clean, and Dwight mentions her strength. Mattie told Josie Lexie always smelled like vanilla and could run faster than anybody he knew except maybe

> Washunga and Allegawaho. Edna told Josie these were the sons of the Kansa Indian who responded so well to her music.
>
> We couldn't imagine how any woman could run faster than men or children in the kind of shoes, or long, bulky skirts we wear, but Edna said she wore men's pants and a shirt that fit her curves. Edna blushed when she said this. Josie was shocked and asked if Lexie was a moral person, and Edna said, "the moralist." She said getting used to Lexie took a while, but she was glad she could finally see beyond her clothes to the woman underneath.
>
> Josie asked why Lexie ran, and Edna said she ran mostly to relieve the heartache of being away from her family and sweetheart.

Lance took the diary and reread the last phrase aloud, "You ran? The sweetheart is me?"

"Yes. I ached with pain, Lance, and the longer I stayed there, the more I believed I'd never see you all again."

> I'm curious to see how Mary, Jesse, Jonathan, and Nathan Johnson describe her. They'll be arriving soon, and I wonder how they'll react when they see me. Both Sean and Dwight tell me I look more like Lexie than the twins.

"What!" Lance's eyes and voice reflected the mirth he felt, "Four of you? I bet seeing their faces when they saw Olivia would have been hilarious. I wouldn't have believed this part of the story had I not been holding a picture of women in your family with strikingly similar looks."

> When I think of Jonathan, Jesse, and Nathan Johnson, my insides shake like jelly. I wonder how they'll react when they see me. Josie and Annie gave me advice, but I'm still nervous about meeting them. Edna said Nate and Lexie didn't get along at all,

"That part is true, Lance. Nate Johnson was a real pain."

> ... so, I hope the man will look beyond my facial likeness to see the real me. If he turns out to be the abrupt, contrary person I envision, I pray I can keep my temper in check and my tongue still.

"I never could keep the words between my teeth when I was around Nate, which is why I stayed away from him as much as I could. The man could light a fire under me this quick," she snapped her fingers.

> Edna gave us all a description of the Johnsons and said Jesse was always full of life and happy, but I wonder if the war changed all that. I can't imagine how he and Jonathan felt knowing they could have killed each other. Such a dreadful, deadly war. Hopefully, they have no hard feelings between them. The atmosphere is so uncomfortable when bitterness and anger are present.

"Jesse and Jonathan fought on different sides of the war?" Lance's brows lifted.

"Apparently. Maybe the other diaries will tell us what happened."

> Even the mention of Jonathan's name is enough to start my heart pounding. He's the one I'm most concerned about meeting. From what Dwight and Sean said, he hasn't gotten over Lexie even after all these years. I think I will know him immediately from everyone's description and by the look in his eyes. Josie and Anne were both drawn to "the look," as I expect I will be. Lexie seemed to pull real men to her, and if he's of the same quality as Sean and Dwight, I would be foolish not to latch on to him. The only sticking point will be if he shares my faith. I won't consider anyone who doesn't.
>
> I hear the wagons now, so I'll stop.

"Wow," was all Lance could say.

"Did you hear that, Lance? Her faith?" Lexie continued reading until she found an entry describing the meeting between Jonathan and Olivia.

"He believed, Lance! Bull-strong, stubborn Jonathan Johnson became a believer. God is so good. I wonder what led to his conversion?"

"Do you know what this means?"

"What?

"You'll see most of them in heaven."

Lexie stood, pulled Lance up, and danced a jig around the room.

Each evening after dinner, Lexie snuggled next to him on the sofa and read the diaries and letters aloud. She laughed, cried, or mourned as she read Annie and Josie's tales of travel on the Oregon Trail, Fergus' death, and Sean West's conversion, or she'd tremble when she read Olivia's account of Jonathan and Jesse's struggle to stay alive as they fought on different sides during the Civil War, and then struggled to rebuild their lives in Oregon. Lance often asked for clarification, and she'd retell certain parts of her time-travel adventures.

Olivia Johnson wrote with such skill that Lexie pictured herself there with her friends and family of the nineteenth century. Her heart overflowed with love as she read the letters that had passed between Mattie, Mary, Peter, Mammy Sue, and Big Tom, and she wished she could grab her phone and call them. She ached to hug them all.

"Feels like we've been watching an epic drama, babe. One in which you had a leading part." Lance said after Lexie closed the last diary. "Who needs to go to a movie?"

She nodded, a far-away expression in her eyes. "Lance, I want to take them with me to Costa Rica and Guatemala."

"What?" Lance looked at the large binders of information stored neatly in the bookcases, and then at her. "You do remember we're taking only four fifty pound suitcases of necessities, and we'll have to pay through the nose for any extra bags?"

"Yes, but if I work like a mad woman and get the rest of this information archived, I can burn everything to a disc or transfer the information to a small backup drive. Do you remember how both the Institute's website and Rudy advised us to bring something from home to help relieve our homesickness and the monotony of rainy days? Hearing and seeing recordings of my people from both centuries would help me so much, love."

"Sounds like a good idea." He played with a lock of her hair. "What do you think Audrey or your mom will say when they see your name in nineteenth-century diaries, assuming they'll take the time to read them?"

Lexie's eyes widened, and she stared at him. "I never thought about the possibility."

She chewed on her bottom lip and shook her head. "They'd never understand, Lance, and would forever bombard me with questions. I know them. They'll get their feelings hurt if I don't answer, yet talking about my experience isn't easy. Just thinking about doing so makes my stomach hurt."

"I remember how you kept choking over your words when you tried to tell me."

"Now you know why."

She closed her eyes and massaged the scar. Finally, she looked at him. "I can't let them see the diaries or letters where my name is mentioned. I'll store those archives separately, and put the originals in a safe deposit box. I'll summarize a few of the diaries for Mom and Grammy, or anyone else who wants to read them."

"That's the best idea."

"Lance, I'd like to have Rudy and Antonia over for dinner soon."

"Why? You're not afraid of the ugly things they might tell you about Guatemala, are you?"

She rubbed the scar. "I don't like hearing about all the danger, violence, and poverty, but I think we'd be wise to find out everything we can, don't you? How else can we plan?"

"Yes. Patty told me one of the Spanish teachers at the nearby high school is from Costa Rica, and her mom lives in San José. Maybe we can schedule a time to chat with her too."

"You know what else?"

"What?"

"Since our passports and visas came, and we're getting closer to the date of departure, one of my greatest fears is I'll get to the field and can't communicate. I have nightmares about this, Lance. I picture us trying to hail a taxi at the airport in San José to take us to the home of the family with whom we'll live, but we won't know how to tell the driver what we want. Sometimes in my dreams, we get to our new home, but we can't talk to the members of our host family to find out where to put things or what we should do. How will we know what we're expected to do before we start classes at the Institute? I don't even know how to ask where the bathroom is."

"Don't worry. Gary said he'd meet us at the airport and take us to meet our family. He'll interpret for us initially, and help us do what we need to do. He'll come with us when we go to the bank to get our account set up too. I'm glad he's our Big Brother."

Lexie massaged the scar with frantic strokes. "Do you think Rudy, Antonia, or this teacher might teach us some survival Spanish?"

"Hey, great idea, hon. You're full of them tonight, aren't you?"

He stood and held out his hand to help her up. With a smile, he pulled her into his arms. His fingers trailed down her cheek and jaw but stopped when they felt the pounding pulse just below her ear. "Wow, you are nervous about this, aren't you?"

She nodded.

He kissed her neck and whispered, "Jesus said, Peace I leave with you, My peace I give to you. Don't let your heart be troubled or afraid, Lexie."

She kissed the palm of his hand. "Keep reminding me, love."

By the first of November, Lexie had scanned and saved all the diaries, letters, and photos, and had cross-referenced them on the spreadsheet. As she stared at some of the pictures, an idea came to her. She opened iMovie and created a new file, then began to import photos and voice files. After that, she opened the word processor and pulled Josie's diary and the letters of Mattie, Mary, and Peter toward her. She typed and printed the text, then picked up her phone and dialed Kimberly.

"Hey, Kim," Lexie held up the photo of the Bells and stared at their images as she spoke, "I'm calling to see if you and Weston would be willing to make voice recordings of some text I'll send you. I want to make a movie with some of the information I learned from the diaries and letters, and I thought your voices would be perfect for Mary and Mattie."

"Sure. Sounds fun. How do you want us to record?"

"Either from your phone or computer, whichever has the best sound quality. Send me the files when you're finished. When the movie's done, I'll send you a DVD."

For the rest of the afternoon, Lexie planned the movie and typed passages from the diaries. She'd sometimes reread what she'd printed, and then stare at the ceiling deep in thought.

Lexie made several calls to people in her church and then went online to search for stock photos and videos to supplement what she had. She found a couple of quality clips of a Civil War battle reenactment, and of a wagon train both on the move and crossing a river.

When Lance got home late that afternoon, he stepped toward the computer to see what she was doing, but she shook her head and stood.

"Don't look yet. I want this to be a surprise."

"Are you going to tell me what you're doing?"

Lexie walked with him toward the kitchen. "I'm making a movie using the photos and audio files of my nineteenth-century people. Friends from the church agreed to read passages from the diaries and letters, and Pastor Jeff said we could use the sound system and microphones after the services next week to make the recordings. To all of this, I'm adding stock images, video footage, and background music to make a movie we can watch over and over when we're away from home. I hope the movie will have that epic feel. The disc won't take up much space in our bags, so we can bring our people with us."

"Who's going to read which letter or diary?"

Lexie told him who she'd asked as they prepared dinner.

"Lance, do you remember when I told you I felt such an urgency to discover my ancestry before something happened to Gran? That what I found might be important to my future?"

He nodded and sipped his soup.

"Well, I've done all of this, and I don't know why or how what I've discovered is important. The sense of urgency hasn't gone away, either. In fact, the feeling is stronger now, and I'm confused. I don't know why I still have this soul-pressing. I don't know how else to describe this sense of urgency.""

He looked at her and spoke softly, "Mine's a burning, hon."

"What? You feel it too?"

"Yes. I have ever since I surrendered to the Lord's command to go to Guatemala."

"Then you don't think what I'm sensing is related to discovering my ancestry?"

"Maybe, but don't you think the Lord would instill in you the same sense of burning, pressing, or urgency he's given me? After all, we're a team now. How can we work together in unity if we don't have the same spirit?"

"What does this burning cause you to feel?" She ate her soup and waited for his answer.

He spoke after several moments of thought, "I feel dissatisfied and discontented at the thought of staying here, because I know this is not where God wants us. I'm restless at the thought of delay, and I'm eager to get going."

In the weeks just before Thanksgiving, Lexie finished her movie and made several copies. She and Lance took more jiu-jitsu and First Aid / CPR classes, took Spanish lessons from the high school Spanish teacher, Señora Garcia, two days a week, bought Rosetta Stone software and began twice-daily lessons on the computer, though Lexie often spent many more hours in front of the screen trying to perfect her accent or learn the phrases whenever her fears of not being able to communicate surfaced. They pumped Antonia and Rudy for information about Guatemala and worked with Olivia to collect and prepare healthy, simple recipes she could cook over a wood-burning stove.

"I've friended Señora Garcia's mom on Facebook. She lives in a little house in one of the suburbs of San José. She's really into using the local plants and herbs as medicine. Señora Garcia says her mother has helped a lot of people in the neighborhood," Lexie explained to Olivia as she added seasoning and vegetables to the simmering chicken broth.

"How do you communicate with her? Does she speak English?" Olivia cubed the chicken breasts and scraped them into a skillet to brown.

"Señora Garcia showed me a fairly good online translator. I type what I want to ask in English, and the program translates immediately. I copy and paste what I want to say into the message box and send. When Señora Baca responds, I copy and paste her Spanish into the program and click the 'translate into English' button. The process is slow, and if I'm not concise with my words, I get a funky translation, but we both catch the drift of each other's meaning."

"What does she say about the availability of fresh vegetables and herbs?"

"She said I can get a variety of fresh fruits and vegetables from any of the farmers' markets. Apparently, the university in San José has an extensive agricultural program, and I can get produce from them too."

"Make sure you wash all fruits and vegetables well with distilled water. You don't want to chance getting Hepatitis, Salmonella, or *E. coli*."

Lexie thought of the innumerable buckets of water she'd heated on Edna's stove. "I don't know if I can buy distilled water, Mom, but with the water purifier Lance and I found online, we can purify almost five thousand gallons of water without iodine, chlorine, or other chemicals. The device doesn't weigh much, and the thing's small enough to fit in a suitcase. This filter will get us through at least two years on the field and'll remove almost one hundred percent of viruses, bacteria, and protozoans. We also have a LifeStraw for each of us. The straw is portable and does the same thing as the purifier."

"You don't have to buy distilled water, Lexie. You can distill the water on the stove with a pot of boiling water, a glass bowl, and ice. I found the instructions online and printed them for you. Distillation sounds easy enough."

"Thanks, Mom, for watching out for us. I appreciate all the help you've given me. I love you so much."

Olivia nodded and brushed tears away with the back of her wrist. "I love you too, sweetheart. I wish ..."

Lexie knew the unspoken words would be ... *you wouldn't go.* She sensed the melancholy of her mother's soul, so she put down the ladle and hugged her. "Give your worry to the Lord, Mommy. He's called Lance and me to go, and he can protect us."

"I know, but thinking about you being so far away for two years really hurts. Dad and I can't protect you. We can't keep you safe."

Lexie stepped back and looked in Olivia's eyes. Her voice was tender when she spoke, "Do you think you can keep me safe now, Mom? Can you stop me from getting injured in a car wreck? Can you prevent me from being mugged in Topeka, or dying from a disease or terrorist attack in the US? I can't stop these from happening to me, Mom, so how can you? My life's in God's hands, and he knows my beginning, middle, and end."

"I know, but my pain will be magnified if any of these things happen to you in a foreign country. I already feel so helpless thinking of you in such a violent place like Guatemala."

Lexie remembered the aching pain in her soul when almost two hundred years had separated her from the people she loved. She groaned, hugged Olivia, and laid her head on her mother's shoulder.

"We are helpless, but God isn't, Mom. That's why you have to cry out to Him. He said the fervent, effective prayers of His righteous people are of great benefit. Don't you remember?"

She nodded.

"Lance and I are counting on our families, and the churches who've committed to support us during this time, to take us before God's throne in prayer on a regular basis."

Lexie kissed Olivia and returned to stirring the contents in the pot. "This morning Lance and I read the eighth chapter of Revelation together before he went to work. In this passage, an angel stood before the altar of God. He was given a censer and incense to be offered upon the golden altar with the prayers of all the saints. When he offered these, the smoke of the incense and the prayers ascended before the Almighty. Though these verses occur during the time of Earth's coming tribulation and judgment, they comforted me to know God hears each and every one of our prayers. None are lost. Think about that, Mom. All believers' prayers are heard, even when we sometimes think God's not listening."

He hears. He knows me. I am His child. Lexie took comfort from her own words.

NINE

The Garrett and Logan families joined each other for Thanksgiving at the Garrett's house. The addition of Patty's gregarious husband, Dan, and their three active children raised the energy and noise levels, and made the house feel unusually small. When leaves were added to each end of the long table to accommodate everyone, and the tablecloth, dishes, and silverware were laid, the dining area shrank to a friendly, barely-enough-space-to-get-by, excuse-me-please room.

Lexie smiled when she heard the conversations and laughter around her as dishes were passed and silverware clinked together. This was family.

"What are you and Lexie taking with you, Lance?" Patty asked. The question focused Lexie's attention.

"We have to travel light, so we're each taking only a week's-worth of clothes. We know the family we'll stay with has laundry facilities.

If we have to get anything else, we'll buy clothing there. The Big Brother assigned to us by the Institute, Gary Davenport, advised us as to what household items to bring."

"Like what?" George Garrett looked with interest at his son.

"Bedding, linens, clothing, rainwear, medicines, toiletries, household items, foodstuff, and electronic items to name a few."

"At least you won't have to worry about snow and cold." Amy spoke as she helped her youngest granddaughter ladle gravy over a slice of turkey.

"The weather can still be chilly, Mom, especially during the rains. Lexie and I plan to take lightweight clothing we can layer if needed. We ordered some light, breathable rain parkas and pants that will roll up and fit into a space no larger than a small umbrella. Cabela's sent them last week."

Lexie joined the conversation, "We've been wearing our new waterproof shoes to break them in. We were warned about the rain and dampness and how much walking we'd be doing, so we're trying to prepare. We know from all the mountain hiking we've done in Colorado, if our feet are happy and dry, we're happy."

"What do you mean, walking?" Amy raised her brows.

Lance answered, "We've been told most Costa Ricans walk, because traffic in San José on the weekdays is terrible. Our home will be a fifteen-minute walk from the Institute. Did you know the last numeral on a vehicle's license plate determines on which day of the week a person can drive? If people drive in the city on the wrong day, they can be fined. They call this road space rationing."

"Hmm. How inconvenient," David commented.

"We'll, I can't see it'll matter much to us, because we'll walk, or take a bus or taxi. We won't be driving."

"What kind of foodstuffs? Seems to me cans and things would add too much weight." David cut his turkey into more manageable bites while waiting for Lance's answer.

"You're right. We don't have to bring much. US products are available, though items like salad dressing mixes, chili and taco mixes, and dry soup mixes are expensive or unavailable. Good thing Lexie and I don't use these. We'll take our favorite spices and seasonings, since they won't take up much room. We'll stock up again when we return here for Christmas next year, before leaving for Guatemala."

Lexie saw the tightening around Olivia's mouth and the tears that came and went.

"Aren't you staying with a family in Costa Rica?" Patty asked, "Won't they provide the food? Isn't that why you're paying room and board?" She looked from Lexie to Lance, and back again.

"Yes, they'll provide three meals a day, but what if Lance and I need a little time to adjust to the food? Gary said we can purchase almost anything we need in local department stores, but I'm bringing several small containers of stevia powder Mom extracted from her plants for sweetening, as well as vitamins and other things we might not be able to find."

Lexie dropped her hand and touched the leather bag hanging from the back of her chair. The bag had traveled with her to 1857, and remained close at hand in the twenty-first century. Since Guatemala sounded a little like primitive Kansas territory, she intended to be better prepared than she had been when God sent her into the past.

"What else will you take?" Greg asked, and looked at Lexie.

"Well, for a wedding gift we got a small, infrared titanium cooktop. A special, nonstick pan and skillet with glass lids were included. The base of the cooktop remains cool, except where the pan touches the center. We'll take these in case we want to do our own cooking, especially in Guatemala. They won't take up too much room, and they aren't heavy."

"Don't you need electricity? Are you going to need an adapter?"

“No. Electrical outlets in Guatemala and Costa Rica are the same as here.”

“What household items did the Institute suggest, Lexie?” Olivia sipped her coffee and watched her face.

“Objects to make us feel at home, or remind us of home. Gary suggested board or card games, and DVDs or CDs. This is where you all come in. I want to do more videotaping before we leave so we can see your faces, hear your voices, and remember the people and places we love. Maybe we won’t get so homesick. I’m also taking the movie I made of my ancestry, which I’d like to show you after dinner.”

“She’s worked on this for months,” Olivia spoke, and glanced around the table at the others. “Knowing how much detail Lexie puts into her projects, I’m sure the movie will be impressive. I wish my mom and grandmother could be here, but neither felt like coming. I’m glad you’re giving each of them a DVD, Lexie.”

“Weston said you had him and Kimberly read some letters for you. Did you get to use what they sent?” Steven finally joined the conversation.

“Yes. They were perfect for the parts. You’ll see.”

By the time everything had been cleaned and put away, the children were sprawled on the bed in the front bedroom, already engrossed in a new adventure video Patty had brought for them. The adults moved into the living room and settled comfortably. Greg dimmed the lights. They watched Lexie slide the disc into the player and push play, and then settle herself close to Lance.

“I’ve been looking forward to this, hon,” he whispered near her ear. “I want to see the diaries and your people come alive.”

She nodded and reached for his hand. “You will.”

The first thing the listeners saw and heard was a black screen and the sound of a violinist playing the opening chords of “Oh,

Shenandoah" with a soft, quiet touch. The black screen dissolved into a lightly textured, leather-like background, and the words, A Journey into the Past: Ties that Bind grew, solidified, and stabilized in the center.

"Are you the one who's playing, honey?" David asked, and everyone looked at her.

"Yes, I played all the music, including the harmonies. I used the violin and synthesizer."

"I like the western-looking font," Olivia said, "The text looks old, but the letters aren't too loopy or hard to read. I like the dark, antique brown color very much." Olivia stopped talking and watched the title change into the introduction of the diaries, and listened as Lexie's recorded voice read the text displayed on the screen.

"You sound like a professional voice artist, babe," Lance whispered.

"I must have recorded the narration pieces fifty times before I liked them," Lexie sighed and leaned into his shoulder.

As the soft strains of "Oh, Shenandoah" faded, the image of the Bell family appeared as if burning through the background, and a sound of trace chains, popping whips, and wagons on the move could be heard as Fergus began to speak. The camera slowly zoomed in to his face as he told who he was, when and where he was born, and what was the most difficult thing to bear as he traveled the trail to Kansas Territory. His familiar, scratchy voice caused Lexie's tears to pool in the corners of her eyes. They spilled down her face when she listened to Jim, Edna, Dwight, Mary, and Mattie tell about themselves and their adventures on the Trail.

"Oh, how I wish I could hug them," Lexie whispered.

Lance drew her closer. "Eventually, you will, babe."

For the next hour, the Garretts and Logans watched the unfolding of Lexie, Steven, and Olivia's ancestral story. When the movie came to an end, no one spoke for a few moments.

"Wow," Patty said. "Hollywood movie-makers don't have anything on you, Lexie. I feel as if I know these people, and could point them out to you on the street. I wish I knew more about what happened to Peter when he got to Oregon. You said slavery was illegal and slaves had to be freed, yet freed slaves weren't allowed to stay in Oregon. What was the quote by that man? I think his name was Jesse Applegate."

Lexie closed her eyes and recited, "Being one of the 'Poor Whites' from a slave state I can speak with some authority for that class—Many of those people hated slavery, but a much larger number of them hated free negroes worse even than slaves."

"Wow," Patty said again. "I hope Peter landed on his feet, whatever happened."

"I'm sure with the help of the Bells and Sean West he would have. People liked Peter."

George laughed. "You speak as if you knew them well."

Lexie shrugged and glanced at Lance.

Steven stood and stretched. "I liked the pictures and music you used with Jonathan and Jesse's battle scenes the most. Knowing they could've killed each other would've been a hard thing to think about before pulling the trigger. I'm glad they were still friends in the end, that they got to Oregon, and that Jonathan started this family."

Amy hugged Lexie. "Well, I liked the tales from the Oregon Trail the best. I learned some things from listening to Edna, Josie, and Annie I didn't know, and I thought Mattie's letters were delightful, though Peter's were more informative." Amy's smile was sincere. "Yours is one of the best movies I've seen, Lexie. What I saw makes me wonder about my ancestry. Thanks for showing the DVD to us. I'd like a copy if you're selling them."

"I'll give you one."

"No, I know you had to buy the DVDs and other supplies, so I want to make a donation. Then you won't be in the hole."

Olivia stood and approached Lexie. "I don't know what to say, sweet girl. I'm amazed at what you were able to do with our story. I feel as if I know Olivia Anne and Alexandria much better. They seem like real people now, and not just names on a piece of paper, or hazy images. The people who read the letters had perfect voices for their parts."

"Do you think Gran and Grammy have watched their DVDs yet, Mom? I asked Kim and Weston to wait to show their family until today, so we all saw the movie on the same day."

"They were supposed to watch the DVD right after dinner at the home. Gran was so excited she talked about the movie to several of the other patients and workers. They wanted to see your movie too."

David bent and kissed Lexie's cheek. "You're amazing, honey. I'm very, very impressed."

"Thanks, Daddy."

David looked from Lexie to Lance. "The big blacksmith, Jim, reminded me a little of you, Lance. I don't know why, really, but he did."

Lance grinned and flexed the bicep of his left arm. Muscles in his shoulder and chest bulged with tension at the movement. "All these impressive muscles, right?"

David laughed, but his tone flattened and became more serious as he appeared to struggle to put his thoughts into words, "Oh, there's no doubt you're strong, Lance, but I think the resemblance has more to do with your attitude about serving and pleasing God, no matter what others think, and no matter the cost, than to the size and hardness of your muscles."

Lexie couldn't tell if her dad thought this was a good thing, or not.

Olivia's phone rang. She glanced at the caller ID. "Excuse me," she looked at the people in the room and said, "Mom's calling."

She answered and walked toward the hallway as she listened to Audrey, but stopped before she completely left the room. She turned back to the people who chatted with each other, and then stood in front of Lexie.

"I'm glad you, Gran, and the other patients in the home loved Lexie's movie, Mom. Here, you should tell her what you told me. Hold on a minute. I'm putting Lexie on." Olivia handed the phone over.

"Hi, Grammy. Happy Thanksgiving."

While Lexie spoke to Audrey, Olivia smiled at the others. "Mom said everyone at the home who watched the movie stayed glued to the large screen until the ending credits. Several of the eldest people started telling stories of their own ancestors, and she said the workers popped popcorn and made hot chocolate. She said the festive atmosphere and the ability to share stories has made everyone happier."

By the time she, Lance, and the Logans rose to bid the Garretts good-bye, and to thank them for their hospitality, Lexie and Olivia had fielded several calls from family members who had either seen or heard about the movie. They all wanted copies.

"Hmm. Seems like your movie's going viral, Lexie," Patty teased as she helped Lexie on with her coat. "Maybe you've missed your real calling of family historian and movie maker."

She smiled. All the praise felt very good.

Suddenly, the scar on her arm stung. She rubbed the wound through the thick material of her coat. For a moment, she returned to the memory of her last day in 1857, when she'd surrendered to God while she sat on the piano bench. She remembered how the room seemed to shrink around her to the size of a great fish's belly. Much like the prophet Jonah, she sensed the movement of the creature as it swam the ocean depths, and she experienced the sensation of burning as the stomach acid touched her skin. The stench of decaying fish nauseated her. She blinked.

Thanks for the reminder, Lord. Thanks for keeping me focused on what's important.

No smile raised the sides of Lexie's mouth when she looked at her sister-in-law. "Oh, I know what my calling is, Patty. At least I do for the next two years. After this time, we'll see."

The sky was dark and full of stars when Lexie and Lance followed David and Steven outside. Olivia had stayed a moment longer to finish her conversation with Amy and George.

Lance put his hand on Lexie's arm to keep her still. She looked at him as he said, "Hon, I want to talk to your mom before she gets in the car. I have to know what I've done to offend her. Will you keep your dad's attention for a couple of minutes?

Lexie glanced at the sliver of moon in the sky before she nodded. "You're going to try to talk to her in this cold? The temperature is below freezing, love. She won't stand for much conversation in the cold and dark."

"I'll see if she'll make time to talk to me tomorrow."

Steven was already belted into his seat in the back, texting his friends, and David had already started the car when Lexie walked to the driver's side window and spoke to him. As she chatted with her dad, she watched Lance and her mom. The porch light gave her a good view of them as they talked, and based on her mother's posture, tight lips, and hard jaw as she walked with Lance toward the car, she didn't think he'd received a favorable response to his request.

He helped Olivia into the car and then turned to Lexie, who'd walked around the car and took Lance's hand.

"What did she say?"

"She said to come over tomorrow morning at ten after Steven and David leave. Your dad is taking your brother to see the office complex. The site is shut down for the holidays until Monday."

"Do you want me to come with you?" she asked, and slid into her seat.

Lance closed her door then walked around to his side of the car. He belted himself in, turned the ignition, and looked at her. "Maybe she won't feel like we're ganging up on her if I go alone, hon. Maybe she'll tell me what's eating her, and why I now seem to be public enemy number one."

When Olivia opened the door to him the next morning, Lance wondered how successful the talk with his mother-in-law would be. Her face was tight and mask-like, and the corners of her mouth didn't curl into a smile of welcome. She looked at him as if she barely knew him. He began to pray silently.

"Come in." She tipped her head and closed the door behind him.

He followed her into the kitchen.

"Do you want something to drink?" Olivia's tone would register somewhere between forty and fifty degrees on a Fahrenheit thermometer.

Lance shook his head and sat next to her at the kitchen table. She stiffened into a queen-like pose, and when he noticed Olivia's tight, forward-thrusting jaw and crossed arms, he fought down the urge to raise his own defenses and respond in like manner.

When Lexie occasionally got upset with him and tightened into a similar unfriendly, uncommunicative, queenly posture, he'd learned his typically male, head-on, in-your-face responses never worked well with her, and they wouldn't work with her mother.

"Thanks for agreeing to see me, Olivia," he kept his voice soft and friendly.

She tilted her head but said nothing.

"I wanted to talk to you, because lately, I've started to get the idea that I've done something to offend you."

He waited for her answer, which was long in coming.

"Why shouldn't I be upset with you?"

Lance noticed she wouldn't even say his name.

"My daughter has given up plans to continue her education and her dreams of playing violin for the Topeka Symphony Orchestra, to follow you to one of the most dangerous countries in the Western Hemisphere. David and I know you understand this, because we and the Monterros have provided you with a ton of information. Still, you insist on going and taking my baby with you. Lexie's got so much potential, but out of her love for you, she'll risk her life and health. For what? Orphans? There are plenty of orphans in this country who need help. Why can't you stay here and work with them?"

Olivia's white-hot anger seared his lungs and left an acrid, bitter taste in his mouth. He yearned to fight fire with sarcastic fire, but he knew this action would result in the total destruction of the already tenuous relationship he had with his mother-in-law, so he begged the Spirit for patience and love, and spoke as gently as he could.

"I know you and David fear for her, Olivia, and I haven't discounted your fears or any information you've provided, but Lexie and I have to be obedient to God. He's the only One who knows why He wants us in Guatemala, and not in the United States. When you talk to Lexie, you should ask her if she is surrendering her plans and dreams to my will, or to the Lord's. Maybe she's going out of her love for Him."

"The results are the same. She'll leave her home and the people she loves."

"Just as Abraham did, Olivia, and God made tremendous promises to him and his descendants. He protected Abraham, and gave him a better dream and future than the man could've ever imagined for himself. He can also do the same for Lexie."

"Don't use an ancient patriarch to support your actions," Olivia's words were impatient.

"Well, if you're unwilling to consider Abraham, then consider your own ancestors. Think of the sacrifices they made in order to receive the blessings of the Almighty."

Olivia's face softened. She must have been replaying some of Lexie's movie in her mind, but then her brow furrowed and her pupils constricted. Lance knew she would not be persuaded. He stood, so she did too.

"I'd better go. I can see myself out."

Olivia nodded but said nothing.

As he walked toward the car, he felt her gaze on him as she watched him from the window.

> *Father, she doesn't want to hear. She's letting fear drive her thoughts, emotions, and actions. I understand why she's acting this way, Lord, but her behavior is still hard to take. Please calm my anger toward her. I ask you'd soften her heart and give her and David an understanding of how faithful, loving, and reliable you are. Help them to understand.*

When Lance stepped through the door of his own living room, he heard the low, prayerful tones of Lexie's violin. The music came from their bedroom. He removed his shoes and listened for several moments. Some of the tenseness left his body as he walked toward the sounds with slow, silent steps.

Lexie looked out the window while she played, her back to the open door where he stood. As he watched her, Olivia's accusations slithered underneath his skin and tied themselves into acidic bundles in his stomach. Had Lexie given up her dreams for the Lord, or for him? When they'd spoken together at the Cousins reunion several months ago, hadn't she said she'd given up her plans, but she trusted God to direct her to bigger dreams? How did she really feel about the actions they were about to take?

Uncertainty dilated the pupils of his eyes and again tightened every muscle in his body.

Lexie finished the last chords of "Nearer, My God, to Thee" and turned toward the door. She studied Lance's posture, put down the violin and bow, and walked to him, arms open. In one fluid motion, he reached for her, wrapped his arms around her, and turned his face into her neck.

"I don't have to ask how it went, love. The answer's obvious."

For several moments, Lexie massaged the tight bands of muscles in his back. Finally, he kissed her neck then looked in her face, his nostrils slightly flared. She fingered the shallow furrows between his dark eyebrows, and then rubbed the pads of her fingertips against the dark stubble on his cheek and chin.

He stilled her hand and brought her fingers to his lips.

"Why have you agreed to come to Guatemala with me, hon?"

Lexie's eyes widened. "Because God gave me another chance to be obedient to His will. What did Mom say to cause you to ask this question?"

Lance relaxed, and his breathing slowed. "Tell me how you truly feel about not being able to complete your master's degree, or play with the Symphony. Your mom holds me responsible for the loss of your dreams. Do you?"

Lexie searched her heart for the truth. "You aren't responsible, Lance. What was the verse we read in Proverbs? Something about the heart of man plans the way he will go, but the Lord establishes his path? Just because I'm going with you now, doesn't mean I can't get my degree, or audition for the Symphony later. Who knows? I may want something different two years from now."

The furrows smoothed from his brow, and his jaw relaxed. The soft look in his brown eyes reflected the emotions in his heart. "Other than Christ's love, you're the best thing that's happened to me, Lexie. I'm so glad you didn't stay in the past with Dwight, Jonathan, or Sean."

She nodded and laid her cheek against his chest. "Lance, what are we going to do about Mom? What can we say to help her understand?"

He stroked her hair. "I don't think anything we say will make much difference right now. Fear, hurt feelings, and anger are tearing at her. God's going to have to deal with your mom, babe. All we can do is love her and pray."

"We're supposed to go to my parents' house for an early Christmas in a few weeks. I hope she and Dad are reconciled to our leaving by the time we get together. I'd hate to have our celebration tainted by anger. If we leave for Costa Rica, and they're still mad ..." Tears choked her words and clouded her eyes.

He kissed the top of her head and held her tight.

"I know, hon. I know."

"Lance, I can't deal with the added stress generated by family issues. I just can't."

He pulled away far enough to reach for her hand then bent toward her ear and whispered, "I can do all things through Christ, who gives me strength."

He repeated Philippians chapter four verse thirteen several times until she joined with him in the recitation. He stopped speaking when he saw her tears had dissipated.

"The Lord is our refuge and strength, Lexie. He's a special help in time of need, so run to him, my darling. His arms are open."

What were the words God had spoken to her heart back in 1857?

> *Lay hold on the anchor, Lexie. I AM the anchor of your soul, both sure and steadfast. I will never leave you nor forsake you, daughter. Lay hold! Lay hold!*

PART TWO

TEN

As Lexie stood in the airline's baggage check line, she looked toward the large glass entry doors and watched travelers coming and going. She chewed on her bottom lip and grasped the handle of her suitcases so hard her knuckles whitened.

"Relax, hon. They'll come," Lance's calm voice reassured her.

"Do you think Mom will come with Dad and Steven? Dad's accepted the fact we're going, but she hasn't. She's still upset."

"Olivia will come, babe. You're her only daughter, and she loves you very much."

Lexie's phone rang. The unique sound of the ring identified Kimberly as the caller.

"Hi, Kim."

"Hey, cousin. I just wanted to tell you good-bye. I hope you'll keep in touch."

"I plan to. Lance got me a new tablet and keyboard for Christmas.

You should see this thin, light-weight piece of technology, Kim. The thing has more bells and whistles than I'll ever use. Hey, maybe we can Skype regularly."

"You'll have good internet connections to do this?"

"Yes. Lance didn't know how reliable service would be in either country, so we've got a small device that will give us our own secure WIFI hotspot. We had to subscribe to a global service."

"I'm sure you and your family will have a little more peace of mind knowing you can communicate quickly and easily."

"I hope so. Grammy installed Skype on her new laptop, so she can take her computer to the nursing home and I can talk with Gran. She's pleased to learn we can see each other's faces, and can talk free of charge, no matter where in the world we are. We've practiced, so she feels comfortable using the program."

"That's good. Hey, Lexie, I wanted to ask you something. I don't quite know how to phrase this question, or how you're going to respond, but I have to ask anyway."

Lexie straightened and turned toward Lance at the hesitancy in Kim's voice.

"What do you want to know?" Goosebumps raised on Lexie's arm under her deep purple jacket, and she brushed a strand of hair out of her eyes. Lance focused on her face when he heard her tone.

"Well, I started reading the scanned copies of the diaries you gave me for safekeeping. I got curious about my history after the family watched your DVD, and I wanted to know more details about Matthew Bell. I started reading some letters and Olivia Johnson's diaries during my vacation, and ..."

Lexie felt the color drain from her face and reached toward the pounding pulse below her ear with her free hand. Kimberly knew! In her haste to finish last minute tasks, Lexie had sent her cousin copies of the full diaries, not the edited versions. And now Kimberly knew.

Lance frowned and mouthed, "What's wrong?"

"I'll tell you in a minute," she whispered.

"Lexie, are you there?"

She swallowed hard before replying, "Yes, I'm here. I know what you're going to ask, Kim, but I don't know if you'll believe my answer."

"Try me."

Lexie looked around and lowered her voice, "I can't talk right now. I'm surrounded by people, and we're getting ready to check in."

"What if I ask you some questions you can answer with yes, no, or short answers, and then we can talk at length later?"

Lexie sighed. "Okay. Ask."

"Are you the Lexie Logan mentioned in Olivia Johnson's diary and Mattie's, Mary's, and Peter's letters?"

"Yes."

"You, a twenty-first century woman, are mentioned in a diary written in 1866, and in letters written in 1858?"

"Yes."

"Then that means you ... traveled through time and visited our ancestors?"

Lexie could almost hear Kim's mental struggle. "Yes."

Her cousin was silent for several moments. "Does Lance know?"

"Yes."

"Anyone else?"

"You."

"When did you go back in time?"

"June 10, 2014."

"When did you arrive in the past?"

"June 10, 1857."

Lance's eyes widened. "She knows?"

Lexie nodded.

"How long were you gone?"

"Three months."

"Three months? But our reunion was July 2014 and you were there. When did you return to the future?"

"June 10, 2014."

"What? How did this happen?"

"God."

More moments passed before Kimberly could speak, "Were any of the voices we heard on the DVD actual voices from the past?"

"Yes."

"Mattie?"

"Yes. Weston read the letters, but the younger voice at the starting of the DVD was Mattie's."

"Fergus?"

"Yes."

"The rest of the Bell family, as well as Sean West, Jesse, Jonathan, and Nathan Johnson?"

"Yes."

"Did the Bells believe you came from the future?"

"Eventually."

"They let you record them?"

"Yes, just before I left."

"Do you have more voice and video recordings that weren't on the DVD?"

"Yes."

"You had your phone with you then?"

"Yes."

"Will you let me listen to them? See them?"

Lexie hesitated. "Maybe."

"Wow, wow, wow."

"Listen, Kim, we're almost to the counter. Can we chat later?"

"Yes. Please promise you'll call when you get settled. In the meantime, I'll finish Olivia Johnson's, Josie's, and Annie's diaries."

"Please don't say anything to anyone else. Not even to Weston. Promise?"

"I promise. Good-bye, Lexie."

"Bye, Kim."

"How did she find out?" Lance asked, as they stepped toward the counter.

"In my hurry to get everything done before we left, I accidentally sent her the complete, unedited versions of the letters and diaries. She's been reading them."

As she turned from the counter, ticket in hand, Lexie adjusted the shoulder strap of the roomy leather bag. Now packed with her "survival" gear, Lexie kept the bag near to hand, much as she'd done in the past. She also clutched the handle of her violin case.

"Lance. Lexie."

She and Lance turned to see Amy, George, and Greg walking toward them.

"Whew. Couldn't find a place to park." Greg smiled and hugged each of them. Amy and George did the same.

"Patty said to tell you she's sorry she couldn't see you off, but the kids started school today and she's back to being the number one chauffeur and gofer, in between all of her online meetings for work."

"We understand." Lexie played with the identification tag hanging from the zipper of her bag. "Amy, did my folks say anything about when they'd be here?"

"They're right behind us. They had to park quite a distance from the elevator."

"There they are, hon." Lance tilted his head toward the glass doors.

"Over here, Mom. Dad," Lexie called and waved. David, Olivia, and Steven wove through the crowd to get to them then they hugged and kissed each other.

"Hey, Stevie, I thought today was your first day back to class. Already starting the new year out by ditching?" Lexie teased, and held on to Olivia's hand.

"Couldn't miss seeing my favorite sister and brother off." He hooked his thumbs into the waistband of his jeans. "Wish I were going with you. Your life sounds more exciting than mine right now. I'd rather be heading to the beaches of a tropical country and seeing new sights than sitting in a chair and listening to teachers talk while the temperature outside doesn't even reach forty degrees."

"You only have one more year, Stevie."

"Actually, I have only half a year, Lex. The counselor said I've got enough credits to graduate early."

Lance looked at George. "You have a lot in common with Steven, Dad. He's very good in math and science, and he's a real hot-shot in his chemistry class."

Steven grinned.

"Hmm," George said, "I'd like to hear about your future plans."

"You and me both, George." David chuckled and clasped Steven's shoulder.

"You can talk about that later, you three," Amy softened the admonition with a smile, and turned to Lexie. "You fly into Dallas Fort Worth?"

"Yes. From there we have a direct flight to San José."

"How long will the flight take?"

"A little over four hours."

Lance joined the conversation, "We have to start classes tomorrow, Mom, so we wanted to get to our new home as soon as we could in order to prepare. Gary's meeting us at the airport."

"I have something for you, Lexie." Olivia squeezed her hand and handed her a package. "Sharon made the gift to my specifications."

Lexie handed Lance the violin then opened the box and lifted out a thin, wide, flesh-toned belt. She looked at Olivia in question.

"The adjustable belt snaps in front, and is supposed to be worn under your clothing. Though the material is breathable and soft, and won't cause you to sweat, the fabric is also very strong. The pocket on the inside front is large enough to carry the tablet Lance got you without creating a noticeable bulge around your middle if you wear loose clothing. There's a place for your passport, visa, and money, and your cell phone if you want to carry the thing there. Maybe you won't be such a target."

Olivia brushed away tears she couldn't stop. "I'm sorry I'm such a wreck."

"I love you, Mommy." She hugged Olivia and whispered in her ear, "Thank you. I'll wear the belt every day, and think of you. As soon as we get through security, I'll find a restroom and put your gift on."

"Lexie and I should head upstairs now. We have plenty of time, but the lines are long, as you can see."

They exchanged last hugs and kisses, and the Garretts and Logans walked toward the door.

Olivia stopped. "David, I need just a couple more minutes. You and Stevie go on. If you'll get the car and wait by the elevator in the parking garage, I'll be right there."

David nodded, and Olivia took Lance by the hand and walked with him and Lexie.

"Can we talk just a minute, Lance?"

"Sure, Olivia. Here?" He indicated a wall near the escalator. "Doesn't look like there are too many people around this area."

Olivia nodded.

"I'm going to the restroom while you two talk, okay?" At Olivia's nod, Lexie kissed her and left.

"I want to apologize for the way I've treated you, Lance. I'm sorry. I just—"

"I know, Olivia. I know why you acted the way you did, and I forgive you."

With a cry like a wounded animal, she wrapped her arms around his neck and buried her face in the soft material of his shirt. "Take care of my baby. Bring her back safely."

"I'll do my best. But put your trust in the Lord and His goodness, Mom." He cupped her face and kissed her cheek. "Good-bye. I love you."

Olivia dropped her arms and walked away.

During the flight from Dallas to San José, Lexie tried to rest, but couldn't. From the moment the stewardess got on the public address system and went through the safety spiel in Spanish and English, Lexie knew she was in trouble. Though she recognized what was said by the hand motions and her previous travel experiences, she didn't understand a word of the woman's Spanish, even after all the hours she'd spent trying to learn the language. The sounds didn't separate themselves into words, but continued in one long string of rolled r's and trills.

She pulled out the card of emergency instructions from the seat back in front of her and flipped to the Spanish text. The only words she understood were cognates similar in English. *Flotación* was obviously the word flotation, and had to be emergency.

Lexie replaced the card behind the barf bag. Between her fear of not understanding and her knowledge of how her stomach responded to turbulence, she was almost certain she would need the bag, which created more stress.

"What's wrong, hon?" Lance turned from talking to the passenger who sat in the window seat to his right and looked at her. "You're almost hyperventilating."

Lexie could feel the panic tightening her throat so she could barely speak. With certainty, she knew the emotion filled her eyes. "I didn't understand a word the stewardess said, Lance. People all around us are speaking Spanish, and I don't understand them, either. I feel sick."

He reached for her hand and whispered in her ear, "Deuteronomy chapter thirty-one verse eight. 'It is the Lord who goes before you. He will be with you; he will not leave you or forsake you. Do not fear or be dismayed.'"

"Lexie, say the words with me."

After she'd repeated the verse three times in a whisper, her fists unclenched and the tenseness left her jaw, neck, and shoulders. She relaxed into the cushions and closed her eyes, though her lips moved in silent prayer. Her breathing returned to normal, but she kept a firm clasp on Lance's hand.

Just about an hour or less before touchdown she dozed for ten minutes, but opened her eyes when the stewardess began to hand out immigration forms.

"Please complete this form before exiting the plane. When you arrive in the terminal, follow the signs and proceed to immigration. Give them this form, and when you are finished there, you may go to baggage claim. Look for your flight number on the carrousel to claim your luggage. You will find shops and a currency exchange desk in this area."

Lexie's eyes widened. Soon, she'd be landing in Costa Rica to begin a new phase of her life.

The stewardess saw the wide-eyed look. "Is this your first time to travel to Costa Rica?"

At Lexie's nod, she smiled. "Don't be afraid. The process is not difficult. After you have your luggage, proceed to Customs and give the agent your declarations form. He or she will check your bags, and then you are free to go."

The plane began its descent, and Lexie gripped Lance's hand. She wondered if he could see the pulse pounding in her neck.

He smiled at her, anticipation and excitement in his eyes.

"Gary can't come into the terminal, but he said he'd be waiting for us near the elevator on the first level of the parking garage. He'll have a sign with our names written in big letters. I'll text him when we're through Customs."

The plane landed and taxied to the terminal.

"Welcome to Juan Santamaría International Airport in Costa Rica. Please remain in your seat with your seatbelt securely fastened until the plane comes to a complete stop." The stewardess gave her welcome and instructions over the public-address system, first in Spanish, and then in English, "The current temperature outside is 24 degrees Celsius. The low tonight is expected to be fifteen degrees."

Lexie blinked. She'd forgotten she'd have to make conversions from US customary units to the metric system, so she did some rapid calculations and determined the temperature was 75 degrees Fahrenheit, and would reach a low in the mid-sixties. Quite balmy compared to Topeka's cold, forty-degree high.

"Current time is 5:35 p.m.," she continued.

Lexie looked at her watch and exhaled in relief. She was in the same time zone as her loved ones back home-the same time zone, and the same century.

Gary waited for them near the elevator. Though he held the sign with their names written in large letters, she knew who he was by the welcoming smile stretching across his mouth and into the corners of his sideburns. The smile lit sparks in his blue eyes. He looked to be in his late fifties, and he'd probably been a blonde in his younger days. The Costa Rican sun had burnished him to a rich shade of tan, and had bleached his hair almost white.

After the introductions, Gary led them toward an older Nissan sedan and helped load their suitcases in the trunk.

"Had to borrow this car from a friend. Today's Monday, so only vehicles with license plates ending in ones or twos can drive in the city now. Mine ends with a six, so I can drive on Wednesdays."

"You're staying long enough in the country to own a car?" Lance asked from the back seat.

"Yes. I work here for an American-based business. Have for six years. I attended the Institute when I first came. The people there helped me a lot, so now I help them by volunteering as a Big Brother."

"The steering wheel is on the same side as the cars in the US," Lexie said and snapped herself into the seatbelt. She met Gary's eyes in the rear-view mirror. "Does this mean Costa Ricans drive on the same side of the road we do?"

He nodded.

As he wove his way through the crazy traffic and turned southeast, he told them about their host family.

"The Mora's are very excited to have you both. Two years ago, they hosted a man from Georgia. He attended the Institute, and then left to serve in Honduras at the end of his year. Javier said having another man in the house was enjoyable, because he didn't have to listen to so much women's chatter, which is why he's glad you're coming, Lance. He hopes you like to tinker with, and fix things, because he does. He has a never-ending list of projects he works on when he comes home from his regular job as a mechanic. Earns some side money by repairing broken things for his neighbors. He's very talented in many areas."

Gary chuckled. "Mariana is the chatter box, but their daughter, Gabriela, is shy and doesn't say much I've ever heard. I know they're pleased a woman will come this time. They're very curious about you, Lexie, and have asked many questions."

"Do they speak English?" Lexie could barely get the words out through the constriction in her throat.

"Most Ticos speak some English, though Mariana's isn't very good, and she's hard to understand. I imagine Gabby's English is better, because she studies the language in school."

"Ticos?" Lance leaned forward to hear Gary's answer.

"The ending *-tico* is an affectionate term they add to the end of words. They use this ending to mean everything in their town. For example, they'll change words like, *chico*, meaning boy child or kid, to *chiquitico*. The word small, *pequeño*, becomes *pequeñitico*."

"How old is Gabriela?" Lexie prayed the girl was old enough to have taken several years of English.

"She's seventeen."

Stevie's age. Lexie smiled, and the constriction in her throat loosened. "I look forward to meeting them. Is there any advice about living with this family you can give Lance and me?"

"Yep. Just remember why you're here. You want to learn Spanish so you can serve in a Spanish-speaking country. The best way to do this is to watch, listen, and try to interact with native Spanish speakers. In your orientation at the Institute these next few days, you'll be told you'll make a million mistakes, and you will, so don't let them bother you. The people here are gracious and patient."

"But how do we communicate with them tonight and find out the basics?" Lance asked before Lexie could.

"They've invited me to stay to dinner. I'll interpret for all of you. Gabriella will walk with you to the Institute tomorrow so you'll know how to get there. Her school is nearby, so taking you won't be out of her way."

As soon as Gary pulled up to the curb in front of their new home and popped the trunk, the Mora's front door opened and Javier stepped out and waved. Tight black curls surrounded his head, and his dark brown eyes sparked pleasantly. He was shorter than she, Lance, and Gary. He walked to meet them and to help with the luggage, while Mariana and Gabriela stood framed in the doorway, watching and waiting, smiles on their faces.

The man shook hands with Gary and said something in rapid Spanish. The only word Lexie recognized was Gary's answer. Sí. Yes.

She clutched the handle of her violin case tighter and held the instrument closer to her middle when Javier turned to her and Lance and said, "*Bienvenidos a nuestra casa.*"

Lexie was certain she had a deer-in-the-headlights look on her face, but she swallowed the lump in her throat and tried to smile.

Lance held out his hand and said, "*Gracias.*"

Gary interpreted, "He said, *Welcome to our home.* Don't look so scared, Lexie. The Mora's won't eat you."

She took a deep breath, released the tension in her shoulders and arms, and offered her hand to Javier. "Gracias." She wondered if he felt the trembling of her fingers, and if he could see the pulse pounding just below the surface of the skin on her neck.

He smiled again, tilted his head toward the women who waited, and made a "come" motion with his hand. He continued talking in rapid Spanish, and Gary interpreted after each phrase.

"Javier says his wife and daughter have been filled with excitement. They tried to guess what you looked like, and how you would be, but none of them expected such tall, handsome, light-skinned people."

Lexie smiled. "Thank you. Gracias."

Javier's eyes widened and he looked from Lexie to Lance. Gary laughed when he interpreted their host's words.

"Lance, Javier said your wife should smile more often. When she does, she lights up like a match."

Lance nodded and looked in Lexie's eyes. "Yes, I know. She lights up my heart with her smile."

Javier chuckled and introduced Lance and Lexie to his wife and daughter.

Mariana greeted Lance with words, but hugged Lexie. The petite, dark-haired, dark-eyed woman's head reached only six inches above Lexie's elbow, and she realized her host mother was the same height as Edna. She returned the hug.

"Come," Gabriela said in heavily accented but understandable English, "Your room."

She and Lance followed the teenager through the small living and dining area. The girl was as petite as her mother and moved with the grace of a dancer. They followed her into the bedroom.

Only three feet of space separated the double bed and a large wooden wardrobe, though only four feet separated the walls and bed. Lexie rolled her suitcases into the space nearest the door, sat her violin on the colorful tropical bedspread, and noted the fresh flowers filling the vases on the nightstands next to the bed. She saw the little touches her host family had added to make them feel welcome, so she turned and smiled.

"Thank you, Gabriela. Please tell your mother the room is lovely."

Lexie recognized the I-didn't-understand-what-you-said look, so she pointed to the flowers and said, "Beautiful. Pretty. Thank you."

Gabriela nodded, and then struggled to make her next words as perfect and understandable as she could, "I am named, Gabby."

She pointed toward the dining room and looked at Lance and Lexie. "You come. *La cena está lista.*" Gabby made eating motions, and the two nodded and followed her.

"Gabby?" The girl stopped and looked at Lexie.

"*Baño*?" Lexie made washing motions.

"Ah, *sí. Perdóneme.*" She pointed to the small bathroom they would all use, and left.

Lance closed the bathroom door, took Lexie into his arms, and nuzzled her neck. "You did well, babe. I'm proud of you."

She leaned her forehead against his then turned toward the sink.

As she lathered her hands, Lexie's eyes met his in the mirror. "How did you know what Javier said when we first arrived?"

"I recognized most of the words from our lessons, and I expected such a greeting. Didn't you?"

Lexie sighed and dried her hands on the towel. "I still can't distinguish the words when they're spoken so fast."

Lance dried then turned her to face him. His hands rested at her waist. "You will. Give yourself time, Lexie. You're such a perfectionist. What's the expression? Rome wasn't built in a day?"

When they walked into the dining area, Javier signaled them all to be seated. He reached for his wife and daughter's hands, and waited for them to join hands with the person seated beside them. He prayed, and Gary interpreted.

Gary's ability to switch from one language to another so easily amazed Lexie. She doubted if she would ever develop such proficiency.

"Mariana and Gabriela are very good cooks. They made this dinner for you, with hopes you would enjoy your first taste of Costa Rican food."

He listened to Mariana's rapid speech, and then pointed out the dishes. "In front of you are black beans and white rice. In the large wooden bowl next to them, you have *picadillo de platano y carne*—a dish made with green bananas, meat, vegetables, and spices, and next to that, you have *orecchiette* with tuna. You'll recognize the vegetable salad and some of the fruits on the other tray. The drink in your glasses is *horchata*. The H at the beginning of this word is silent. *Horchata* is a traditional drink Mariana makes from ground almonds, coconut milk, sesame seeds, nutmeg, and vanilla."

Lexie took small portions to see how her stomach would handle the new food, but Lance dug in without hesitation.

With Gary interpreting, the table conversation was relaxed. By the end of the meal, they knew about each other's' backgrounds and families. They discussed expectations, and set bathroom schedules. After Lexie helped Mariana and Gabriela clear the table, she thanked everyone and asked to be excused so she could call her family. The Mora's nodded and smiled.

"*Buenas noches, Lexie.*"

"I'll come in just a minute, hon," Lance said.

Lexie laid on the bedspread and created a group text.

> Made it to Costa Rica w/o problems. Had good dinner with Big Brother Gary and host family. Start school tomorrow, 7:30 a.m. Classes end 12:30 p.m. Lance will send text soon. Will call tomorrow afternoon. Very tired now. Love. Lexie.

ELEVEN

Mariana had lunch prepared when Lexie and Lance finished their first day of classes and, for this, Lexie was thankful. Exhausted, she could barely keep her eyes open. She hadn't slept well last night, even as tired as she'd been, because she couldn't stop predicting what would happen on the first day of class. Fortunately, none of her predictions had come true. The teachers and other students were kind and helpful.

Gabby arrived shortly after she and Lance returned to the house, so they all sat down to more black beans, rice, salad, fruit, and spaghetti in white sauce. Mariana asked them many questions in both Spanish and English, but Lexie understood none of the questions in either language. She shook her head and often repeated the words burned into her brain by fear: *Lo siento. No entiendo. I'm sorry, I don't understand.* Gabby struggled to translate, but couldn't keep up. Only Lance's friendly attempts to communicate kept everyone's stress levels from reaching the rupture-a-blood-vessel point.

"Gracias, Mariana." Lexie made eating motions. Why can't I remember the word for food or lunch? I feel like such a baby.

"*De nada.*" Mariana nodded then stood and began to clear the table.

Lexie and Lance helped, though Mariana and Gabby both looked startled when Lance took his dishes to the sink, rinsed them, and then returned to the table to remove more dishes.

He didn't see the look, but Lexie did, and she wondered if he'd overstepped some unknown, invisible line of acceptable behavior. Everyone in both the Garrett and Logan homes were expected to help clear the table, no matter if they were men, women, or children, and this expectation translated into an ingrained response.

Mariana said something, and Gabby turned to Lexie. "You play *violín*? *Mamá* ask you play, please."

Lexie nodded and went to the bedroom for the instrument. When she returned to the living area, Mariana and Gabby were laughing at something Lance said, and the unexpected twitch of envy she felt at her husband's ability to communicate with their new family so easily surprised her.

They settled themselves on the sofa and watched Lexie remove the violin and bow. Anticipation sparked in their brown eyes. Lance smiled.

The smooth feel of the wood as she raised the violin to her shoulder and placed her chin in the rest, and the familiar, friendly feel of the bow between her fingers relaxed the tension in her body. Oh, how she wished she could express herself in Spanish as fluently as she could share her emotions with a musical instrument.

She closed her eyes. For several minutes, the music voiced her fear and turmoil, but soon softened into melodies of praise and joy. She opened her eyes and looked at Mariana as she played notes easily recognizable as "thank you for opening your home. Please be patient with us."

Mariana and Gabby clapped enthusiastically and jumped up to hug Lexie after she'd returned the instrument to the case. Lexie returned their hugs. Though she didn't understand what they said, the caresses and praise in their voices, and the way they patted her arms soothed her fears. Her breathing returned to normal.

Lance drew her to him for a kiss. "I'll never get tired of hearing you play, babe. How many other men get to enjoy their own private concerts?"

Gabby and Mariana watched their interactions with interest and laughed when Lance pulled away, kissed his fingertips toward Lexie, and exclaimed in a dramatic voice, "*Ella es ¡fantástica! ¿No?*"

"*Sí. ¡Fantástica!*"

Lexie took a deep breath and pointed to her room. With hand and arm movements to aid and supplement her Spanish, she pointed to herself and said, "Tired. Sleep. Okay?"

Even though Lexie knew she hadn't conjugated the verb *sleep* using the correct form, but had left the verb in the infinitive form, *to sleep*, Mariana understood, nodded, and made a good-bye motion. She turned to the kitchen and indicated to Gabby she could start her homework.

"I'm coming with you, hon. Snuggling with a time-traveler and taking a power nap sound better than anything I can think of right now." Lance walked with her into the bedroom and closed the door.

Lexie reread what she'd written to friends, family, and supporters before adding more lines to the first of the monthly newsletters she promised to send.

We arrived safely and started classes today. The experience wasn't as frightening as I imagined. Lance and I have classes for five hours every day, with breaks between each. In the morning, we go to a pronunciation class. Today, we tried to produce all the sounds of the language. My tongue has a hard time making the double r trill, and I wonder if I'll ever be able to get this right. Our homework is to listen to the CDs and practice the drills. Soon we'll learn phrasing patterns, and proper intonation. Then we go to Basic Grammar and Oral Expression classes. These are mostly taught in Spanish, which is stressful, but I'm praying Lance and I will be fast learners. For some reason, the language seems to come to him more easily than to me. There are other new Spanish learners in our classes, and they struggle with the same fears we have, so in a way, I feel better knowing we're not the only ones. The teachers are wonderful, caring people who want us to be successful, and all the students in our classes are attending the Institute because they plan to serve the Lord in Spanish-speaking countries. Already, I feel a sense of camaraderie.

The Institute is located in a middle-class neighborhood. As you can see from the photos, the vegetation is green and lush, and the crimson bougainvilleas are gorgeous. There are mountains to the south, and two weekends from now, Lance and I plan to travel with our host family to a nearby beach located an hour away on the west coast. We've already been cautioned to protect ourselves from the tropical sun, and our Big Brother has warned us of the

> dangerous riptides that have carried strong swimmers out to sea. Sometimes warnings are posted, but sometimes they're not, which has curtailed my desire to swim in the ocean.
>
> Please continue to pray for us on a regular basis. We know prayer can move the hand of God.

Lexie double-checked the newsletter before pressing send, looked at her watch, then opened Skype and called Olivia and David. When they answered the video call, she saw Steven had crowded next to them to get in on the conversation.

"Hi, honey," David said, "You're looking good. How is everything?"

Lexie gave them details of her experience to date, and toured the house with the tablet. She returned to the dining room table and looked toward the door. "Just a minute. Javier and Lance just came in from outside. Lance has been helping him with a project, and Gabby and Mariana just came in from the market. I want you to meet them."

The Moras moved toward the computer and smiled when they saw their images in a little box near the top of the screen.

"Hey, Lance." Steven waved, and Lance greeted him and his in-laws.

Lexie pointed to her hosts. "Mom, Dad, this is Mariana and her husband, Javier. Mariana, Javier, these are *mis padres*, Olivia *y* David *y mi hermano*, Steven."

She signaled for Gabby to step closer. "This is their daughter, Gabriela, but we call her Gabby."

The families greeted each other with smiles and head nods, and the words, *nice to meet you, or mucho gusto*.

After the Moras moved away, Olivia asked, "Have you been sterilizing the water?"

"We've started water through the filtration system. We'll have about nine liters ready to drink in an hour. I boiled water before we went to school this morning, and let the water cool while we got ready. We've been drinking this through our LifeStraws."

"How old is Gabby?" Steven tried to sound nonchalant, but Lexie saw his interest.

She grinned. "Seventeen."

"Does she speak English?"

"A little."

"Pretty girl. Maybe I'll have to pay more attention in my Spanish classes."

Lexie laughed.

After several minutes, she signed off and called Kimberly. Her cousin answered the video call on the first ring.

"You're right on time, Lexie. Hey, how are things?"

Lexie told her, gave her a video tour of her new home, and then waited for the questions she knew Kimberly wanted to ask.

"I finished all the letters and diaries. Are you ready to answer questions now?"

Lexie saw the excitement in her cousin's eyes. "Yes, I suppose so, but you'll find everything I tell you hard to believe. I'm warning you up front."

"Start at the beginning, and tell me everything."

"I won't have time to give you all the details, but I'll give you as much as I can in the next hour before dinner."

"Will you call in the evenings when you don't have much homework?"

"Yes."

"Okay, tell me."

"Well, my journey started on June 9, 2014, when Lance and I broke up."

Kimberly rested her elbows on the table, leaned closer to the camera, and listened to Lexie's tale unfold, an expression of delight and wonder on her face.

Part way through their hour, Lexie chuckled and said, "You look like you're sitting in an IMAX theater watching a tale of adventure so riveting, you can't look away."

"I am riveted. Go on. What happened after you got to the box supper?"

Lexie continued until she smelled dinner. "I better go, Kim. We're getting ready to eat."

"Do you know what you should do, Lexie?"

"What?"

"Write your story. Even if no others except the two of us and Lance read what's written, at least your memories will be preserved."

"Maybe. I'll think about it. See you tomorrow."

By the time Saturday came, Lexie thought her brain would explode from listening to Spanish all week. In the evenings, she'd focus so intently on trying to understand Mariana's chatter, she often gave herself a headache. Had Gabby not been there to help, and without Lance's encouragement, she would've given up. Her discomfort intensified when she saw how quickly her husband conversed with those around him, and she wondered if he'd be moved to a higher class at the end of the trimester, and she'd be left behind.

What's wrong with me? Why is this so hard?

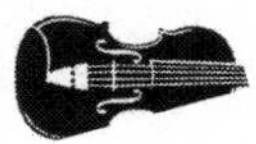

"Hey, what do you think about going to the gym on the campus and getting in a workout? The kids from the Academy often use the place for basketball, but maybe we can find an unoccupied corner."

"Sounds like a good idea. Let's go for a run first. Will you tell Javier and Mariana what we're doing?"

Lance nodded.

When she and Lance entered the gym dressed in their comfortable sweats, several of the teens smiled, but continued chatting over the sounds of bouncing basketballs, squeaking shoes, and laughter.

Some stopped talking to watch her and Lance pull a mat toward the corner, and several eased in their direction to watch when they took up stances and move into martial arts actions and counter-actions.

"Whew, you're pushing me hard today, hon." After thirty minutes, Lance wiped away the sheen of sweat dampening his forehead.

"Got a lot of frustration to work out of my system," Lexie answered and struck. She ignored the comments and words of encouragement from the cluster of teens surrounding them, and focused on Lance's counter-actions.

Finally, the stress of the week had worked itself out of her body and she could smile again.

"Hey, do either of you two play?" A tall, thin, sandy-haired boy looked at them and spun a basketball on the tip of his index finger. He introduced himself.

"Yep. Both of us." Lance smiled at Gene's enthusiastic response to his answer, but looked at Lexie. "Are you up for a game?"

"I guess."

By the time the scrimmage was over, Lance and Lexie had a new, younger group of friends who begged them to return when they could.

"Next time, you'll have to play on opposite sides to balance things up more. That game was too lop-sided." Gene ran his fingers through his sandy hair. He looked at Lexie. "You can be on my team any day."

She grinned. "Thanks."

"*De nada*. How'd you learn to play like that?" He walked with them outside.

"I've played in school, and then I often shoot hoops with my brother, Steven. He's seventeen and plays varsity basketball."

"Well, if he ever comes to visit, you can tell him he's invited to play with us."

Gene interpreted for his friend, Tomás, another tall, lanky, brown-skinned player who nodded enthusiastically.

Lance spoke, "I think your parents are in our classes. They talk about a son named Gene, and you look like them. Is your last name Getty?"

"Yes."

"You're going to Bolivia when you finish here?"

The teen nodded again.

"How do you speak Spanish so well?" Lexie hooked the strap of her leather bag over her shoulder and waited for his answer.

"Oh, I had Spanish since I was in middle school. I attended an International Baccalaureate school from middle- to high school, and we were required to be proficient in another language. I've picked up more here."

Lexie released the breath she'd held while waiting for his answer. She was prepared, but dreading to hear he'd learned to speak so fluently only in the time he was in Costa Rica.

On Sunday, everyone in the Mora house slept a little later, but then got up, ate, and prepared for church. Javier had invited them to attend last night during dinner, and Lance asked Lexie if she wanted to go.

"He said they go to a small mission church several blocks from here. Only about fifty people attend."

Lexie had agreed.

When Javier opened the door for them to enter the church, Lexie adjusted the strap of the leather bag, and clutched her computer tablet against her body.

"Relax, babe. You look like you're holding a shield, and we're about to enter an enemy encampment. These are brothers and sisters, remember?"

Lexie nodded and forced herself to release the death-grip on her tablet.

The Moras greeted their friends and pastor and introduced them to Lance and Lexie. The people seemed very interested to learn about them, and began to talk and ask questions at the same time. Lexie couldn't distinguish words in all the sounds, so she smiled and grasped Lance's hand so tightly he removed her fingers and tucked her palm under his elbow. Her fingers curled around his bicep.

"Come." Gabby signaled, and they followed her to padded chairs in the third row from the front, in the middle of the small sanctuary. Lexie wished they could've sat on the back row, because when she glanced around, she saw she and Lance were the only light-skinned people in the place. With her light brown hair and golden skin, she stood out like a beacon. Several people seated to their right and left and slightly in front, tried not to stare, but they appeared to struggle with controlling their curiosity.

A drummer took his place at the drums, and Lexie smiled to see Tomás from the gym, pick up the guitar. He nodded and returned her smile.

The music leader greeted everyone and opened the service with prayer. He led them in praise and worship songs, many of which Lexie recognized. When she was able to follow the Spanish words projected on the screen, and could add her alto voice to those of others, she forgot about herself and turned her heart to worship.

When the pastor moved to the lectern and opened the Scripture, Lexie opened her tablet and pulled up the bilingual Bible. She recognized *Efesios* as the book of Ephesians, and she understood the words *capítulo seis* to be chapter six. She didn't know at which verse he would begin, so she read the whole chapter in English then listened for words she knew to help her figure out where he was in the Spanish Bible. When she heard *del diablo*, Lexie knew the pastor spoke to the congregation about putting on the whole armor of God so they could stand against the wiles of the devil, so she scrolled down to verse ten. Lance whispered for her to enlarge the screen so he could see the words.

Lexie followed the pastor when he read, and then reread the English and summed up the ideas.

> Be strong in the Lord and in the power of His might. Put on the whole armor of God, so you can stand against the schemes and trickery of Satan. You don't fight against flesh and blood, but against spiritual forces of evil. Stand with the belt of truth fastened. Put on the breastplate of righteousness, and the shoes of readiness to share the gospel. Most importantly, use the shield of faith. With this shield, you can extinguish all the flaming darts of the evil one. Put on the helmet of salvation, and take up the sword of the Spirit, which is the word of God.

The words spoke comfort to her heart.

At the closing of the service, Javier questioned Lexie, "*¿Entendiste?*"

Lexie nodded. "*Un poco.*"

Lance's eyebrows rose. "Did I just hear you tell Javier you

understood a little of the message?"

"Yes."

But then a stream of Spanish left Javier's mouth. She didn't understand much, but thought he said Mariana and Gabriela had gone to *la cocina* for some reason. He wanted Lance to follow him outside. She didn't know why Mariana and Gabriela were in the kitchen, but several other laughing, chattering women had gone with them.

Lexie looked around the empty room and took a deep breath. She released the air in her lungs. Space. Clean, empty, quiet space. She climbed the steps to the small stage and ran her fingers over the lid of the old piano. Why had no one played today? Was the piano out of tune? Is that why the instrument was shoved up against the wall and pushed out of the way?

She sat down on the bench, her back to the sanctuary, and opened the cover. Her fingers moved up and down the keys in a quick set of scales. The piano was in tune. Lexie smiled and pressed the keys with love. She played only for herself and the Lord, and time faded.

Her eyes opened when the sound of a softly-played guitar joined her in the hymn of praise. Tomás smiled but didn't speak. He pulled his stool near, and together they moved from one song to another. Their music-speech was fluent and harmonious, and didn't require words in any language.

Only the insistent grumbling of Lexie's stomach recalled her attention to the time and place. She smiled at Tomás and closed the lid. Someone coughed and they both spun around. Several members of the congregation watched and listened, then rose and clapped.

With a sheepish grin, Tomás returned his guitar to the stand and then waited to see what Lexie would do. She took a deep breath and reached for her leather bag.

"*Adiós*, Tomás."

"Lexie, *¿quieres tocar el piano con nosotros el próximo domingo?*"

Tomás must have recognized the lost expression in her eyes, so he pointed to the piano and made playing motions, then pointed to her, himself, and the drums and asked, "*¿Domingo?*"

"He wants me to play with them next Sunday?" Lexie looked at Lance and the Moras. They all nodded.

"*¿Práctica?*" Lexie hoped she asked when they practiced.

"*Practicamos los miércoles a las cinco.*"

In class, they had worked with calendars and clocks. *We practice on Wednesdays at five o'clock.*

Mariana spoke to Tomás, and the only word Lexie understood was violín. The teen raised his brows in question, made the motion of playing a violin, and asked, "You play?"

"Yes. Sí."

"You bring *violín a la práctica*?"

She nodded again.

"*Bien.*"

Throughout the next weeks, the anticipation Lexie felt for Wednesday practices and Sunday morning worship always surprised her. Playing with Tomás and the drummer, Daniel, recharged her drained emotional batteries. When she was with them, her attempts to speak Spanish weren't such an ordeal. They made as many mistakes in English as she did in Spanish, but they were able to accomplish what needed to be done. Sometimes, they played for an additional thirty minutes after practice just because they wanted to.

Lance linked his fingers with hers as they left practice together.

"Your Spanish is getting much better, hon. When you were telling Tomás and Daniel about your brother, you produced several perfectly constructed sentences, and your pronunciation sounded native-like. I'm proud of you."

"Did I really?"

"Yes."

"I don't know why, but they're just easier to talk to. Talking to Mariana is still a task."

Lance's praise warmed her, but this lasted only until the afternoon of the next day. She and Mariana were in the kitchen preparing dinner, while Javier and Lance rebuilt a motor. Gabby had returned to school for an activity, so Lexie had no language support. She struggled to keep up with her host mother's conversation.

When Mariana asked her why she didn't swim in the ocean like others from the United States, Lexie tried to tell her she was afraid of the riptides, but only got as far as "I am afraid," before she saw Mariana's eyes widen. Then the woman started laughing until tears ran down her face.

Heat raced up Lexie's neck and colored her cheeks. What had she said? Whatever words she'd used must have been wrong to get such a response. Lexie put down the knife, washed her hands, went into the bedroom and shut the door. When her hands stopped shaking, she opened the translator and typed the words she'd used in Spanish and read the English translation.

"Oh, no. God, why is this so hard?" Lexie flung herself on the bed and wept. After a bit, she took out the violin, propped herself up with pillows, and began to play. When Lance came in the room, a look of concern in his eyes, she said nothing, but continued to the end of the song.

"What's wrong, Lexie? Mariana told Javier she'd upset you, and Javier told me I should check on you. What happened?"

"I'm never going to be able to function well in Spanish, Lance. Not here. Not in Guatemala. All I do is embarrass myself and slow you down."

"Don't say that. What happened?" He sat on the edge of the bed and took her hand.

"When Mariana asked why I didn't swim in the ocean, I tried to tell her I was afraid. Instead of using the correct verb phrase, to have fear, I used the verb, I am. Then I couldn't remember the exact word for afraid, so I accidentally added an extra letter and the wrong vowel to the end, and basically told her the reason I didn't swim in the ocean was because I was ... I was feces."

Lexie saw the look in Lance's eyes. "Go ahead. Laugh."

"I'm not laughing at you, hon. Don't you remember we'll make a million mistakes? This is just one of them."

"One among many. I think I've already made my million and am starting on the next. Today wasn't the only time. Yesterday, I tried to tell Mariana and Gabby I was embarrassed about something, and Gabby asked when the baby was due."

"You used the false cognate *embarazada*, pregnant, instead of *avergonzado*, embarrassed?"

She nodded.

"I've done the same thing many times, babe. The other day, I told Javier I wanted cherries, *cerezas*, but I said *cervezas*, beers, instead. He looked at me strangely, but told me where the nearest liquor store was."

Lexie's jaw remained rigid.

"We talked about this, hon. We knew we'd have problems, but decided that the most important thing would be how we handled them. Remember?"

At her lack of response, he asked, "Do you want to quit and go back home?"

Did she?

Not your will, but Mine, the Spirit reminded her, and waited for her response.

The scar tingled and she ran her index finger up and down the fading red welt. She relaxed and shook her head. "No."

He stretched out on the bed next to her, clasped his hands behind his head, and began to pray.

"Lord, I ask you to give Lexie peace. Her heart is troubled and afraid. Please remind her she has access to the peace only you can give, and she doesn't have to fear. You're the fount of all wisdom, the Calmer of the storm, the Prince of Peace. Lexie and I both know the important things in life are not easily gained without a lot of effort and tears, but learning Spanish seems to be an insurmountable hurdle. I don't ask you to remove the obstacle, but I do ask you to increase our wisdom and understanding. In the name of your precious Son, I ask this. Amen."

"Amen," she agreed.

Lexie turned on her side and put her arm across his chest. When he rolled to his side and smiled, she touched his cheek, kissed him, and said, "Thanks, love."

His arms went around her and pulled her close. As she snuggled and listened to his heartbeat, she thought of the first sermon she'd heard at the mission church. Though she'd been saved from the moment she'd accepted God's mercy and grace provided on a bloody cross on Mount Calvary, she hadn't been putting on the protective helmet of salvation to guard her mind from doubts and fears. Since before she'd come to Costa Rica, these fears had almost hamstrung her, and she was tired of this.

She thought of the strength Edna Bell showed when she left everything and followed her husband, first to Kansas, and then to Oregon. Life was hard, but she'd carved out a place of comfort and security for her family, and Lexie had never heard her whine about how difficult her situation was.

Mammy Sue lived within the tight bonds of slavery, yet she didn't complain or feel sorry for herself. Her focus was always on the comfort and well-being of others and, as much as she could be in her situation, she was a happy person.

Then she remembered her ancestors, Alexandria and Olivia Ann. Alexandria had raised three children during the hand-to-mouth days of the Great Depression, and though great pain and sorrow peppered her life, she held things together and survived. Not only that, but she and her family had thrived. Olivia Ann left the comforts of an established life to follow her husband to the mission field to minister to people who had every right to hate them, but through the power of God and their desire to obey, they overcame. Olivia Anne's lack of knowledge of the Cherokee language at the beginning hadn't stopped her from loving the people and doing her best to serve them.

Now here she, Lexie, was, choosing to isolate herself just because Mariana had laughed. She'd pulled into her shell, and for the past two months, she'd been mentally sniveling about how hard Spanish was. She'd focused on her shortcomings instead of on the strengths God had given her to get the job done.

No more. Enough is enough.

Lexie rolled over the top of Lance and knelt beside the bed.

"God, please forgive me for my selfishness and pride. If you can use the silly mistakes I make, and the laughter these cause, to bring others close to you, please do so."

The mattress squeaked and Lance knelt beside her. For the next several minutes, they poured out their fears to the only One who could do something about them.

When Lexie stood, she felt lighter. She smiled and reached for Lance's hand. "Let's go see what's for dinner."

Mariana stopped talking to Gabby and Javier when the two entered the kitchen area. She dropped the slotted spoon onto a dish on the stove, and rushed to Lexie. She put her arms around her and said, "*Lo siento, hija.*"

Lexie accepted the apology by returning the small woman's hug, and by kissing her on the forehead. "*No importa, Mariana.*"

The incident really wasn't important, and she knew Mariana hadn't meant to laugh and make her feel bad.

Over dinner, Lexie forced herself to participate in the conversation. She'd slipped into the bad habit of letting Lance do most of the interpreting for her, with the result that he spoke better and more fluently than she did. Not anymore.

When she made errors, and saw the Moras trying to stifle their laughter, Lexie adjusted her mental helmet and said, "Please. Explain me how to say correctly."

Though Spanish didn't seem to get any easier in the following days, the bonds of friendship developed and trust grew. The relationship Lexie soon enjoyed with Mariana more closely resembled the one she'd had with Edna, and Lexie's heart rejoiced.

TWELVE

"Mariana, Javier. I want talk to you about my brother, Steven." Lexie waited until everyone had finished their meal before bringing up the subject. She spoke to them in her best Spanish, but knew her sentences were not quite right. Holes punctured the construction, and these gaps continued to bother her.

"Yes?" Javier smiled his encouragement.

"Steven not in school from thirteenth of March until twenty-first for his Spring Recess. He wants to come here for visit. Mom and Dad say if you let him stay with us, they will provide additional money for his food and bed. Steven say he okay to sleep on sofa or floor."

Gabby chuckled and looked at her mother. "On the computer, he looks tall, Mamá. I don't know if our sofa is sufficiently long."

Lance laughed. "Steven is as tall as I am."

Mariana nodded at Lexie. "Javier and I will talk, and then we will speak to you tomorrow. ¿Sí?"

Lexie agreed.

Gabby pointed to the DVD Lexie held, and looked to her parents. "May we watch Lexie's movie now? The one about her ancestors?"

"Yes." Javier inserted the disc into the player.

Though they didn't understand much of the English, they sat and watched with the same attention her family members had when she showed the movie at Thanksgiving. When the show was over, Lexie was hard-pressed to answer the Moras' questions, but she did her best and they were satisfied.

Early the next morning, Javier said, "Please tell your brother he is welcome to stay with us during his vacation, Lexie."

"Great! I will Skype them this afternoon."

Gene and Tomás received Lexie's news about her brother's visit with enthusiasm. They wanted him to play basketball with them on Saturday, the day after he arrived, and Gene wanted him to visit his classes at the Academy for as many days as he could. He intended to arrange this with his teachers right away.

"I'll go with you, Gene, to make sure they're okay with this. How about Lance and I stop by after class? We'll have to talk to the principal before we mention Steven's visit to the teachers."

"I hope your brother won't get bored. Our trimester break isn't until April 25, so there's not much we can do during the weekdays. I have a couple hours of homework in the afternoons, and my folks want me home before dark. At least he'll visit before the rainy season starts in May. Tomás says the rains last until November, and the worst storms happen in September and October."

Lexie didn't know if Steven's ability to fit into her life in Costa Rica so easily was due to youth, ignorance, or an excess of courage, but from the moment he entered the Moras' home, he was comfortable with everyone, and they with him. He laughed at his mistakes, though Lexie didn't hear many of them, he kept Gabby and Mariana in stitches, he earned Javier's respect with his ability to identify, understand, and solve problems, and he used the subjunctive mood of the verbs without even thinking. She still struggled with the subjunctive.

Lexie yanked out the stinging darts of envy and adjusted the helmet of her thinking as she, Lance, and Steven entered the gym on Saturday. Several teens greeted them and clustered around. Lexie introduced her brother to the students, and they eyed Steven with respect and friendship.

"Heard about you. Lexie says you play on the varsity team. Tomás and the rest of us have been looking forward to playing with you. Are you ready?" Gene asked.

Steven nodded.

Gene grinned and said, "Well, you can't play on Lexie's team, because she's really good, so how about you play on my team? We'll have to balance things out if Lance is on the same team as your sister. He's really good too."

Once the teams were as equal as Gene could make them, they played basketball for two fast-paced hours.

"That was fun." Lexie wiped her face with a towel and reached for her water bottle. She glanced at Lance. "Because we've been coming to the gym at least three times a week, and because I regularly hear commands like jump, pass, catch, or shoot in Spanish, I'm getting the command forms of those verbs down a little better."

She watched her brother, Tomás, and Gene saunter toward them. "Stevie sure looks like Dad."

Lance nodded and tilted his head toward the cluster of admiring girls who remained a few steps behind Steven and his friends. "The señoritas like him too."

"He makes functioning in another language and culture look easy, doesn't he?" Lexie plucked out another dart of jealousy, mentally flung the thing away from her, and then firmed her jaw. "I'm proud of him."

On Monday, Steven shadowed Gene in his classes and came home relating how fun the experience was. "Wish my classes were as interesting."

He helped clear the table, and Lexie saw the raised eyebrows and grins passing between Mariana and Gabby. Steven's actions had been as ingrained as Lance's, so the women said nothing, but let him help.

Javier and Lance went back outside to work on the motor, Mariana stayed in the kitchen, and Gabby laid her books and papers on the table to begin her homework. Steven asked what she was working on, and Gabby frowned and made a face.

"Chemistry. Sometimes I don't understand the way my teacher explains the new concepts."

"May I see?"

Lexie lounged on the sofa, violin in hand, playing runs and pieces of tunes as she watched Steven explain how to find the masses of molecules. Gabby smiled when she understood, and then flipped to another section of her textbook and asked him to explain how electrons fill orbitals.

In Lexie's relaxed state, she ignored the words in both languages, but listened for the rhythm, pitch, and tone of their words. She wondered if she could make the violin strings duplicate what she heard, and Lexie got the whimsical notion if she listened well enough, she could create a new song.

Charmed with the idea, she closed her eyes and listened carefully. After each phrase, she replicated what she heard and smiled when she made the violin strings sound close to Gabby's or Steven's voice.

When Mariana called to Gabby from the kitchen, Lexie matched her tones. As she listened to the music in the words, she suddenly jerked upright.

"Mariana!" Lexie leaped to her feet, violin in hand, and rushed to the kitchen area. Her host mother stared at her in obvious alarm, but Lexie smiled and said, "I need your help. Wait here, please. I'll be back in a moment."

Lexie returned to the kitchen and laid her Spanish books on the counter. She opened to phrases containing the subjunctive forms. Her English notes were written in the margins.

"Say each sentence and then wait for me."

Mariana read the first phrase, "*Me gustaría pintar más a menudo si tuviera más tiempo.*"

Lexie knew the phrase meant I would like to paint more often if I had more time.

She closed her eyes and replicated the speed, tone, and pitch of Mariana's words with the violin then repeated the phrases with the correct intonation and pronunciation.

Mariana clapped.

"*El médico le recomienda que tome las pastillas con la comida.*"

The doctor recommends he take the pills with food.

"*La ley requiere que usted tenga dieciocho años de edad para votar.*"

The law requires you to be eighteen years old to vote.

"*Si yo fuera un hombre rico, no tendría que trabajar duro.*"

If I were a rich man, I wouldn't have to work hard.

She understood!

Lexie lowered her violin and bow to the counter, turned and grabbed Mariana's hands, and danced with her around the kitchen. Then she picked up the violin and pointed to every object in the kitchen with the bow, including the hinges on the cabinet doors.

Mariana gave her the words and Lexie listened for the music in each. She played their unique sounds, and when she finished, she looked at Mariana, smiled, pointed to each object in the order they'd been spoken, and said their names correctly. Then she repeated the process in the rest of the rooms of the house.

In the days following, Lexie couldn't get enough. The insurmountable wall of fear she'd raised in her mind collapsed. In class, she listened to the music in her teachers' words, and soaked in the accents and intonation. At home, she'd follow Lance and Javier outside to learn more words and phrases, or she'd go to the market with Gabby and Mariana just to listen to the harmonies surrounding her.

The Moras, Lance, and Steven watched in astonishment as her Spanish abilities rocketed.

"She reminds me of that musical genius kid in the movie, *August Rush*," Steven said.

"You've far outpaced me, hon." The admiration in Lance's voice warmed Lexie even more than the jog they were taking around the neighborhood.

"I still struggle. I'm only good if I'm in familiar territory."

"You did fine when you chatted with Manuel."

"Who's Manuel?" Steven jogged beside them.

Lance answered, "He's a man from Mexico who now lives in Costa Rica with his daughter and son-in-law. He works at the *mercado*—the market—as a janitor. Lexie talks to him every chance she gets. Tell your brother what he said the last time you talked."

Lexie shrugged. "He said if he knew the words I know, he could talk to doctors and lawyers. He wouldn't be a janitor."

"Wow. That's impressive, Lex."

"What he didn't know is how hard I struggled to express myself. I used cognates because they were close in English, and I knew the meaning, but he considered them to be very educated words. Then when two of the owners of the mercado approached us, I got really nervous. They knew Manuel didn't speak English, so they figured I must understand Spanish. For several minutes, we talked about everyday things, then they started a more serious discussion about politics and business in the United States. I had a hard time staying up with three people—well, two really, because Manuel didn't talk when the bosses were around—who sometimes interrupted each other, or who asked me questions so quickly their words sounded like machine gun fire. If you'd taken my blood pressure just after I left the conversation, you'd think I needed medication."

"But this conversation happened before your big breakthrough. I'm guessing you could hold your own now."

"Maybe. I still can't express myself as easily in Spanish as I can in English, even after my breakthrough."

"Of course not, hon. Fluency takes time."

During the night, Lexie dreamed she worked at the orphanage in Guatemala. She'd been given the responsibility of supervising six-to-nine-year-olds as they played outside in the fenced yard. She was chatting easily and happily in Spanish as the well-behaved children waited in line for her to push them on the swings. Then she looked around and noticed the open gate. She knew she'd latched the latch when they entered, but the gate now stood wide open. When she made a quick head count, she realized one of the children was missing-the girl who wore protective head gear because she had seizures.

Trying to stem the panic quickening her heart and constricting her throat, Lexie questioned the other children. They stared at her, no comprehension in their eyes. The more she spoke to them in Spanish, the more they looked at each other and backed away.

Lexie couldn't stop the tears as she struggled to make herself understood. They turned and ran from her, fear in their eyes.

"No! Come back!" She yelled and went after them. They screamed, ran out the gate, and bolted in all directions.

Then the scene faded, and she returned to the Kansas prairie at the moment she'd identified the rumbling earth as a buffalo stampede. The animals were headed straight toward her and Matthew Bell.

"Run, Mattie. Run!"

The boy frowned and looked at her as if he didn't understand. Lexie realized she'd spoken in Spanish, but he didn't understand. She picked him up and ran. He cried and resisted, and she fell into the eroded crack in the earth as the buffalo herd stampeded over the top of them. She lifted her left arm to protect Mattie, and the glancing blow from a calf's hoof gashed her arm from the outside of the left elbow to the inside a few inches above her wrist. She screamed.

"Lexie, wake up. You're having a nightmare. Wake up, babe."

The dream evaporated and Lexie realized she was sitting up in bed, her wounded left arm crushed against her ribcage and her right arm cradling the left.

"They didn't understand me, Lance. As hard as I tried to speak in Spanish, they didn't understand."

Brick by brick the tumbled wall of fear rebuilt itself, though the form of the fear took on a different shape. Lexie wondered if she'd remember her Spanish in emotionally tense situations. The few times she'd been upset, she wasn't able to remember how to say things, which created more frustration. Lexie knew she couldn't control all the problems coming her way, no matter how well she planned, but knowing in ten months the well-being of several children would become her responsibility frightened her.

Lexie built the wall during her dreamtime, but forced herself to tear the stones down in the mornings with prayer, extra effort, and the use of her violin. She visualized several emergency situations in which she'd need to know Spanish, and asked Mariana or Javier how to say what needed to be said. She'd first listen to the music in their words, replicate the sounds on the violin strings, and then repeat the phrases several times until she'd committed them to memory.

When she remembered the violence in Guatemala, she'd repeat phrases in her mind as she and Lance practiced their martial arts movements at the gym. Moving and speaking in rhythm helped her remember the phrases almost as well as she could with the violin.

On Saturday, Gary drove Lexie and Lance to the airport so they could say good-bye to Steven. They couldn't go into the terminal with him, so they stood next to the elevator in the parking garage.

"I wish I could stay longer." Steven shook hands with Lance then hugged Lexie.

"I wish you could too, little brother."

"When you're on Skype, make sure you do so at a time when Gabby and I can talk afterwards, okay?"

Lance raised his brows. "Did Javier and Mariana give you their permission?"

"Yes. We're just friends, so don't make our talking sound like some kind of mushy romance. I like Gabby because she's quiet and doesn't act silly like most of the girls I know. She's smart, and we can actually have a decent conversation."

"You sound like Dad. He never liked silliness very much either. Kiss him and Mom for me when you get home, Stevie. Tell them I love them."

"Will do. Bye, Lex. Lance."

In the car on the way home, Gary talked with them about their upcoming conversation class they'd chosen for the second trimester starting in April.

"I learned a lot when I chose to get out in the community for conversation instead of taking the conversation class."

"Tell us more about how this option works." Lance kept his eyes on the traffic, but listened to Gary's answer.

"Well, you'll have a facilitator who'll lend direction and encourage you. This'll be one of the staff members from the Institute, and you'll be accountable to him or her. Then you'll work with a native speaker who will help you prepare and practice texts. You'll have to memorize these."

"Do these Spanish speakers know English?" Lexie wondered why her throat tightened. So what if they didn't speak English? She now knew enough Spanish to communicate with them. She forced her jaw to relax.

"Some. Often, they want to improve their English, so they'll swap help with you. Are you up to teaching someone English?"

Lexie smiled. Mattie and Peter had profited from her instruction, even though she hadn't thought she knew how to teach them.

"Yes," Lexie replied.

"What do we have to do in the community?" Lance breathed easier when they left the big-city traffic and turned onto quieter streets.

"You'll have a group of ten to fifteen people in the community you'll visit twice a week. They can be your neighbors, store owners, or others."

"What do we do when we meet them? I heard we have to spend six hours a week either talking to them or participating in some planned activity. This doesn't include the two hours a week with our native speakers."

"Part of what you're expected to do is listen and observe. Then you'll meet three times a week with either your facilitator or your small group to discuss your learning. The great part about this option, is you can be creative and can decide what you want to do and how you'll use what you've learned."

"Well, the next trimester starts April 29, so Lance and I have time to try and figure out what we want to do."

That evening after dinner, Lexie handed Lance her computer.

"Here," she said, "Read what I've written so far."

"What's this?" He looked at the document on the screen.

"My story. The story began on June 9 of this year, when I tried to dodge my destiny as a missionary's wife and was sent back to 1857."

Lexie watched his face as he read the first three chapters.

He finally looked up. "Wow. There's even more of your story here than what you've told me. This is like the movie you made. When I read your words, I feel like I traveled to the past with you."

"Kim keeps begging for more details, so I decided to write a blow-by-blow account. I'll send her what I have."

"Great, hon. Maybe the story you'll write from the time of your return to the present will highlight how you're now following your destiny."

"You mean how we're following our destiny, Lance? What do you think our destiny really is?"

He thought for several moments. "To be conformed to the image of Christ. To love God and others."

"You make it sound easy."

"It's never easy, babe, but don't you think the end results are worth the pain? Don't you want to hear the Lord say, 'Well done, good and faithful servant. You've been faithful over a little, and I will set you over much. Enter into the joy of your Lord.'?"

"Yes, very much."

His arm went around her, and she bent her head and laid her cheek over his heart.

For several minutes, she listened to the comforting beat, but sat up and smiled when her host father entered the room.

Javier shared the news that a wealthy businessman on the other side of the city had heard of the quality of his work and wanted to hire him to repair his car. A blind man could see how eager he was to accept the job.

"He said he would bring the vehicle here tonight so I can work on his car after my regular job. He will pay me well."

"That's great news, Javier."

The man nodded, but the intent look in his eyes told them more important information followed.

"The news is good only if I finish the repairs in three days. He needs the car no later than Saturday afternoon."

"Can you be finished by then?"

Javier grimaced and shrugged. "Only if I have a helper. Will you help? You have more knowledge of motors than others I would ask, Lance."

Lance looked at Lexie, and she nodded.

"Sure," he said, but turned back to Lexie.

"What about practice tomorrow, hon? I don't want you to walk home by yourself."

"I'll be okay, Lance."

"Maybe, but I'd feel better if you'd get Tomás to walk with you. Promise, Lexie? Our house is only a block out of his way."

"I promise."

"Make sure you have your phone before you leave."

She nodded again, picked up the computer, and went to the bedroom to work on more of her story before she sent the document to Kim.

Music practice went so well the next evening she, Daniel, and Tomás stayed an extra half hour playing together.

Then her phone beeped and Lexie saw Lance's text message. She sent a quick reply.

"I'd better go, hombres. Lance is wondering if he needs to send out the marines to search for me."

They nodded then shut down and locked up. "Thanks for agreeing to walk me home, Tomás. I don't believe your escort is necessary, but I made a promise."

"To keep a promise is important, Lexie. I am happy to walk with you."

They chatted together for two blocks before Lexie realized she would have to change her beliefs about necessities.

As soon as the two young men stepped from the deepest shadows and began to follow them in the twilight, Lexie knew their intentions were evil. Adrenalin-laced blood flooded her system, and her senses soared to high alert. She fought down the panic threatening to turn her knees to jelly.

"Tomás, don't look, but we're being followed. Is there a safe place nearby?"

He tensed but didn't turn. "My aunt lives one block from here."

She and the teen increased their speed, but so did the men. She heard the excitement in their heavy breathing and in the staccato sound their shoes made on the pavement.

"They're gaining, Tomás. We have to face them, because we're not going to get to your aunt's before they grab us."

Please, God! Help!

Suddenly, Lexie stopped, spun around, and sidestepped.

One of the men swerved to follow, knife in hand, but he couldn't stop his forward movement in time to prevent Lexie from pushing him hard in the chest. He stumbled backward.

When the man bent his right elbow to begin a slicing motion toward her face, Lexie's martial arts training took over. She covered, moved inside the knife's arc, blocked the arm, and punched the forearm of his knife hand with her right fist. The man groaned and struggled to hold the weapon. He sliced at her again, though he was slow, and Lexie covered, moved in, bent with most of her weight on her left leg, and then blasted through his left shin with the instep of her angled right foot. When he cried in agony and bent over in pain, she threw her right elbow and whacked him on the back of the neck, kicked his knee, and whacked the back of his neck again. He fell and curled up in a fetal position on the ground, groaning.

Lexie picked up the knife and turned toward the other man and Tomás. Her friend fought bravely, but blood covered the front of his shirt and dripped from a thin razor cut along the left side of his jaw and neck. He wobbled in exhaustion.

His opponent, box cutter in hand, stepped back and turned slightly so he could see both her and Tomás. His eyes slid to the groaning ball on the ground before they moved back to his intended victims.

Lexie thought to tell him to put down the knife, but she couldn't think in Spanish and focus on his movements at the same time, so she did the next best thing. She opened her mouth and screamed as loudly and as long as her lungs and throat would let her. Though the high-pitched scream didn't wake the dead, the sound did rouse the neighbors. A few porch lights flipped on and curtains moved.

Before the last notes ended, a large, dark, growling mass moved past her and barreled into their assailant. The man hit the ground so hard she thought he cracked the pavement. The mass rose from the ground and took form. Lance.

Lexie fell into his arms.

"Are you okay, sweetheart?" He searched for wounds. "Are you hurt?"

"I'm fine, Lance, but Tomás isn't. We need to get help."

Moments later, they heard sirens and saw the flashing lights of police cars. Someone had called for help.

The two men were handcuffed and placed in the back seat of one of the cars, while officers questioned Lexie, Lance, and Tomás.

The teen had collapsed, but was lucid enough to answer questions. When an ambulance and emergency personal arrived, he adamantly refused to go to the hospital. He said his aunt, who lived nearby, was a nurse and could stitch him up.

Lexie struggled to understand and answer the questions the officers asked, and she had to close her eyes several times and try to focus on the music in the words. Deep down, she wondered if her halting speech would be used against her by the police who may, or may not turn out to be crooked.

As she, Lance, and Tomás climbed into the back of the police car to be driven to his aunt's house, Tomás leaned toward them and whispered, "Those two men who attacked us belong to one of the gangs who operate in a different part of the city. I have heard of them. I do not know why they are here in our part of town, but they steal, kill, and find great joy when they can terrorize others."

He grimaced in pain when he tried to smile at Lexie. "Perhaps they will think twice before they try to rob a light-haired, light-skinned American woman again."

Tomás glanced at Lance. "I'm sorry my escort did not stop an attack."

"I don't think anything would have stopped them, Tomás."

He remained quiet for a few moments. "Me, I do not think this. If I were your opponent and saw a man of your size and strength walking with Lexie, I would not attempt an attack." He chuckled. "I have seen how well you use both fists and feet, when you practice in the gym. Had they seen this, they would not now be feeling like a truck ran over them."

After they delivered Tomás to his aunt's house and helped her clean and stitch him up, Lexie and Lance walked the remaining distance to the Moras' house where the three of them waited anxiously.

"We could not imagine what had delayed you," Javier said, after Lance told them of the fight.

Lexie listened to the conversation and her agitation grew.

"Javier, do you think the police will question us further? Do you think this case will go to trial, and we'll have to testify?"

Javier was slow to answer. "Perhaps."

Lance touched her arm. "Why are you worried?"

"You know how long the legal process takes in the US. What if we're expected to testify in December, when we need to return home? Our visas don't allow us to stay longer. Will the police ask the government to extend our stay? Can they force us to stay?"

No one knew the answer, so she continued, "And you know the men are going to lie and tell a different story. Will the police doubt us?"

"I don't know how they could, hon. From what Tomás says, the men are known criminals with violent records. They picked on two smaller, unarmed people who were minding their own business. Why would they doubt?"

"Because my fingerprints are on the knife, and I took the man down without getting hurt. He now knows I've had martial arts training. What if the man says the knife is mine, and I was the aggressor? What if the two say they were minding their own business and Tomás and I attacked them?"

Mariana and Gabriela gave each other wide-eyed looks and waited for Lance's answer.

"I don't think anyone could believe such a story, babe, especially not police investigators."

Lexie wondered if Lance assumed too much. After hearing the Monterros' tales of the astounding corruption of police and military in other Latin American countries, she wasn't certain things would turn out right for her. Innocent people all over the world had been punished for crimes they didn't commit, and she wondered if she would be one of them.

THIRTEEN

When would the police come? Would they find her at school? At home? Would they stop her on the street, or would they demand she come to the police station like she'd seen on some of the cop shows on television? Were the law enforcement officials trustworthy, or were they corrupt? How well would she understand the questions put to her in Spanish? Would an interpreter be provided? What if she and Lance were detained and couldn't return home in December? The what-ifs grew into a shadowy Goliath who waited on the battlefield of her mind. Lexie fought to release her fears to the Lord and to calm the bile that occasionally pushed its way into her throat as she moved through the following days and nights, but her weight dropped.

Mariana tried to coax the return of her appetite by preparing the most tempting meals she could, but no matter what Lexie put in her mouth, the food was seasoned with too much worry.

"You have to stop thinking about this, hon. You're making yourself sick." Lance frowned and caressed her arm. Javier and Gabriela nodded.

"I'm trying, Lance, but I can't seem to stop."

He said nothing for several moments as he studied her face. "What would Alexandria do?"

Lexie closed her eyes and pushed the mental replay button on everything she knew about her ancestor. She straightened, opened her eyes, and gave him a watery smile. "She'd march into the police station and demand to know what was happening with the case and where she stood."

"And what would Edna do?"

Lexie's smile widened. "She wouldn't go to the police, but she wouldn't allow her thoughts to debilitate her, either. She'd reach for a darning needle or a soup ladle and get to work."

"Sounds to me like you have good models."

She nodded, and he quoted Second Corinthians chapter twelve, verse nine, "And He said unto me, My grace is sufficient for you: for my power is made perfect in weakness."

Lexie's nod was slow and thoughtful, and when she caressed the laugh lines at the corner of his eyes, he reminded her of Matthew chapter six, verse thirty-four. "Therefore do not worry about tomorrow, for tomorrow will worry about itself. Each day has enough trouble of its own."

"That's true. Thanks for being here for me, Lance." She turned to her host family and smiled. "Something smells delicious, Mariana."

As April slid into May with no visit from the police, Lexie relaxed. She focused on her community activities and on completing the story of her time-travel experience. Whenever Goliath suggested the case was not forgotten or finished, she'd wind up her mental slingshot and fire scripture-stones at him. This strategy worked until the day she returned to the Moras' and found an official-looking letter addressed to her and Lance.

She nodded for Lance to pick up the envelope. Her hands shook, so she clasped them and stared at the flowing script of the sender.

Javier pointed to the name. "Jorge de la Cruz. He is a well-known prosecutor."

Lance opened the document and read the letter aloud in Spanish, with help from Javier.

Lexie summarized in English while she searched Lance's face "We're required to go to this attorney's office next week where our depositions will be taken?"

He nodded and she felt the blood rush from her face. The specter of Goliath rose and mocked her. "Will they provide an interpreter? Do we need an attorney?"

They both looked to Javier, who shrugged. "I have a friend. I will ask."

Over the next few days, Lexie wrote down every little detail about the attack and asked Javier and Mariana to check her grammar and usage. She rehearsed the words until she memorized them, and asked her host parents and Lance to think of questions the attorney might ask.

She couldn't eat on the morning of the appointment, but downed half a glass of orange juice at Lance's urging, though the fluid didn't rest easily in her stomach. Every few minutes, she looked out the window and frowned at the dark clouds and pelting rain.

What a miserable day. Lord, I know this is the day you have made. I'm trying to rejoice and be glad for your blessings, but can this day get any worse?

When her phone rang with her mom's special tone, Lexie's stomach lurched. Mom never called her, and when they visited on Skype, they spoke on Saturdays, not Wednesdays.

"Mom?" Lexie couldn't control the tremor as her voice rose in question, and Lance straightened in his chair and turned toward her.

"Lexie?" The tears in her mother's voice and the way she struggled to speak frightened her.

"Mom, what's wrong?"

"Granny Becky's in the hospital. She's not expected to live through the night."

"Oh, Mom, no." Lexie brushed at the tears tracking down her cheeks and reached for a tissue Mariana held out to her. "How's Grammy?"

"When I left the hospital, Mama was holding Gran's hand and telling her how much she loves her. I had to leave when she started to say what a good mother she'd been." Olivia gasped and again struggled for words, "My heart almost broke when I saw Mama holding on to Gran. She looked old, Lexie, old and weak—not like the strong woman I know her to be, and her looks made me realize how quickly we're all moving up in the appointment line every day."

"The appointment line?"

"Yes. Don't you remember the verse in the ninth chapter of Hebrews Pastor talked about the Sunday before you left? 'It is appointed unto men once to die, but after this the judgment?'"

"I remember."

"That verse pops into my mind every time I find a new wrinkle, gray hair, or age spot. I'm reminded of my mortality. I hate this aging and dying stuff, Lexie."

"I know, Mom."

"Wish you were here, honey."

"I wish I were too. I'd give you a hug and kiss and tell you what a great mom you are."

Olivia's uncontrolled sobbing tore at Lexie's heart and she couldn't speak for several moments.

"Give Dad, Stevie, Gran, and Grammy a hug from me. Tell them I love them."

As soon as she hung up, Lance wrapped her in his arms and she turned her face into his neck.

"Gran's dying."

"I know. I could hear part of the conversation. I'm sorry, hon."

The Moras huddled around her and offered comfort through touch and kind words, but they all looked up at the knock on the door.

"Ah, that will be my friend, Esteban Araya. He is the attorney I spoke of. He has offered to accompany us to your appointment, though you will be using a court-appointed interpreter. Esteban's mamá is from the United States." Javier opened the door.

Lexie clutched Lance's hand and studied the man who entered. Though he appeared to be in his late thirties, the man carried himself with the assurance of someone who knew who he was and what he could do. His thick black hair spoke of his Costa Rican ancestry, but his clear blue eyes and light skin were comfortably American.

She dabbed her eyes with the tissue and gave him a watery smile when they were introduced.

"Lexie has received sad news from home, Esteban. Perhaps we should give her time to collect herself before we chat. Would you like something to drink?"

Javier nodded, and Mariana and Gabriela scurried into the kitchen and returned with drinks and snacks before they sat down to listen.

Esteban asked her to tell her story. She related the events of the attack in the order she remembered them, then waited for him to speak.

"Your Spanish is very good. I doubt you will need the interpreter, Señora Garrett."

Comfort seeped through her brain at his words. "Thank you, Señor Araya, but I struggle to remember Spanish in an emotionally-charged situation. I'm not familiar with legal terms in your language either, so I'm sincerely grateful for the interpreter."

Esteban nodded and asked Lance to tell his side of the story. When he finished, he looked at the attorney.

"What do we need to know about the deposition process, Señor? Neither Lexie nor I have ever had to do this."

"The defense and prosecuting attorneys for both young men will be present to question you. The court reporter will record your statements while you are under oath. The purpose of this process is to find out what you observed and to preserve your testimony. Each side wants to learn all the facts before the trial so there are no unpleasant surprises. They look for weaknesses in their respective cases, and then prepare for ways to avoid or rebut them at trial."

"Is there anything else we should know?" Lexie wished she hadn't drunk the orange juice. The audible gurgling in her midsection embarrassed her.

"In general, questions can be broader than what is allowed in court, and you'll be expected to answer all of them. Unless you are asking for interpretation, you should not ask other questions. You should listen carefully and answer precisely. Depositions are serious matters and false statements made under oath carry both civil and criminal penalties."

"Excuse me please." Lexie jumped up and raced to the bathroom where she emptied the contents of her stomach.

"You grace is sufficient for me, Lord. Your power is made perfect in my weakness," Lexie repeated the truth over and over in her mind until calm returned.

She sat next to Lance and accepted the bottled water Gabriela handed her. She looked at Esteban. Did she see amusement sparkling in the depths of his eyes? Her chin firmed. “How long will this meeting last?”

“Some last fifteen minutes, some a week or more.”

“Once we give our statements, then what?” Lance asked.

Esteban shrugged. “The time you may be expected to wait to learn if you will be required to testify in court depends on the prosecutor and how long he wants to drag out the process. I have known cases to extend to the very end of the statutes of limitations.”

Lexie blinked to stop the threatening black spots from spreading across her vision. “What’s the usual time frame for the statutes of limitations?”

“Three years or more, depending on the crime.”

Lexie inhaled until her diaphragm filled then exhaled slowly. Okay, Lord, you know the beginning from the end. Your thoughts and ways are higher than mine, so all I can do is trust you’ll work all things out for good.

They rose and Esteban gestured toward their cell phones. “You should leave those here until you have finished the interview. Señor de la Cruz does not permit them in his office.”

Leaving her phone, even for an hour or two, felt like abandoning the life rope securing her to her family, but at least she was still in the twenty-first century and could contact them when she returned.

Two hours later, Gabby opened the door to her and Lance as soon as Esteban pulled away from the curb. The sober look on her host sister’s face as she handed Lexie her cell phone caused an immediate plummeting in Lexie’s midsection.

“Your mamá wishes to speak to you. She cries much.”

Lexie handed Gabby her dripping rain jacket before speaking into the phone, “Mom?”

Several moments passed before Olivia could form the words Lexie expected, but dreaded, “Granny Becky passed an hour ago,

Lexie."

Tears pooled and fell, and Lance moved up behind her, encircling her within the comfort of his arms.

"She was ready to go, Mom. Every time I visited, I had to sing to her about heaven."

"I know, honey. Grammy and I were with her to the end. We'd been chatting, when Gran's eyes suddenly widened and she smiled. She reached for my hand and told me to 'tell Lexie, good-bye. After I greet my Lord and my loved ones, I'm going to look for Fergus and the others. I'm planning to have a long sit-down chat with them about you.' Then she closed her eyes and sighed out her last."

Lexie hiccupped in an effort to talk around the tears. "How's Gran?"

"Mama's sad, of course, but she's glad she was with her. The look of peace on Gran's face comforted her."

"Have you made arrangements?"

"Yes, which is why I called. Granny wanted you to play the violin at her memorial service."

Lexie leaned against Lance's chest. "You want me to come home?"

Olivia sniffed. "I do, but Gran didn't. She said she wanted us to set up the computer and a video camera and Skype the service at a time you weren't in class."

Lexie finished making arrangements and faced her host family. She accepted the tissue and hug Mariana offered, and the gentle pats of sympathy Gabby and Javier gave her.

Lance kissed the top of her head and whispered, "I'm so sorry, babe," before releasing his arms and stepping back so she could turn and face him.

"Death sucks."

"Totally," he agreed.

They stood in silence for several moments until Gabby's timid words refocused their attention.

"What happened at the deposition, Lexie? Are you finished with lawyers and courts?" Gabriela put her hand in Lexie's.

Lexie sighed and shook her head. "I gave my testimony and waited for Lance to give his. I don't know if we're finished, Gabby. We'll have to wait and see what happens next, but I'm not going to let the uncertainty bother me. God has set out his plans for us. If he wants us to stay longer in the country, we'll stay longer. He can work out all the details. I'm tired of trying to figure out everything on my own."

The next Saturday, Lexie joined the memorial service via computer. The gray, rainy day matched her mood. As she played the songs Gran loved, she imagined her great-grandmother conversing with the Bells, Johnsons, and Wests about her. Did they know of her struggles to be obedient and to walk without fear? If so, did they beseech the Lord on her behalf?

In the weeks and months following, Lexie determined to be more like Alexandria and Edna. She poured her energy and time into studying the Bible in both Spanish and English, strengthening her bonds with Lance and her host family, aiding the mission church with their services and projects, and getting to know people in the community better. She played basketball and soccer with the younger set and worked to better her martial arts skills. She also completed the tale of her time-traveling adventures and sent the final copy to Kimberly for her comments. Her cousin responded with, "Wow! Wow! Wow!"

Lexie's investments paid off in a closer relationship with the Lord, Lance, and the Moras, a variety of friendships with people of all ages, and requests to play the violin or piano wherever she went. She marveled at the power of music, especially the songs of worship and praise, to soften hearts and move people to action.

When she and the other band members from the mission church gave impromptu concerts in the park or in the community building, they always played to a packed audience. People began to bring and share food, and soon, curious passersby stopped to see what was happening. They usually stayed and joined the fun.

The shadowy Goliath of fear remained buried until the letter from the court resurrected him again. Lexie and Lance were required to give their testimony at the attackers' trials. One trial began the first week in November, only a week away, the other began the second week of December.

"But we're supposed to return home the third week of December, Lance. What if-?" She firmed her jaw and forced down the panic rising into her throat. "No, I'm not going to ask that question. Never mind."

He kissed her. "Good girl. Let's take the Moras to dinner tonight as a way of thanking them for all they've done for us."

"Listen to yourself, Lexie," Javier spoke as they waited for dessert after dinner. "I have listened to you speak to different people throughout the evening. You had no trouble understanding or responding to the waiters or other community members who stopped by our table to take your order or to say how much they enjoyed your concerts. When Doctor Quintana and his wife spoke of your help at their clinic, you neither stumbled nor grasped for words when you answered. "Do you remember your first day here?"

Lexie grimaced. "Don't remind me, Javier."

"But you should be reminded, hija. How else will you see the progress you have made?"

"And you inspired mamá to try harder to learn English." Gabriela smiled at Mariana, who nodded emphatically. "When she saw how you struggled and overcame, she decided she should try to be better, especially since we plan to travel to your home for a visit in a couple of years."

In heavily accented, but understandable English, Mariana patted Lexie's hand and said, "In whatever country you live, Lexie, you will always be *hija de mi corazón*—the daughter of my heart. You and Lance are always welcome in our home."

Lexie wiped away the escaping tears and looked at each of them as she spoke, "Had I known what a wonderful family I'd live with here, I would never have been so frightened. Thank you for your kindness."

Would Guatemala contain such friends? The country remained shrouded in a veil of darkness too thick for Lexie's emotions to penetrate. Nearing the end of her stay in the past, the Lord had asked her if she'd be willing to go to the "people who sat in darkness in Guatemala." She'd agreed, but at what price? What awaited her? She shivered and rubbed the scar.

The trial dates approached, and Lexie rehearsed her testimony multiple times a day. She planned to use the court-provided interpreters so she could hear each question twice-the original question in Spanish, and the translation in English. The extra time this allowed would give her time to think of her answers.

As she sat on a bench outside the closed courtroom doors and waited for Tomás to finish his testimony, Lexie's stomach gurgled.

"Be quiet, beast!" She rubbed her abdomen and muttered, "You'd better not embarrass me today."

Lance reached for her hand. "Let's talk to the Lord while we wait. Shall we, hon?"

A few minutes later, the doors opened and Tomás exited. The court official signaled for Lexie to enter and told her where to sit. She forced herself to walk to the witness stand with as much grace and dignity as she could muster. Out of the corners of her eyes, she scanned the faces of the jury members as their gazes took in her appearance. She was certain they tried to reconcile the information from previous testimony with their perception of her physical ability to stop an attack by larger, armed men.

Lexie glanced toward her attacker, who stared at her with a sullen expression.

Soon the questioning began. She was told to state her name and physical address in the United States, and to give her current address in Costa Rica.

"Please explain to the court why you are in this country, Señora Garrett," Señor de la Cruz spoke.

She answered, relieved her voice didn't tremble. The prosecutor reviewed her testimony, which she confirmed, then turned the questioning over to the defense attorney.

"Señora Garrett, describe your martial arts training." The attorney listened intently to each of Lexie's carefully spoken words. Fear grew as the questioning continued. The man seemed intent on casting doubt on her story. His suggestive questions implied the weight of blame rested with her and Tomás-just as she had predicted they would.

When the judge dismissed her, she fought to control her tears and to keep her face emotionless. She walked through the double doors just as the court officer signaled Lance to enter. As he passed, she whispered, "They tried to blame us."

They discussed the trial with the Moras at dinner.

"The defense attorney bent the situation and my answers into something unrecognizable as the truth," Lexie heard the hopeless tone in her words, and wasn't surprised when Lance frowned and shook his head.

"No juror is going to believe his take on the situation, babe. The attorney was trying to shift attention away from his client in any conceivable way, but the idea you and Tomás instigated the attack against notorious gang members isn't plausible. You'll see. The jury will probably convict your attacker."

Lance was right, and though the second trial proceeded in a similar manner, both young men were blamed for the attack. They also faced further litigation and more serious charges for their criminal involvement with drugs and illegal gang activity.

With Goliath firmly buried again, Lexie enjoyed the graduation celebration the Moras hosted for her and Lance at the mission church. The standing-room-only crowd showered them with best wishes, hugs, and requests to return to Costa Rica when they could. Yet as much as she loved these people, Lexie longed to return to her loved ones for their hugs and kisses before she boarded another plane and flew into the darkness of Guatemala.

PART THREE

FOURTEEN

"Are you okay, babe?" Lexie opened her eyes at Lance's question.

"Yes." She tilted her head to look around him at the passenger in the aisle seat. "I never imagined Mom and Dad would let Stevie come to Guatemala with us. I wonder how he convinced them?"

Lance glanced at his brother-in-law., "Maybe your parents think the more males to guard you, the safer you'll be."

"I heard you." Steven leaned forward so he could see her. "Why shouldn't I come? I graduated in December, and I'm a free man. I knew I wanted to serve with you when you left for Costa Rica, so I made sure my passport and immunizations were up-to-date. I took extra Spanish classes at the Junior College at night too."

Lexie stared at her brother. Why couldn't she respond to these new challenges with the same eagerness and excitement? Did five more years of life instill a greater degree of caution and fear, or was she naturally timid? She'd never thought of herself as a scaredy-cat.

"Why are you looking at me like I've grown two heads, Lex?"

Both he and Lance waited for her answer. "I'm so proud of you, little brother. So very proud. I wish I could be more like you."

Steven laughed, and Lance reached for her hand. "You're more like him than you think, hon."

"Based on his initial reactions when compared to mine, I'm not so sure, Lance."

"You and Mom are such worry-warts, Lex. You're always expecting bad things to happen when, most of the time, they don't." Steven's grin indicated he meant no harm with his words.

Did she indeed fall so quickly into negative thinking? She listened to the hum of the plane's engines and digested her brother's words.

"You may be right, but if I don't try to envision possibilities, I can't make plans to avoid some of the unpleasant situations."

Her husband and brother stared at her.

"Don't look at me like *I'm* the one who's grown two heads."

Lance caressed her face with an index finger. "How many days of joy did you lose, babe, because you worried so much about the trials in Costa Rica? In the end, nothing happened to stop us from going home. We made all the Christmas celebrations with family and friends, and had time to rest."

"Yes, and now, in ten hours, we'll land in the most dangerous country in the Western Hemisphere. You don't think I have anything to worry about?" Lexie grimaced. "Lance, I read the papers Rudy brought with him from Guatemala when he returned from his mother's funeral in December. Stories of beheadings, assassinations, and brutality filled almost every page."

Lexie placed her fingertips over the pounding pulse at the base of her jaw. "I'd like to keep my head."

Lance touched the scar on her arm. "Jonathan and Jesse Johnson knew fear. For years, images of violent death and destruction surrounded them. What advice would they give you?"

Lexie dropped her fingers from her neck and took a deep breath. She closed her eyes and thought of the two brothers before speaking. "Jesse would recommend I take one day at a time and not borrow tomorrow's trouble. He always lived in the moment. Jonathan would tell me, in no uncertain terms, to quit stalling and get the job done." She grinned. Her eyes remained closed as she looked at her mental pictures. "He'd enjoy telling me too, in payback for all the grief I gave him."

"You what? What did you say?"

Lexie's eyes snapped open at Steven's startled questions. Her throat constricted. She and Lance had grown so comfortable speaking of the past she'd forgotten her brother listened.

"I … I …" She rubbed her forehead. What had she done?

"You what, Lexie?" Steven frowned and looked from her to Lance and back.

Lance shook his head., "The tale is hers to tell, Steve, not mine."

"Lexie?" Steven leaned closer and waited.

"I traveled through time," she whispered.

"You did what?"

She reached into her leather bag and handed him the USB drive. "Read."

He removed his small laptop from the case, powered up, and inserted the portable drive into the port.

Lexie looked out the window as he began to read.

Lance spoke next to her ear, "I wondered how long we'd be able to keep your story secret, hon."

She turned. "No one else can know, Lance. I can't afford to make more stupid slips. Promise me, if I start to say things that might lead to situations such as this, you'll stop me."

"Promise," he whispered and leaned back in his seat. She rested her head on his shoulder. He stroked her hair with his other hand and closed his eyes.

Lexie watched Steven read of her attempt to run from God. Her brother appeared to be as mesmerized as Kimberly had been. He didn't hear the flight attendant when she asked him what he wanted to drink, so Lexie ordered for him.

Several hours later, he looked up. "Can I copy this to my computer, Lex? I want to read the story again."

She hesitated, but finally nodded. "Only on the condition that you don't share the information with anybody. Do you hear me, Stevie? No one else can know."

"I promise. Here." He ejected the USB and returned the drive to her before shutting down the laptop.

"Lance obviously knows your story, Lex, but does anyone else?"

"Kimberly found out when I accidentally sent her the electronic copy of the original diaries. She's the person who convinced me to write about my adventures."

"So, some of the voices we heard on the DVD were our people from the past, weren't they?"

"Yes."

"Do you have more recordings?"

"Yes."

"May I listen to them?"

Kimberly had asked the same question. What motivated both her cousin and brother to want to hear more? Lexie realized she often listened to the recordings to keep the people from her past alive. Maybe they wanted to feel the connections too.

Without saying anything, she opened the first recording and

handed her phone and attached earbuds to her brother.

His smile was a gift.

She enjoyed his changing expressions as he listened to Fergus' stories, and then to the tales told by little Ray Roberts, her elderly box supper companion. She replayed the stories in her mind as Steven scrolled through the rest of her voice files and viewed the videos she'd taken of the Bells.

His eyes glowed when he returned her phone. "Wow," was all he could say.

"Kimberly said the same."

"Lexie, of the four reasons you gave as to why you couldn't go to Guatemala with Lance, which one, if any, is still a problem?"

She dropped her eyes and began to finger the scar. She looked at her brother when he reached across Lance and touched the wound.

"The Mark of Jonah?" He examined the pink line.

"Yes, a daily reminder of the consequences of trying to run from God."

"So?" He waited for her to answer his question.

Lexie sighed. "Maybe I'm a slow learner, Stevie, but all of the reasons continue to be issues, depending on the circumstances."

"You're not running now." Lance opened his eyes and joined the conversation, "That's what counts."

"And you speak Spanish fluently, so the lack of language abilities shouldn't be a problem anymore, Lex."

Their sincere concern touched her heart. She smiled and said, "So I can mark one excuse off my list and focus on the other three?"

"Better let the Lord take care of the others, love, and you concentrate on the work ahead."

"You're right, Lance. Keep reminding me."

The hideous newspaper images sprang to mind at his words and, with firmer jaw and tightened lips, Lexie pushed them away and reached into her bag for something to distract her. Her Bible rested in the overhead bin, so she contented herself with Guide to Essential Oils and Plant Therapy, Olivia's Christmas gift to her. She completed the last page of the guide when the pilot spoke to the passengers over the public-address system and warned they'd be landing soon at La Aurora International Airport in Guatemala City.

Lexie replaced the book and looked out the window. She noted the three volcanos and the tightly packed houses of the millions of people who lived in the city. Crime. Violence. Death. A real need for the saving power of Jesus Christ. She clasped Lance's hand and sighed.

Okay, Lord. I'm here and want to do my best for you. I'm counting on you to protect us so we can do your will. Please keep Goliath buried.

The giant of fear threatened to resurrect the moment she stepped out the glass doors to wait for Rachel and Bob Richardson, the orphanage directors. More than a hundred people stood around with seemingly nothing better to do than accost travelers who exited the terminal. Children offered to shine her shoes, though she wore tennis shoes. Official-looking men, unassociated with the airport, offered Lance the opportunity to use their cell phones to call his ride "for a small fee."

She and Lance declined all offers as politely as they could and stepped toward the curb when they spotted the Richardson's blue van.

"Lance, Lexie, and Steve?" Bob raised an eyebrow and, at their nods, opened the van's back doors and loaded their suitcases into spaces not occupied by large boxes of diapers, infant formula, and other supplies. "I'm Bob. Rachel and I've been looking forward to your stay with us. Hop in."

The couple looked to be a decade older than she and Lance, but Lexie had never been a good judge of age. They both had brown hair and brown eyes, and both appeared to be in good physical condition.

Rachel eyed them and then smiled. "Buckle up. We'll talk more when we get out of the city. Traffic is horrendous. You'll see why we come here only once a month for supplies."

The hair on the back of Lexie's neck raised the moment they left the airport and got into traffic.

"This is madness. I hope pilots are more concerned with the rules than these drivers," Lance whispered and leaned forward to help Bob watch. Steven overheard his words to her and nodded before returning his attention to the road.

The muscles in Lexie's middle clenched and wouldn't release. She pinched her lips together and covered her mouth to keep the bile from rising any further. Lance had earned his international pilot's license before they left Costa Rica "just in case," but her heart throbbed in panic when she thought of him flying over the jungles and volcanos of Guatemala.

No one appeared to pay attention to any traffic rules. Speed limits, lane markings, and stop signs were frequently ignored, and instead of using signals to alert others, either the driver or passenger would stick a hand out the window and wave to indicate they intended to do something unpredictable. Cars and trucks stalled in the middle of the road and pedestrians darted through busy traffic to cross the street.

"Why don't they use crosswalks?" Lexie gasped as the van almost hit a woman who seemed to appear from nowhere.

"Aren't any," Rachel said keeping her eyes on the road. She gripped the safety handle on the door until her knuckles whitened. "You now see why using a cell phone while driving is against the law."

On the highway, drivers drove as fast as the condition of their vehicles permitted. Some reached only twenty miles per hour.

"Look at the buses, Lex. Chicken buses." Steven pointed to the brightly painted, recycled school buses.

"You know about the chicken buses?" Rachel turned to look at her passengers for only a moment.

"Yes, friends from Guatemala told us about them," Steven replied.

Rob spoke but didn't look back, "They serve almost every town in the country because their fares are cheap, but criminal activity and frequent fatal accidents make them particularly dangerous. The modern inter-city buses offer more security from highway violence, but you still must be careful. Armed attacks are increasing."

They began to climb in altitude as they traveled the twisting roads toward Antigua. Rachel barked a warning as the driver in the vehicle in front of them decided to pass a tractor-trailer straining to make the climb. The driver passed on a blind curve and almost plowed, head-on, into another car.

Lexie yelped and flung her arms in front of Lance and Steven as if to restrain them from flying forward.

"You see this kind of careless driving all the time." Bob glanced in the rear-view mirror and grimaced. "Fatal head-on collisions are quite common."

"Has anyone hit you?" Lance asked and stared at the road ahead as if to see what danger lurked around the next bend.

"No. We've been fortunate. We can't afford the consequences."

"Consequences?" Steven leaned forward and waited for Bob to explain.

"When drivers are involved in accidents resulting in injury, they may be detained and held in protective custody pending investigation. If a person dies in an accident, the officer takes every driver involved into custody and impounds their vehicles. The judge won't release them until he determines who's at fault and how much money they have to pay in damages."

Lexie shuddered. She wouldn't be driving Guatemalan roads in the foreseeable future.

"Is that a roadside stand?" Steven turned to stare as they passed.

"Yes," Rachel said. She fanned the heat away from her face with a piece of mail as she glanced at the stand.

"Looks abandoned." Steven turned to her for an explanation. "Yes. Guatemala's suffered from drought and flooding in the last few years. The *campesinos* are having a hard time making ends meet."

Lexie thought of the base word, campo, before speaking, "Campesinos? People who live in the country?"

Bob spoke without turning his head, "Most of them work small plots of marginal land. To keep body and soul together, many of these poor people work on the large coffee and sugar plantations. From November through May, there's no rain, so they can't grow crops during these months. Food is predictably scarce."

Lexie prayed as she watched a thin young man zip by them on a motorcycle. He wore no helmet.

How am I ever going to make a difference in the lives of these people, Father? What do I have to offer?

You have nothing; I have everything.

She straightened. What, Lord?

All you have, I gave you.

Lexie thought about his words all the way to Antigua.

"We can't take the time today to show you around, but hopefully you'll have an opportunity to get back later," Rachel smiled her apology as the van bumped over the cobbled-stone streets and out of the city.

From the moment Bob passed through the gates announcing their arrival at the orphanage and parked the van in front of the long, two-story building several kilometers outside of Antigua, time seemed to speed up.

Rachel greeted a small, dark-skinned man. He returned her greeting then smiled and nodded at Lexie and her companions before reaching for the boxes of diapers Bob handed him.

"Nico is our grounds keeper and general handyman." Rachel tilted her head toward the man and juggled an armful of groceries. "He keeps the jungle from encroaching into the yard."

Lexie glanced at the lush vegetation surrounding the coral-colored stucco building then grasped the handles of her suitcases and followed Rachel and Nico toward a side door. She glanced over her shoulder. Lance and Steven helped Bob unload more boxes and bags before they grabbed the other suitcase handles and hauled the heavy bags forward.

"First order of business is to get the supplies unloaded, and then to show you to your rooms." Rachel's practical instructions reminded Lexie of Edna. Once Edna resolved herself to living in a soddy dug into the side of a hill, she marshaled her emotions and brought order out of chaos.

"Space is at a premium here, so Nico offered the extra twin bed in his room to you, Steven."

Nico looked at them when he heard his name but didn't pause in his unloading task.

"Great." Steven smiled and nodded at his new roommate.

Bob grinned. "He asked me to tell you he doesn't snore or speak English."

"We'll get along just fine then." Steven left his luggage and walked toward the man. He offered his hand and said in Spanish, "I don't snore either, Nico, and I'm sure my English literature teacher wonders if I've mastered English. The scores I got on a few of my essay papers didn't impress her."

Nico's eyes widened, and a barrage of happy Spanish accompanied his hand movements as he put groceries in the cupboard. Lexie guessed he was only a few years older than her brother.

Steven offered to help Nico with the supplies, and the look on the man's face indicated Steven had gained good friend status.

Lexie hoped she would make friends as quickly.

"We'll leave them to finish. Come, I'll show you your room." Rachel started up the tiled stairs.

"I'm going to work on the truck." Bob nodded at his wife and headed toward the door they'd just entered. Rachel tipped her head to acknowledge his words.

"Give me a moment to get the suitcases into the room, and I'll come with you." Lance turned to Lexie. "Do I need to help you unload the bags first, hon?"

"No, go ahead. I'll put our things away and see what jobs Rachel has for me."

The room was as small and clean as their room in Costa Rica.

"Come down to the kitchen when you've finished, Lexie. I have to help Adela get the babies' bottles ready. Turn left at the bottom of the stairs. The kitchen is down the hall to the right."

The kitchen was larger than Lexie expected, and she smiled at the sight of the industrial gas range. No wood-burning stove. No dried buffalo chips. Thank you, God.

Her smile slipped when she overheard Rachel and two other women speaking about her. One heavier-set woman washed dishes. Soap suds climbed to her elbows as she chatted with Rachel and the other woman as they poured formula into bottles. Their backs were to Lexie, and they hadn't heard her approach.

"Does she speak Spanish?" the woman at the sink asked.

"I don't know, Alma," Rachel said, "but her brother doesn't have a problem communicating with Nico."

"All the Americans I know speak with a strange accent, if they know Spanish at all," the other, thinner woman spoke, disdain lacing her tone.

Al'ma laughed. "So how many Americans do you know, Adela?"

The woman shrugged and filled another bottle. "I listen to the tourists when I visit my family in Antigua. The town is full of Americans and other English speakers."

"What does she look like?" Alma rinsed the dishes and put them on a drying rack.

Rachel glanced over her shoulder and noticed Lexie. She smiled and said, "Turn around, sisters, and you can see for yourselves."

The women turned. She swallowed and moved forward for introductions. The way the women studied her reminded Lexie of the expressions on the jurors' faces as she'd walked into the courtroom to testify at both trials. She forced herself not to tense.

"Hello," she spoke using her best Spanish intonation. "I hope my accent isn't so strange you can't understand me."

Adela blushed. She had the saddest eyes Lexie had ever seen, and a mouth unused to smiling.

Rachel's eyebrows lifted. "Your accent is almost perfect, Lexie. Better than mine, and certainly better than Bob's. How can this be? I've lived in the country for almost two decades. Have you been to Guatemala before? Did you live here?"

"No. I learned how to listen to the music in words."

All three women stared at her as if she'd said something they'd never heard. The expression in their eyes indicated they understood her words, but not the meaning.

Before Lexie could explain, a timer rang, and the women hustled to get the bottles on a stainless-steel cart.

"Come, Lexie. We need to feed the babies."

Lexie gulped. Babies. She'd spent most of her life in school learning, but classes for caring for tiny little people never showed up on her course schedule.

She followed Rachel into a large room. Three women looked up but continued to rock the infants in their arms. They smiled at Lexie, and she smiled back. Six other babies slept or played in the cribs lining the three walls across from the nannies.

"This room houses the newborns and babies up to crawling age, Lexie. Each nanny cares for three children."

She pointed toward another section of the building. "Twenty other children under the age of six live next door."

Adela and Alma handed bottles to the waiting nannies, while Rachel picked up a baby and walked toward Lexie.

"This young man is Oscar. He enjoys his bottle, and he doesn't mind who feeds him. I think you'll do well with him."

"You want me to feed him?" The inside of Lexie's mouth dried.

Rachel grinned. "Yes."

"Should I wash first?"

"You'll find hand sanitizer on the table next to the empty rocker."

Lexie sat, and Rachel placed Oscar in her arms. He wriggled and she almost dropped him.

"You don't have experience with little ones, do you, Lexie?"

"No, but I'm willing to learn."

Did the tiniest of sighs escape from between Rachel's lips?

"Okay. First, hold him the way you see Rosa, Tina, and Valeria holding their babies."

Lexie adjusted Oscar's position and he relaxed.

"Now give him his bottle. Burp him after he gets halfway, then give him the rest. He'll be ready for a nap afterward." Rachel tilted her head toward Adela and Alma. "We're going to prepare lunch for the other children. The nannies will show you what to do. We eat while the older ones play."

Lexie studied the baby in her arms. He stared at her face and hair as he nursed.

She smiled and caressed his cheek with a finger.

"You're a handsome boy, aren't you, Oscar? I wish my eyelashes were as long and dark as yours. I'd never have to wear mascara."

"Señora?"

Lexie looked up at Valeria.

"So sorry. Oscar, he no understand English. You speak the Spanish?"

"Yes. I told the baby how handsome I thought him."

The three women smiled and nodded, then began to question Lexie about herself and those who traveled with her.

"Tell me about Oscar," she asked when the nannies placed cotton cloths over their shoulders and lifted the newborns. They began to pat the babies' backs, so Lexie copied their movements. Oscar burped and smiled, and Lexie kissed the top of his soft head.

"He came to us in a box." Tina continued to feed her baby after the little girl burped.

"What?" She searched their faces to see if the woman joked, but the seriousness of their expressions told her she didn't.

"A box?"

"Yes. Someone left the pobrecito on the steps of a hospital in Guatemala City in a cardboard box. The hospital contacted us, and Rachel brought him home. He has been with us for three months."

Tears slipped from the corners of Lexie's eyes as she snuggled Oscar close and continued his feeding. She brushed the drops away, then caressed the skin near his temple with the back of her knuckles.

"I'm so glad you're here, little one," Lexie whispered in English near his ear.

Oscar stared a moment, let go of the nipple, and grinned. A dribble of milk trickled out the side of his mouth.

The tightness in Lexie loosened and fierce protectiveness filled the space when she returned his smile.

"Perhaps the little one thinks you are an angel." Rosa watched her and the baby.

"An angel?"

"None of the nannies have skin as light as yours. Neither does their hair glow like a halo in the light."

"See," Tina said, "even now he reaches to touch your face."

Lexie kissed the tiny fingers. Oscar's eyes never left her face as he nursed. He did seem to be mesmerized by her looks.

Soon Oscar's lashes fluttered and his eyes closed. His body relaxed into sleep. Lexie had never seen such an enchanting sight.

"Burp him again before you put him in his crib," Valeria instructed. "I will check on him after we eat."

Adela came to sit with the babies while she and the nannies enjoyed their half-hour lunch.

Lexie followed her mentors to the dining room, though she wished she could've held Oscar a while longer.

The men stood when they entered, and Lance kissed her cheek before seating her.

Steven and Nico talked and laughed like they were the best of friends already, and she again marveled at her brother's ability with people.

"I hope you aren't too tired from your travel." Rachel looked a her, Lance, and Steven. "The nannies who watch the older children asked for you to come and play. The little ones who are old enough to understand always enjoy our visiting guests, especially those strong enough to push them high on the swings."

Lance asked, "Do you have many guests?"

Bob nodded. "Mission groups will come for a week and help out now and then. They often bring needed supplies from the States."

Alma and Nico brought in platters of rice, black beans, corn tortillas, and vegetables and set them in the middle of the table.

When they sat, Bob asked the blessing then handed dishes around the table.

Lexie had learned to like black beans, rice, and the fried, banana-like, *plátanos*, in Costa Rica but, deep down, she wished for a taste of slow-roasted turkey breast.

After lunch, each person took his or her dirty dishes to the kitchen and rinsed them.

"Yay! Play time," Steven sounded enthusiastic and ready for anything.

Lance held Lexie's hand as they walked toward the back yard, but she stumbled when she saw the gate to the fenced yard.

"Lance," she hissed and tightened her hold, "that's the same gate I saw in my nightmare."

She looked toward the group of waiting children. One child wore a protective helmet, and Lexie's heart threatened to pound through her chest. She wanted to turn and run.

"This can't be happening, Lance."

"Don't jump to conclusions, hon."

"Can a person have a nightmare while the sun shines and her eyes are wide open?" The acid in her stomach simmered.

"Come on. I'll keep an eye on the gate, okay?"

Lexie squeezed his hand. "All right, let's go."

FIFTEEN

The first few weeks of January passed in a blur. Caring for babies and toddlers filled Lexie's days. She, like the other nannies, sterilized bottles, laundered bedding and clothing and participated in the hundred-and-one activities needed to keep the orphanage running. Her favorite times of the day included feeding and rocking Oscar and the other babies, playing games with the toddlers, and singing or playing her violin for the children before they went to bed. When Bob or Nico didn't need Steven or Lance's help, they joined her. At first, the nannies looked suspicious when Lance plopped himself into the rocker next to her and asked to hold Oscar, but they soon accepted his presence after he'd convinced them he'd had ample practice caring for his nieces and nephews.

"Sanitize first, love." Lexie waited until the sanitizer dried and placed Oscar in his arms.

"Look at you, big guy." Lance tickled the baby's belly.

Oscar grinned and flailed his arms. "Hey, look at his bottom teeth. He's cut his first two already."

"Yes, and he was cranky for several days until they came in." She handed him a bottle, "Here, he's ready to eat. Will you feed him while I grab Patricia? She's rattling the bars of her crib with impatience."

"Sure."

Tina, Patricia's primary caregiver, smiled her thanks and continued feeding Jaime.

"What have you and Steven been doing?" Lexie snuggled Patricia in her arms and gave her the bottle.

Lance spoke, his eyes on Oscar, "We've been digging drain ditches, strengthening fences, and helping Bob put the motor of his truck back together. The five-year-olds wanted Steven to play ball with them, so he's outside now."

He glanced at Lexie. "How are things inside?"

"I'm catching on, Lance. The nannies don't roll their eyes as much or give each other the look when my inexperience surfaces. I get on well with Tina, Valeria, Rosa and most of the other nannies."

"Alma and Adela?"

Lexie hesitated. "They're polite, but not as friendly as the others."

"Any idea why?"

"Not a clue, Lance. I sensed their reserve the first day when I overheard them talking about me."

She put Patricia to her shoulder and patted the baby's back. "If I walk up to the women while they're chatting, they'll stop talking and turn away. Their expressions and responses remind me of Edna's initial reactions."

"In what way?" Lance made a silly face, and Oscar grinned and reached for Lance's mouth.

"Edna disapproved of my appearance, outspokenness, and ignorance. At first, she'd respond to my questions in the same cool tones Alma and Adela use with me. Polite but nothing more."

"What caused Edna to change toward you?"

Lexie closed her eyes and replayed her time in the nineteenth century. "She started to thaw after I began to teach Mattie to read."

Lance didn't speak, and she wondered if he processed her words. She watched him, hoping he'd come up with ideas she could use to improve her relationship with the two women.

"So, you invested in Edna's life. You gave of your time and energy to meet a need she couldn't, right?"

"Yes."

"Well?"

"Hmm. You've given me something to think about, love."

Lexie reread her manuscript later that evening, pondering her life with the Bells to see where the relational shifts occurred. She agreed with Lance's assessment, but how could she invest herself in Alma and Adela's lives? They didn't need reading instruction and didn't appear to be interested in learning to play the violin. She already helped them cook, clean, and tend babies, so what more could she do?

The queasiness and cramping in her stomach finally made Lexie look up from the text. She glanced at the clock and then at Lance. He smiled and patted the bed next to him.

"Coming." She logged off the computer and headed for the bathroom. Her pace increased as the bile climbed into her throat. She dropped to the floor in front of the toilet and heaved up her dinner. The pain ripped at her middle and twisted her insides. Her skin cooled, and the shakes began.

She stood and stumbled to the sink to brush her teeth. What had she eaten to cause such stomach upset? Had she touched a contaminated surface and somehow ingested a nasty virus or bacteria in her food or drink? Even after she'd been so careful? Images of death by cholera popped into her thoughts, as well as the remembrance of her words to Steven.

I've never been out of the United States. I've read enough to know that the living standards in Guatemala are not those I'm used to. What if I get sick and need medical attention? What would I do? I'd probably die!

Her teeth chattered as she crawled under the sheets.

"What's wrong, hon?" Lance frowned when he saw her face.

Lexie snuggled into his warmth. "Caught a stomach bug. Maybe I'll feel better after a good night's sleep."

She didn't feel better in the morning, and neither did several of the five-year-olds who had played outside in the newly fenced play area. The children suffered from diarrhea and fevers, so the nannies isolated them, and Rachel called the doctor.

Lexie spent her time rushing from the bed to the toilet and back again. She pulled the covers up to her neck and curled into a ball.

Lance brought her a glass of water and felt her forehead. "No fever. Good. Dr. Carlos Naranjo came from Antigua to check on the kids, so I asked him to examine you before he leaves."

Dr. Naranjo's professional demeanor and kind eyes eased Lexie's discomfort. She answered his questions and allowed him to draw her blood, but frowned when he asked for permission to do a more thorough exam.

"My nurse is not here," he said and looked at Lance, "so I must ask you to remain in the room with your wife, Señor Garrett."

"Is something wrong? Why do I need a pelvic exam?" Lexie sat up so quickly her stomach protested.

"Please, Señora Garrett. You are ill but do not exhibit the same symptoms as the children. I took samples from the little ones and am confident the test results will show they came into contact with human fecal material in the newly turned soil of the playground. During the last rainy season, a nearby waste pit overflowed and saturated the adjacent land. I saw this when I came for one of my visits. You did not come into contact with this soil, correct?"

She nodded.

"Then I must look further for the cause of your sickness."

She nodded again and lay down.

When he finished the exam, he removed his gloves and tossed them in the trashcan.

"You are pregnant, Señora Garrett."

"Pregnant!" Her voice and Lance's sounded like one.

"Are your sure, Doctor?" Lexie's palms began to sweat, yet chills crawled up and down her spine.

Dr. Naranjo nodded. "You are not far along at this time, but of this I am certain. The results of the blood test will confirm your condition. Congratulations."

Pregnant. A baby. In October or November. In Guatemala. Lexie threw back the covers, hand over her mouth, and ran for the toilet.

Lance waited for her return, but Dr. Naranjo had left. "Are you all right, babe?"

"I don't know." Lexie slid under the covers and pulled them toward her chin. She stared into his face. "What are we going to do, Lance?"

He caressed her face. "We prepare for a new addition to our family. What else can we do?"

"I don't want our baby to be born in Guatemala." The words left her mouth before she could stop them.

Lance leaned back and remained silent for several moments. "How and when the baby is born is in the Lord's hands. He makes no mistakes, Lexie."

When she said nothing, his eyebrows lifted. "Do you doubt this?"

> *For as the heavens are higher than the earth, so are my ways higher than your ways, and my thoughts than your thoughts, Lexie.*

The Lord spoke to her heart through the fifty-fifth chapter of Isaiah. She and Lance had discussed verse nine after they'd come across the passage in their Bible study two weeks ago.

She sighed. "No, but I sure wish he'd give me a little more insight into his thinking."

They both turned when someone knocked, and Lance opened the door. Alma walked toward Lexie with a cup of steaming liquid.

"The doctor said I should bring you something to calm your stomach." Alma waited for Lexie to sit up before handing her the cup. She grinned when Lexie sniffed the steam.

"Ginger, peppermint, and lemon balm. The herbs will soothe the queasiness without harming the baby."

"The doctor told you I was pregnant?"

"No. I guessed." She tilted her head toward the door. "I must return to prepare lunch. Adios."

Lance closed the door behind her.

"I suppose the news will be all over the orphanage by noon." She sipped the tea and waited to see what would happen when the liquid reached her stomach.

Lance grinned as he walked toward the bed. He placed his hand over her abdomen. "A baby. We're having a baby."

Delight lightened his eyes and deepened his voice. Her spirit lifted at his response. Truly, Lance was the best man on the planet.

Lexie didn't know how she endured the next fourteen weeks of digestive upheaval and distress. Certain smells or foods triggered an immediate and unpleasant response in her midsection and would send her rushing to the restroom at the most inconvenient times. When she finished heaving, she'd return to her chores, pale and shaking.

The nannies made sympathetic noises and called her *pobrecita*-poor little one. They offered all sorts of morning sickness remedies and advice which didn't seem to help, though she tried them all. In desperation, Lexie pulled out her essential oils reference guide and the small bottles of essential oils Olivia had given her for Christmas and tried a few of them. Lance suggested she get more exercise and, between the oils and moderate workouts, the sickness lessened.

"Did you see Alma, hon? She waved at you." His eyebrows raised in question as he glanced at her before pushing one of the five-year-olds in the swing. Lexie pushed another child on the swing beside him. Both children squealed and asked to be pushed higher.

She glanced at Alma and smiled. The woman nodded and returned Lexie's smile before stepping into the house.

"She's changed. What happened?"

"I'm not sure, Lance. She began to warm toward me during my sickest, most miserable days. She'd bring me teas and hot soup. Each time, she'd stay a few minutes longer and talk."

He chuckled and quipped, "Maybe misery loves company?"

"Maybe."

"What about Adela? Has she come around yet?"

Lexie helped the waiting Dulce into the swing, placed a safety belt around her, and adjusted the little girl's protective helmet before answering.

"Not totally. She's friendlier but still reserved. I can't seem to make much headway with her."

Lexie pushed the swing and watched Steven give horseback rides around the new play area. The men had moved the swings and slides away from the contaminated ground and put up a new fence.

"Stevie's such a natural at making friends, isn't he? Look at him with the children. He always seems to know what to do or say at just the right time. You remember how the Moras accepted him into their family almost immediately? And think how he and Nico became best friends from the moment Stevie shook hands. Rachel and Bob act like he's their favorite son. I don't understand how he does this so easily, Lance. I'm sure they didn't offer Friendship Building 101 at his school."

Lance looked toward his brother-in-law and smiled at Steven's enthusiasm and the children's joyful squeals as they urged their human mount to increased speed.

"He's a lot like your dad, hon."

"And I'm more like Mom. We don't make friends as quickly."

"Speaking of your mother, how did she take our news?"

The corner of Lexie's mouth tipped into a half grin. "Just the way I told you she would. She's ecstatic she'll be a grandmother but disappointed she won't be at the birth, or that she won't be able to hold our baby in a clean, US hospital room. She urged me to come home early."

His body stilled. "What did you say?"

Lexie gave him her best smile, and his eyes widened. "You know how that smile makes my stomach turn flips and my heart pound, don't you, hon?"

She reached toward him and caressed his cheek. "I said I couldn't leave the best, most handsome man on the planet."

The expression in his eyes showed her how much her words meant to him.

He caught and kissed her fingers. "Thank you, Lexie. I know you could've chosen either Dwight, Jonathan, or Sean, but you chose me. You chose us. I'm humbled, and I love you so much."

"I love you too, Lance."

At his mention of the men she left behind, she tilted her head and gave the swing another gentle push. "I'd like to be a little bird sitting on one of heaven's bushes listening to the conversation Gran said she intended to have with Fergus, Edna, Jim, and the others. I can only imagine that get-together."

"I'd like to eavesdrop on their conversation too."

Lexie unstrapped Dulce and led the four-year-old toward the sandbox where her age mates played with shovels, buckets, and plastic toys. She eyed the gate latch before releasing the girl's hand.

"Go play now, love. We'll eat dinner soon."

She waited until Nanny Lucia nodded at her and took Dulce's hand.

"Did Rachel tell you we have guests this week, hon? Missionaries with a heart to reach the jungle tribes in the Maya Biosphere Reserve in the Petén region?"

"Yes, the nannies talked about them."

"Well, I think they just arrived. I heard the van in the drive. Let's get the rest of these little ones to their nannies so we can go and meet our guests."

Both couples, Isaac and Jaiden Winters and Neil and Denise Lockley, exhibited the same energy and enthusiasm Lance and Steven showed when they finally touched down in Guatemala. The couples were in their mid-twenties, athletically built, and tanned. Excitement lit their eyes as they spoke at dinner that evening.

"What made you decide on the people of the Petén region?" Bob asked.

The dark-haired man, Isaac, answered, "Jaiden and I are both children of missionary parents. We grew up in Mexico but traveled to northern Guatemala several times. The place is fantastic. When we asked God where he wanted us to serve and he led us here, you can't imagine our pleasure."

Jaiden, his dainty blond-haired wife, nodded and continued eating.

Denise Lockley pushed a strand of red hair away from her face and glanced around the table. "Neil and I visited the region several times over the past ten years, and when we felt the Lord's tug on our hearts, we prayed and fasted until we knew where he wanted us. We met Isaac and Jaiden soon after, and knew the Lord intended us to minister together. Here we are."

Lexie hadn't responded to God's calling as enthusiastically as these couples, and their excitement pierced her with darts of guilt and jealousy. She lowered her eyes to her plate and picked at the food with her fork. Though she willingly served with Lance and Steven, earlier fears had robbed her of the joy she could've had.

"What are your plans?" Rachel looked at the missionary couples as she passed Bob the bowl of black beans he'd requested.

Neil answered, "In a few days, we'll head back to the airport in Guatemala City. Before we leave, we intend to visit a Christian sister who ministers to the people who live in the Guatemala City Dump. From there, we'll fly to the international airport in Flores. Our team will meet us there."

"People actually live in a dump? Really?" Steven stared at their faces to see if they joked.

Neil nodded. "Yes. Generations are born, live, marry, have children, and die in the stench and filth of this dump. From what I've heard, violence and death surround the inhabitants twenty-four-seven."

"We're taking the missionary food and clothing sent by believers in the States."

"Wow. Sounds like those dump-people live in a fourth world," Steven spoke and glanced at Lexie. "We've sure led a sheltered life, huh, Lex?"

She nodded and fingered the scar. *Sheltered. Comfortable. Easy. Blind. Oh, God, I see and hear of such tremendous needs that I'm overwhelmed. Stomp out my fear. Show me what to do. Open my eyes to the doors of opportunities you want me to walk through for your honor and glory.*

The conversation moved gracefully from one topic to another and, by the end of dinner, Lexie again admired Stevie and Lance's ability to make friends wherever they went. Once Isaac discovered Lance was both a civil engineer and a pilot, comments bounced from one side of the table to another like popcorn in a hot skillet.

"We sure could use someone like you, Lance." Isaac's intent expression sent chills up and down Lexie's spine.

"Why?"

"Not only will we be privileged to share the love and mercy of Jesus Christ, but we'll support the indigenous tribes' efforts to improve the sustainability of their lands. We also plan to provide whatever health care we can. Jaiden's degree and my work have been in agriculture, and Denise is a medical doctor. Neil's a carpenter."

Lexie stared. *What am I, Lord?*

> *You're mine. If the whole body were an eye, where were the hearing? If the whole were hearing, where were the smelling? Think on these things, Daughter.*

Think on these things. She'd heard those words somewhere in Paul's first letter to the church at Corinth. Lexie determined to find the passage as soon as she could.

The conversation continued into the evening, long after they cleared the table. Lexie could tell neither Lance nor Stevie wanted to leave, but tiredness gripped her. She rose and signaled Lance to remain seated.

"I'll see you all in the morning."

She walked toward the stairs but paused when she looked down the hall and saw Adela stooped over the sink as if she were crying.

"Adela?"

The woman spun around and wiped her eyes.

"What's wrong?"

Adela's lips tightened and her spine straightened. She didn't speak for a long count of ten. Finally, her shoulders sagged, and tears seeped out the corners of her eyes.

"I do not know what to do, Señora."

"Adela, after our months together, can't you call me Lexie?"

She sniffed and nodded. "Lexie."

"What can I do to help you, Adela?"

"I do not think you will be able to help me with my problem, but I am grateful for your offer."

"Perhaps you would feel better if you shared your burden?"

"The burdens I carry are many, but sharing one might lighten the load." She sighed and sustained eye contact with Lexie. "Have you ever lacked sufficient money to buy food or clothing? Have you watched a loved one suffer because no one in the family has money to buy medicine?"

Lexie shook her head.

"Have you been threatened with eviction from the only place you know because you cannot pay the rent?"

"No."

"I did not think so. Thank you for listening." Adela turned back to the sink.

Lexie recognized the dismissal in Adela's tone but chose not to leave.

"Though I haven't suffered financially, Adela, I've experienced the heartache and pain of separation. I can't give you the details, but I can tell you I woke up every morning for three months wondering if I'd ever see my loved ones again. The separation felt like death."

Adela turned, her expression strange. "What did you do?"

Lexie closed her eyes and massaged the scar. "I begged God every day to give me a second chance to obey him, but I lost hope as the months passed. I prepared myself the best I could for permanent separation."

"You disobeyed?"

Something in Adela's tone opened Lexie's eyes. "Yes, God told me to come to Guatemala, but I had other plans. Though I knew his will, I disobeyed."

"Why?"

"Fear." She pointed to the inside of her forearm. "See this? The scar reminds me I can't run from God."

They stood in silence for several moments.

"Adela, what are your options? What would help your situation?"

She grimaced. "To discover I had a wealthy uncle who died and left his fortune to my family would be a start."

"Would you accept money from Lance and me?"

"I am grateful, but my family has no way to repay such a loan."

"What if we offered the money as a gift with no expectation of payback?"

Tears flooded Adela's eyes. "You would do this? For me?"

Lexie nodded.

"My pride forbids me to accept such a gift, but my heart longs to say yes for the sake of my family."

"Then listen to your heart, Adela."

"Why would you offer such a gift?"

"If I were in the same situation, I'd hope someone would care enough about me to help."

Lexie opened her arms, and Adela stepped into her embrace.

"You did well, babe." Lance snuggled against Lexie's back and whispered into her ear.

She turned to face him. "I hoped you'd think so, Lance. What we gave Adela is all we had for this month's expenses."

"So? We've put ourselves in the position of receiving blessings from heaven, just like the widow who gave her whole living to God. Jesus said she gave more than those who gave out of their abundance. I don't think we can ever out-give God."

She caressed the stubble on his jaw. "You're going to be an excellent father, love. You'll teach our son or daughter so many life lessons."

The gleam of his white teeth in the moonlight reflected the smile in his next words, "I wonder what our baby will look like? I hope he or she has your dark brown eyes and light hair and smells as good as you do."

When Lexie laughed and rolled to her back, he stroked the palm-sized baby. "Good-night, little one."

"Does the fact that I'll have the baby in Guatemala bother you, Lance?"

"No. He or she'll be born with dual citizenship. So what?"

At her silence, he rolled to his elbow and looked at her. "Lexie?"

"I'm nervous about all this. What if I have trouble? What if-"

He placed a finger across her lips. "Shh, you're biting off future trouble again, sweetheart."

"I call my concerns long-term planning, Lance, not biting off trouble." She couldn't stop the irritated nip from entering her voice. "I'm sorry. You're right."

"Doctor Naranjo returns for his regular visit tomorrow. He plans to see you after he checks on the children. We need to be certain you're getting the proper nutrition for a healthy delivery."

She nodded and kissed him. "Goodnight, love."

Lexie waited for Lance's breathing to deepen and his muscles to relax before she knelt beside the bed.

"Lord, you know my fears and reservations. You already know I don't want the baby to be born in Guatemala, but if this is your will, I will submit to you."

"Lexie?" Adela entered the kitchen and moved with purpose to the table where Lexie wrote letters home.

"Hi, Adela. You look well today."

"Yes, I am happy and so thankful to you and Lance. My family has food to eat and a roof to shelter them from the approaching rainy season. My grandfather lives because he got the medicine he needed. The words thank you in any language are not sufficient to speak what is in my heart."

"I understand. Shall I show you what I do when words aren't enough?"

"Yes."

"Wait here. I'll be back in a moment."

Lexie returned to the kitchen, violin in hand, and began to play for the two women. She closed her eyes and allowed the soft music to speak to her heart and theirs.

For several moments after she finished, silence surrounded them.

"You told the truth," Adela finally spoke. "Those are the words I would speak if I could."

Alma stood and tied on her apron. "When you first came, you

mentioned using the violin to help you learn Spanish. Show us how you did this, Lexie."

Did their smiles hint at disbelief when she told of her frustration and battles to learn their language?

"But you speak Spanish so well," Adela's skepticism seeped into her voice, "as if you were born in Guatemala."

"Let me show you how I felt before I learned to hear the music in Spanish words." She played the first dramatic introduction of Beethoven's Fifth Symphony. *Ta-ta-ta-taa! Ta-ta-ta-taa!*

The women stared.

Lexie explained and demonstrated how she learned the language after she heard the music.

"Do you think this method would work for Spanish speakers who wish to learn English?" The intensity of Adela's question indicated something more lay at the root of her words.

"Possibly. Do you wish to learn English, Adela?"

She tensed then nodded. "If I could learn English even half as well as you learned Spanish, Lexie, I could become a tour guide for the English-speaking visitors to Guatemala. I would have one of the highest paying jobs, so my family would have enough food, shelter, clothing, and medicine."

"Well, let's see how this works with you. I'll point to things in the kitchen. Then I'll say the word in English and will try to play the sounds on the violin. You repeat, okay?"

The language game engaged them for almost two hours. Lexie had never laughed so much, and she was certain Adela and Alma hadn't either.

"What's going on in here? I heard you laughing all the way outside." Rachel entered the kitchen, eyebrows raised.

"English lessons." Adela smiled at how well her new words sounded. She pointed to objects in the kitchen and said their names.

Rachel blinked. "How did you do that? You don't have much of an accent."

Adela didn't try to hide her pleasure or gratitude. She smiled and tilted her head in Lexie's direction. "She taught me to hear the music in the words. Soon I hope to learn how to put the words together in sentences."

The change in Adela's attitude lifted Lexie's spirit. The look in the woman's eyes reminded her of the expression in Edna's eyes after she saved Mattie from being trampled in the buffalo stampede. The thought warmed her. Hadn't she impacted her friends and family in the nineteenth century without knowing the extent of her influence? Maybe she didn't have to be a doctor, carpenter, agriculturist, or engineer to make a difference. Maybe she could be herself and impact one person at a time using the gifts God gave her. Yes, she thought she could.

SIXTEEN

The impromptu English lessons continued throughout the following days. Alma gained in skill, but didn't come close to the progress Adela made. The woman's need to better herself for her family's sake drove her. Lexie demonstrated how to use body movements in conjunction with phrasing to help her remember, and Adela absorbed the instruction like a sponge. She practiced throughout the day, and insisted Lexie, Lance, and Steven speak to her in English.

"Wow, Lex. Adela reminds me of you after you had your breakthrough." Steven listened to Adela practicing her sentences as she filled bottles. "She wants every word to be perfect and insists we correct her if she makes a mistake."

She looked up and smiled when Lexie, Lance, and Steven joined her in the kitchen. Without pausing in her work, she quoted Second Peter chapter three verse nine then looked at Lexie.

The Lord is not slack concerning his promise, as some count slackness; but is long suffering toward us, not willing that any should perish, but that all should come to repentance.

Lexie knew what Adela expected. They'd developed this game early in the language lessons. She scrambled to remember the same verse in Spanish and recited, her words hesitant.

El Señor no retarda su promesa, según algunos la tiene por tardanza; sino que es paciente para con nosotros, no queriendo que ninguno perezca, sino que todos procedan al arrepentimiento.

Adela then quoted John Chapter three verse sixteen and pointed to Steven.

For God so loved the world that He gave His only begotten Son, that whoever believes in Him should not perish but have everlasting life.

Her brother grinned and immediately recited.

Before Adela could point at him, Lance quoted a verse they had studied during their evening Bible study with those who remained at the orphanage at night and waited for her to respond.

Adela's brow furrowed but she finally came up with the correct translation. Her smile, so unused in earlier days, spread across her face.

"I want to learn to read and write in English. Will you help me,

Lexie?"

Lexie nodded.

They all turned toward the door when Bob clumped down the hall. He spoke into his cell phone.

"Just a minute, Neil, Lance is right here."

"Hello?"

Lance listened as the missionary spoke. The excitement on her husband's face disturbed Lexie. She'd seen the same expression when he engaged in his more daring activities-like skydiving, bungee jumping, and rappelling. Her stomach lurched, and she put her hand over her expanding middle.

"Let me chat with Lexie and I'll get back with you. Can you wait a half hour? Okay. Bye."

Lance returned Bob's phone and held out his hand for her. "Let's take a walk, hon."

"What's wrong? Tell me now." The writhing in her stomach told Lexie she wasn't going to like what he was about to say. She drew her sweater closer to ward off the chill.

"Neil is in Guatemala City waiting to fly back to the Petén with supplies and medicine for the villagers. The pilot they chartered got in a car accident on his way to the airport and won't be able to get him home, so he asked me to fly him. He's by himself. What do you think?"

Lexie couldn't get the words around the lump in her throat. She lowered her eyes so he wouldn't read the thoughts in her mind.

"Hon?" He tipped her face toward his.

"I'm afraid, Lance."

"Why?"

She pointed at the gathering storm clouds. "This is the first week of May. The worst of the rainy season begins soon. Flying in this kind of weather is crazy. What would I do if something happened to you?"

He remained silent for several moments. "I'd expect you to take care of yourself and our child."

Tears slipped from the corners of her eyes as he caressed her middle. He bent and kissed the baby mound. "Daddy loves you, little one."

Lance drew her into his arms and against his heart. "I'll be gone for a week at the most, babe. Once we land, I'll help Neil unload and transport the supplies into the jungle, and then I'll fly the plane back to Guatemala City and head this way."

Agreeing to let him go was the hardest thing she'd ever done.

"I'm coming into Guatemala City with you, Lance."

"No, Lexie. I planned to catch a ride to Antigua with Bob. He has a dentist appointment. From there, I intend to take a bus into the city."

"A bus? No, Lance. They're too dangerous."

"Which is why you shouldn't come. You'd have to return by yourself, and that's not an option."

"Stevie can come with me." Her jaw firmed. "I want to see you off. Please don't say no."

The muscles in his jaws worked as he gritted his teeth. "All right. Get ready. We have to leave in twenty minutes."

Both Lance and Steven remained on high alert as they traveled through the rain-drenched city to the airport. They watched every turn their bus driver made and sighed in relief when they saw their ride from the Fixed Base Operator waiting for them at the designated location. The driver took them to the waiting plane. Neil waved but continued to help with the cargo-loading.

Lance leaned over and kissed her. "Be safe, sweetheart. I'll see you when I get back."

Rain pelted her when he opened the door. "Lance," she choked on his name, "please don't-" she couldn't continue. Words failed her. She hugged him with all her strength, and he kissed her again.

"Neil's signaling for you to come, Lance," Steven said as he watched the loading, "looks like they're ready."

Lance squeezed Steven's shoulder. "Keep my girl safe."

Her brother nodded.

They waited in the car until the small plane lifted above the end of the runway and banked for the flight to the northeast.

Lexie released the air she'd been holding in a long sigh.

"Do you want to eat here, Lex, or head back to the orphanage?"

"I don't feel like eating now, Stevie. Let's get back."

"How? Are we going by taxi, shuttle, or bus?"

"Do you have any money?"

Steven searched his pockets. "Only ten Quetzals-less than a dollar fifty American money. Do you?"

"About the same. I forgot to ask Lance for more before he left."

"Not good." Steven's lips tightened, and he looked into the churning mass of dark clouds. "This means we'll have to take a chicken bus instead of what we rode earlier."

Lexie gulped and nodded before asking the driver to take them where they needed to go. Her jaw firmed. They had no other choice.

He said *¡Cuidado!—be careful*, but dropped them off near the bus stop.

Lexie buttoned her rain jacket to her chin and covered her hair with the hood before exiting the car. She opened her small umbrella and tilted the fabric to cover most of her face. Steven did the same. She didn't want her coloring to draw unwanted attention. Several passengers waited for the bright red bus known as *Rojo Diablo*—Devil Red, so she and Steven got in line. Lexie looked at her watch. Two-fifty-five p.m. She glanced down the street. The buses left every fifteen minutes, so she assumed the next one would arrive shortly.

She texted Rachel and asked to be picked up in Antiqua in an hour.

> *Dr. Naranjo is coming for his regular visit at that time, but I'll make sure someone will meet you in Antigua at four. Probably Nico. See you soon. Rachel.*

Without being obvious, Lexie studied the other passengers. None looked like terrorists or assassins, but then she'd never seen a real terrorist or assassin before. These people looked tired and ready to go home to their families.

The seats were taken, so she and Steven stood at the back of the bus in the aisle with a few others and clutched the ceiling rail. The odors of unwashed bodies and animals sickened her, so Lexie buried her nose in Steven's back and closed her eyes.

"You all right, Lex?" he whispered over his shoulder.

"I feel sick, Stevie. I don't know how I'm going to survive an hour of this."

He dug a plastic bag out of his pocket. "Here. If you're going to puke, use this."

"Why do you carry around a plastic bag?"

"I used the thing to protect some of my stuff when Lance and I worked outside."

"Oh." Her heart raced at the thought of Lance flying into a thunderstorm. *God, please keep him safe. Keep us safe.*

With a lurch, they pulled away from the curb. Lexie's knuckles whitened in her effort to stay upright. She bumped a seated passenger with her elbow and immediately mumbled her apology.

"*Lo siento.*"

The man leaned forward and tried to see into her face. The towel-wrapped hen resting on his lap squawked her displeasure.

Lexie lowered her eyelids and tugged at her hood, but the man had seen her eyes and light cheeks.

"You are American? From the United States?"

Steven turned his head and looked at the passenger. He tilted his head.

The man studied Steven's features and whispered to the woman seated beside him, "Americans."

The woman looked from Lexie to Steven and back to Lexie and smiled.

"What makes you think we are from the United States?" Lexie spoke as softly as she could and focused on her accent.

He grinned. "You do not smell like the rest of us."

Lexie blinked. She didn't expect her scent to betray her citizenship to others.

The man and woman stared at her for several moments before looking at each other.

"I am certain your smile lights the heart of your husband," the man said. He seemed to expect a response from Steven, and when her brother didn't say anything, he frowned.

Lexie chuckled. "He is my brother."

"Ahh."

The heat from tightly packed bodies nauseated Lexie. She lowered the hood and unsnapped the rain jacket to cool herself. The man's startled glance moved from her light hair toward her expanding belly.

He questioned them for several stops, and either she or Steven answered. The conversation focused her attention away from the discomfort in her midsection, though the pain increased when they left the city behind. The bus swayed at each bend in the road, and she grasped the plastic bag with whitened knuckles.

Suddenly, as they began their ascent up Las Cañas, the driver increased his speed and glared into his side mirror. Passengers grabbed the handlebars on the seat backs in front of them and craned their necks to see what or who the driver tried to outrun.

Another chicken bus approached and attempted to pass. Lexie gasped to see people holding onto the baggage railing on top of their bus.

"What does our driver think this stretch of road is? Daytona Beach?" Steven mumbled, "Hang on, Lex."

Their velocity increased and Lexie glanced to her right. An abyss yawned only a few feet from the edge of the road. She closed her eyes and placed both arms around Steven's waist.

God be merciful!

The game of chicken seemed to last for hours though, in reality, only a few minutes passed before the driver in the second bus slowed and fell in behind their bus. The driver continued to glare into his mirror until he knew the other bus driver had no more grandiose ideas of passing. He then tuned the radio to a soccer game and seemed to mellow as Lexie watched.

She tried to control her shuddering breaths, but they didn't cooperate until the bus topped the hill at San Lucas and they started downhill. Maybe they would get to Antigua after all.

Her thought changed the moment she saw young men on motorcycles approaching the bus on the loneliest strip of road between San Lucas and Antigua. Something about them reminded her of the Costa Rican attackers.

"Stevie, they intend harm," she whispered and pointed as a motorcycle got close and the young man seated behind the driver forced the door open and entered while they moved. In a matter of moments, another had boarded and forced the chicken bus driver to a stop at the side of the road.

"Stay behind me, Lex."

One of the men held a pistol to the driver's head while the other waved his weapon at the passengers.

"Today is your lucky day." His smile didn't reach his dark eyes. "My friend and I are here to solicit donations for two of our disabled companions. Voluntary gifts are greatly appreciated. If you give, you will live to see your families in Antigua."

"Yeah, I bet," Steven muttered.

"Now, you know I could be like those other guys who steal and take all you have, but I'm not going to do that-at least not today."

God help! You are my strength in troublous times.

He began at the first-row seats and handed an empty offering plate to the passengers. When they had given, he moved to the next row and gave them the plate.

"Probably stole the thing from a local church," her brother mumbled only loudly enough for her to hear.

When the thief's eyes landed on her and Steven, they widened.

"Oh, we are indeed blessed today. Wealthy visitors chose to visit our country today of all days. I am certain they are more than willing to donate to the needy."

He smirked when he held the plate toward her and Steven. They gave the only coins they had—less than a dollar in American money. His smirk morphed into a frown.

"Come now. You must do better."

"That's all the money we have." The muscles in Steven's jaw worked.

The man looked beyond Steven into Lexie's eyes. His gazed wandered over her from head to toe, and lust warred with greed when their eyes met again.

"Let us see what the beautiful lady has to say."

Steven glared. "Leave her alone."

Without blinking, the thief hit Steven on the head with the pistol. Her brother crumpled into the laps of the passengers in the closest row.

"No!" she cried as blood streamed from a cut on her brother's head.

The man laughed and pointed the pistol at her belly. "Perhaps the family of such a pretty lady would pay well to have her and the baby safely returned to them, no?"

He hurt her brother, and now he threatened her child? He intended to take her hostage?

Lexi's hands moved faster than they ever had. Before the man knew what happened, she disarmed him and kneed him in the groin. He screamed and doubled over. She rapped his skull with the pistol and, as he dropped, looked up in time to see the bus driver boot the other watching thug out the open door as hard as he could.

The driver watched for a few moments, then grinned his satisfaction. "He will not rob anyone else again." Lexie's heart twisted and broke. The young thief, no older than Steven, had lost his chance at redemption and had now opened his eyes in the torments of hell. Tears filled her eyes.

Men and women poured from their seats and grabbed the robber at her feet. They pummeled his unconscious form with punches and kicks as they booted him out the door. He landed next to his dead friend, and the driver closed the door and put the bus in gear.

Lexie tripped on a market bag in her haste to check Stevie and lost her balance. She fell, stomach first, against the hard edge of a seat. The searing pain in her belly sent agonizing waves of liquid fire through her, and she screamed and crumpled. She couldn't see through the haze glazing her eyes, so she closed them.

Gentle hands lifted her, and someone asked her a question, but she couldn't seem to find the music in the words. She didn't understand. She closed her eyes and let the pain take her.

"Lexie, can you hear me?"

The weights holding down her lids lifted, and Lexie opened her eyes. She looked in Steven's anxious face. She reached toward his bandaged head.

"You're okay?" The words scratched her as they left her throat.

He nodded, and she saw movement behind him. Dr. Naranjo stepped near and took her pulse.

"How do you feel, Señora Garrett?"

"I can't keep my eyes open."

"That is the medicine I gave you. Do you have pain?"

"Some cramping in my back and stomach." Lexie felt for the baby mound and stopped. Her hands shook.

"My baby! Where is my baby?" she cried.

Stevie's sad eyes answered her question.

"No, no, no!" she sobbed, and Stevie held her hand.

Tears tracked down his cheeks as they now raced down hers.

"He's gone. I'm sorry, Lex."

She'd had a son. Lance's son. The sobs strengthened as they tore from her throat. "Why, God? Why?"

She didn't know how long she wept or tore at the covers, but when exhaustion finally stilled her movements, she stared at the ceiling through puffy, unfocused eyes.

"Lexie?"

She turned toward the sound and squinted her eyes in the murky darkness. Next to her bed, Stevie lifted his face from his hands and looked toward the door. Lexie wanted to cry again. Her brother had remained at her side for hours.

"Adela?" Lexie whispered.

The woman stepped into the halo of gold cast by the nightstand light, a tea tray in her hands. "Sí. I have brought you something to soothe your pain, though I know this tea will never soothe the ache in your heart."

Through the haze of hurt, Lexie recognized Adela's empathy. She stared into the woman's equally puffy eyes.

"I, too, have lost a child. Human traffickers stole my ten-year-old daughter a year ago. We found her abused body a month later."

"Oh, Adela, I'm so sorry."

She nodded and placed the tray on the nightstand. Steven stood and indicated Adela should sit.

"How did you get through her death?" Lexie pushed herself up on her pillow and reached for her friend's hand.

Adela's mouth worked as she struggled to get the words out. "Alma lost her baby to sickness at the same time, so we held on to each other and got through the pain together. My husband could not handle the situation, so he started drinking. He eventually committed suicide. Alma's husband left. She has not seen him since."

Lexie didn't know how to respond, so she said nothing.

"When these bad things happen, Lexie, I often question God. I wonder if he cares what happens to us. How much pain can we bear?" She rose and poured the tea. "Drink. This will help."

Lexie obeyed and watched her leave the room. She glanced at her brother. "Go to bed, Stevie. You need the rest as much as I do. I'll see you in the morning."

He tucked her in and kissed her cheek.

"Stevie, don't say anything to Mom and Dad yet, okay? I want to tell Lance first."

"I'm sorry, Lex, but when you were bleeding so heavily, and I thought we might lose you, I texted Mom."

"She knows about the baby?"

"No. I didn't give her the details. Here. Read." He held up his cell phone.

Pray! Pray for Lexie now!

"If that message doesn't get her on the next plane to Guatemala, Stevie, nothing will." Lexie sighed, "Does Lance know?"

"No. Too many thunderstorms between here and there. We can't reach him yet. I'll keep trying."

He bent and kissed her cheek before leaving the room.

Lexie snuggled into her blankets and listened to the continuous rumble of thunder as the raindrops pelted the window glass. The strobe-like flashes of nearby lightning strikes lit up the scenes playing behind her closed eyelids. She relived every moment of the day's tragic events until she tossed and turned in her bed. Sweat and tears drenched her pillow and sheets.

"Stop," she commanded her thoughts and reached for her violin.

Lexie played until she was so tired she couldn't hold the bow. She put the violin in the case and turned her face to the wall. She sobbed and cradled her stomach. Her limbs automatically drew together in a fetal position.

> *Edna curled up like a newborn babe, same as you, when her two young'uns died. Stayed that way for more than a week. Mary and me had to force her to eat and drink, and then she was sick for a long time after.*

Fergus' gravelly voice played through Lexie's thoughts. Poor Edna. She'd lost two children within a day of each other during the cholera epidemic. How had she survived?

"I miss you, Edna. I wish I could talk to you."

Near dawn, Lexie fell into an uneasy sleep. She woke up screaming.

Alma, Adela, and Rachel rushed into the room with Steven only a step behind.

Lexie opened her eyes, disoriented.

"Lexie, what's wrong. Did you see another scorpion?" Rachel looked around the room.

"Lex, are you okay?" Steven sat by her bed and took her hand.

She shook her head. Several moments passed before she could force the words out her throat. "I had a terrible dream. We were all standing in a huge, sprawling line-you know, like the lines outside big department stores just before they open for Black Friday sales?"

He nodded.

"This was bigger. Some people didn't seem to realize they were in the line, but they continued to move forward at a snail's pace with the rest of us. Men, women, and children from every nation and linguistic group were ahead, beside, and behind me. Gran and Grammy were ahead of me somewhere, and so were Mom and Dad. You were behind with your friends. Stevie, I couldn't find Lance anywhere, though I knew he'd been beside me only moments before."

Lexie tried to control her breathing. "The line didn't appear to move, but I knew we had inched along, because I was farther up the street than the day before. People surrounded me: soldiers in camouflage, politicians, reporters, movie stars, artists, cowboys, teens on skateboards, and musicians. The press of so many bodies gave me a terrible headache and nausea."

"Why were you in such a line?" Steven handed her a glass of water with a straw. "Here, drink first."

She touched the pulsing flesh near her jaw. "I don't know. After I shut down my computer, I watched the people around me. An Arabic speaker screamed at a Hebrew man, who returned what sounded like insults. Bystanders raised their fists and urged both to more violent actions. None of the soldiers or politicians standing nearby attempted to stop them, so I turned away and looked for my family.

"Lance stood in the shadows of a building and spoke to a gathering of street people. I wasn't close enough to hear what he said, but he seemed to plead with them. A few stayed to listen, but most turned away. He saw me and lifted a finger to tell me he'd come to me in a moment.

"I rested at the base of a gigantic clock and watched a group of men and women of different ages and ethnicities gaming and drinking together on the sidewalk. The intent, feverish stares in their eyes as they watched the toss of the dice, and the tenseness of their bodies reminded me of that drug addict who stopped at the food kitchen for a meal. Remember, Stevie, the time we worked in the soup kitchen at Christmas three years ago?"

He nodded and waited.

"Our line rounded another corner of the broad avenue, and I noticed a large American flag. The flag hung at half-mast, and I wondered what new disaster had hit our country. At that moment, the pain in my midsection doubled me over, and I fell to the ground. People clustered so tightly around me I couldn't breathe. An ambulance, red and blue lights flashing, pulled up beside me, and a paramedic cleared space.

"'Come on, folks, give the lady room,' he said, and he and another paramedic placed me on a gurney. Before they could get me in the ambulance, though, I had the baby. Several of my line-mates cheered. One man told me I had a son.

"As soon as he spoke, a man in a dark blue or black uniform snatched the baby from the paramedic's arms without saying a word and raced toward the front of the line. I begged and cried for him to bring my baby back, but he acted as if he didn't hear me. People on each side of me raised their fists, cursed, and moved toward the man in black who ignored everyone. He had to stop, though, when a large, white-clad officer blocked his way. The man in the white uniforrm wore shiny gold bars on his shoulders. He held out his arms, and the man with my baby gave him up as if against his will. The crowd closed in around me again, and I—"

Her voice cracked and let the sobs through. "I never saw my child again."

The four of them stood around her and offered what comfort they could.

Lexie reached for the tissue on the nightstand and looked at her friends and brother. "I want to see my baby before he— before he—"

They all looked at Rachel, who finally nodded. "We'll bring him."

Alma laid her son in her palms. Her friend had wrapped him in a soft blue washcloth. Lexie pushed the cloth aside and touched the baby's tiny fingers and toes. She kissed the little face.

"So perfect already." She stared long and hard to imprint her son's features on her memory. "I'll see you in heaven, little one. Mommy loves you."

When Alma rewrapped the baby, Lexie turned her face to the wall. She couldn't watch him leave the room.

"Lex?" Tears thickened Steven's voice as he stroked her hair.

She didn't turn before speaking, "His name is Matthew David Garrett. Will you take care of the arrangements, Stevie? I'm not up to watching his burial."

"Sure." He kissed the side of her head. "Get some rest if you can."

"Wait, Stevie." Lexie twisted her head to look at him. "Will you tell Mom and Dad? I can't talk about anything yet, but they'll need to know."

He nodded.

"Tell them I love them and will call when I feel better."

"Okay. Love you, Lex."

"I love you too."

She waited for the door to close before she turned on her back and stared at the ceiling.

"God, are you here? Did you take my baby because you knew I didn't want him to be born in Guatemala? Was I so wrong you had to teach me another lesson? Why Lord?"

God's answer came to her from Isaiah fifty-five and Jeremiah eighteen.

> *For as the heavens are higher than the earth, so are my ways higher than your ways, Lexie, and my thoughts than your thoughts. Do I, the Potter, not have the right to make what I wish out of the clay? Do you not remember the words of my prophet, Jeremiah, who wrote, 'And the vessel he was making of clay was spoiled in the potter's hand, and he reworked it into another vessel, as it seemed good to the potter to do?' What is your answer, Daughter? Have I the right?*

Lexie didn't want to answer, but his Spirit waited.

"Yes, Abba," she sighed, "You have the right."

> *Feed my sheep, Lexie.*

"What, Lord?"

> *Are you the only one who carries a heavy burden? Feed my lambs, beloved. Let your light so shine before others that they may see your good works. Then they will give me the glory for how you live before them. Come, Lexie, my yoke is easy, and*

my burden is light.

Two days later, Lexie arose early in the morning and showered. She made the bed and went downstairs to the dining room. She greeted the astonishment of the others with as much of a smile as she could muster.

"Good morning," she said. Her smile wobbled but remained in place.

Steven pushed away from the table and hurried to her. "Do you want breakfast, Lex?"

Bob and Nico both stood and watched her approach the nearest chair.

"I think I'll try a bite." She looked at all of them after Steven pushed in her chair. "I want to thank you for all your kindness to me."

They nodded and returned to eating.

"You're one of us now," Adela whispered as she sat a dish next to Lexie.

"I am?"

"Yes. No longer are you another advantaged American in my eyes. You have become a sister in pain." Adela squeezed Lexie's shoulder and left the room.

Lexie stared at Adela's retreating back.

"Do you feel well enough to help in the nursery today, Lexie?" Rachel asked.

"I think so."

Rachel seemed to struggle with her next words, "I need to warn you about something first, though."

"What?"

"None of these Guatemalan babies can be adopted out of the country. This is the law."

"So?"

Rachel's mouth worked, and moisture came and went in her eyes. Her voice filled with softness and caring when she spoke, "Don't get too fond of Oscar or the other little ones, okay?"

Oh, how wise Rachel was to warn her. The moment Lexie snuggled Oscar into her arms for his feeding, her heart wrapped around him so tightly in yearning her middle ached. He smiled and reached for her mouth. Lexie kissed his fingers and caressed his soft skin. Every few moments she brushed her tears off his face.

She looked at the other three nannies after she put Oscar in his crib. "I'm going to rest now. I need to call my parents."

They nodded.

Lexie moved as if her whole body ached, though the ache originated in her heart, not her muscles. What would she tell her folks? How would she handle her mother's expected response? Her emotional batteries were drained already, and she hadn't picked up the phone yet.

Stevie. She'd get her brother to come with her so he could help carry some of the conversational load. She looked at her watch, and then moved to the window. He would normally be outside with Nico now, but the rain had started an hour ago. Where was he?

Movement near the garage caught her eyes, and the sight of her brother yelling, crying, and striking a tree repeatedly with his fists drained her remaining reserve. His hands bled. She grasped the windowsill and shook uncontrollably. As she watched, Nico and Rob stepped near and put supporting arms around Stevie. Her brother crumpled into his friends' arms as sobs shook his body.

Lexie flung herself out the door and into the drenching rain.

"Stevie? What's wrong?" the pitch of her words rose almost an octave.

Nico and Rob stepped back as she grasped her brother's arms.

He couldn't speak through the sobs, so he shook his head and pulled her close.

"I'm so sorry, Lex," he said when he could speak. "Neil just got through to me. Lance—he—Lex—" He choked on his tears. "Lance was caught in a mud slide that wiped out most of the village where he delivered supplies. Neil's phone connection wasn't good, but I'm sure he said they'll be weeks digging out bodies."

Lexie struggled to remain upright as the darkness swallowed her vision. Stevie held her as she screamed until she had no voice, then he picked her up and carried her to her room.

SEVENTEEN

Lexie sat by her bedroom window and stared as lightning bolts ripped through the night sky and turned the black clouds to an eerie greenish-purple. Rain dripped from every roof and puddled on the saturated ground.

She closed Olivia Johnson's diary and placed the book on the bed next to her open suitcase and Bible. The diary was the only one she'd brought of all the others, and she'd read the entries several times during the last three weeks.

Lance's clothing lay in a pile next to hers. The sight of his favorite blue shirt tortured her. She groaned and fell to her knees, burying her face in the material and inhaling, hoping to catch any hint of his scent.

What do you choose, Daughter?

"Do I have a choice, Lord?"

You always have a choice.

The Spirit waited.

"Mom and Dad want Stevie and me to come home."

Did not my servant, Matthew, quote the words of my Son in his gospel? 'Whoever loves father or mother more than me is not worthy of me, and whoever loves son or daughter more than me is not worthy of me. And whoever does not take his cross and follow me is not worthy of me?'

"Yes, Lord."

Am I worthy?

Images of Christ's suffering and the pain he endured because of her sins gutted her.

"You are worthy."

Lexie's jaw firmed and she stood. She hung Lance's clothes back on the hanger, replaced hers in the drawers, and zipped the suitcases. She pushed the luggage into the closet and closed the door.

Praying she had enough signal to get through the disturbance created by the storm, she dialed her mother.

"Lexie!" Olivia answered on the first ring.

"Hi, Mom."

"When are you coming home, sweetheart? We'll pick you and Stevie up at the airport whenever you say. The Garretts will plan a memorial service when you get back."

"I'll be home in December."

"December?" The shock in her mother's voice traveled through every nerve in Lexie's body.

"Yes."

The silence lasted several moments.

"Mom, are you still there? Did I lose you? Hello?" She looked at the phone screen. Still connected.

"Put Stevie on, Lexie."

"Okay, just a minute. I'll get him."

She lowered the phone and whispered in her brother's ear the words she'd said to their mother.

He nodded and took the phone.

"Mom?"

Steven didn't say much but listened patiently as his mother vented.

"Lexie is thinking clearly, Mom. We still have work to do here," he said as gently as he could.

He listened for several more moments. "Okay, I'll tell her. We love you too. Bye."

"Here." He hung up and gave her the phone. "You already know she's unhappy with our decision."

"Yes, she lives in fear, like I used to."

"What do you mean?"

"Do you remember how Dad and Mom always warned us not to use those bad, four-letter-words?"

Steven grinned and nodded. "Dad washed my mouth out with soap one time when he caught me using them."

"Well, they forgot to warn us that F-E-A-R is the worst one of all: The manifestation of this word cripples. No wonder God constantly reminded his people not to be afraid, but to trust in him."

She stared at her hands. "Though as bad as fear is, Stevie, I think the words I need to watch out for all have five letters: P-R-I-D-E and A-N-G-E-R. I always mess up when I act under their influence."

"I love you, Lex. You're the best sister any brother could ever have." He kissed her forehead and pulled her toward the door. "Come on. The rain's stopped, and I smell something cooking. Let's find out what's for dinner."

They helped set the table and Alma and Adela eyed Lexie from the corners of their eyes. They touched her hair, cheek, or shoulder as they passed, and she smiled at them.

"I'm okay. Don't worry."

Bob's cell phone rang in the middle of the meal.

"What? I can't hear you. Try again. Who is this? Dr. Naranjo? What?" His eyes widened. "I'm on my way. Be there soon."

He rose from the table and looked at Rachel. "I have to go into Antigua. I'll be back as soon as I can."

"Why?" She rose and followed him. "What's happened?"

Lexie strained to hear.

He kissed his wife and shrugged into his rain jacket. "Don't worry."

"I am worried. Take Nico with you, please."

The young man stood and waited for Bob's response.

"Okay. Get your jacket, Nico."

Bob looked at their concerned faces. "Pray the rain doesn't start again until after we get home."

No one ate much after Bob left, so they cleared the table and sat in the darkened living room and listened to Lexie play above the thunder's rumbling lullaby. Time seemed to slow as they tried to count the lightning bolts as they streaked across the sky. Rachel glanced at the clock every two minutes and fidgeted with a tissue.

"I can't stand this. I'm going to check on the babies." She stood, and Alma and Adela nodded and followed.

Lexie understood. Waiting frayed the nerves.

"Lex, I'm going to run upstairs for a few minutes and Skype with Gabby if the storm lets me get through. You'll be all right?"

"Yes. Will you open the window near the door a little before you go up? The air is stuffy in here."

"Sure."

She listened to his footsteps as he climbed the stairs before raising the violin to her shoulder. She stood near the living room window and, as she'd done so many times before, allowed the touch of the bow on the strings to draw out her loneliness and pain.

As she played with her eyes closed, Lance's scent seemed to grow stronger in the cool draft from the open window. She groaned.

Oh, Lance, I miss you so much. How am I going to get through life without you?

"Lexie."

Her eyes snapped open at the sound of her name whispered beside her ear. She'd longed to hear that voice for the past several weeks.

"Lance?" She sobbed and turned into his arms. He pulled her close and kissed the air out of her lungs.

Joy squeezed her heart as she searched his face.

"Just a second." She laid the bow and violin in the case and rushed back into his arms.

She buried her face in the material of his shirt and took a deep breath. The scent was all Lance. To ensure he wasn't a dream, she opened her hands and ran them over his hair, face, neck, and shoulders. Solid. Real.

Tears flowed unchecked as she wrapped her arms around him and leaned back just enough to look in his face. "We thought you were dead. Pain and grief have filled my every waking moment since I heard about the mudslide."

He stroked her cheek. "Oh, Lexie, I've missed you so much.

Every time I tried to get home, some major problem prevented me. My texts came back as undeliverable, and then I lost the phone in the slide. I've never felt so helpless or frantic."

His hands encircled her waist, and he dropped his face into her neck and sobbed. "I'm so sorry about the baby, sweetheart. Dr. Naranjo told me."

She held him, and her tears mingled with his. "Our son was so beautiful, Lance. I wish you could have seen him before-before they took him away."

Neither could speak for several moments. Lance picked her up and carried her to the couch. He snuggled her in his lap, and she rested her cheek over his heart.

"Tell me what happened, babe. Dr. Naranjo didn't know all the details." Lance kissed her temple.

She closed her eyes and gave him a blow-by-blow account of her trip home via chicken bus. The memory, branded on her brain by fear, lost some of its intensity now that Lance held her.

Lexie looked up when Steven's door opened and he rushed down the stairs in his usual manner.

"Why are you still sitting in the dark, Lex? Why—?" he flipped the light switch and gaped. "Lance?"

Lexie moved off Lance's lap as he rose to meet Steven's headlong rush.

"How? When? Wow, I'm so glad you aren't dead." Steven brushed tears from his eyes and hugged Lance. Her brother's back pats were enthusiastic and hard enough to make Lexie wince, but Lance just smiled and returned them. "You've got to call home, bro. Your folks are planning a memorial service soon."

The others returned to the room for a joyful reunion, and an hour passed before Lexie took Lance's hands and said goodnight. "We'll see you in the morning."

Lexie closed their bedroom door and handed Lance her phone. "Here, love, call your folks."

Lance put the phone on speaker, leaned against the closed door, and watched her move around the room as she prepared for bed. His eyes glistened.

"Lexie?" Amy Garrett answered on the second ring, "What's wrong?"

"Mom." Lance didn't hide the tears in his voice.

Amy started yelling and crying, "George, pick up the phone now! Lance is on the line. He's alive, praise God!"

Thirty minutes later, Lance handed Lexie the phone and slipped into bed beside her. "Your turn, hon."

Olivia and David reacted much like Amy and George.

Lexie hung up and faced Lance. She caressed his cheek. "Our mourning has turned to joy."

He smiled and drew her close. "More joy awaits, sweetheart."

"Do you see them, Lance?" Lexie shivered and grasped the violin case as they entered baggage claim. According to her phone's weather app, the daytime high had reached a balmy minus four degrees below zero. The nighttime temperature now hovered near minus twelve degrees below zero Fahrenheit. Brr! After two years in a tropical climate, she'd forgotten how cold Topeka could get in December, even in the heated terminal. She couldn't clamp her teeth together hard enough to stop their chattering.

"Not yet, babe. You and Steve keep an eye out for them, and I'll watch for our bags. Here, Lexie." He draped his coat around her.

"Dad said they'll pick us up just outside baggage claim, Lex. I texted them when we landed, so they should be here anytime.

They're riding with the Garretts in their van."

"Look, Lance, there's one of our bags." Lexie pointed as the luggage moved around the carousel.

He and Steven captured their suitcases just as David called to them.

"Lance, Lexie, Steve. Over here."

Lexie rushed into her father's arms.

"Oh, Daddy, I'm so glad to see you."

He kissed her and brushed at his eyes. "I'm happy to see you too, kiddo. Look how tanned you are, though you're bundled up like someone who lives in the Arctic. How many layers do you have on?"

"Three, and Lance just gave me his coat."

"Hi, Dad."

David pounded Steven's back in the bone-jarring way the males in her family tended to use to show deep affection, and Lexie smiled.

"Come on," David said, and grabbed two of the suitcase handles. "Your ride awaits."

The cold seeped into Lexie's bones the moment she stepped outside, and she thought she saw her breath vapor turn into icicles before they shattered and fell.

George slid the door open and helped her into the van. He squeezed her gloved hand, "I'll give you a proper hug as soon as we're in the warmest place we can find in the restaurant."

Then he turned and hugged Lance as tightly as he could. They both brushed tears away before loading the luggage.

"Lexie? Oh, my darling, I'm so glad you're home."

Lexie slid next to Olivia and kissed her. "I missed you, Mommy. During my darkest days, I knew you prayed for me."

Olivia nodded and held Lexie's hand. "Those were black days for your dad and me too. Some of our worst."

Oh, if only you knew how much of the 'worst' I didn't tell you,

Mom.

"Welcome home, Lexie." Amy peered around the front passenger seat and smiled.

"Thanks, Amy. I'm delighted to be home, but I'm having a hard time appreciating this cold."

"You and me both, girl."

Steven folded his tall frame into the seat behind Lexie and leaned over to kiss Olivia's cheek. "Hi, Mom. Amy."

Olivia caressed his face with one hand and brushed at tears in her eyes with the other, "Ah, to have both my children safe and sound and at home with me again. What a Christmas gift."

Lance closed the door after David sat next to Steven, and then slid into the seat beside Lexie. She handed him his coat but he shook his head and draped the warmth over her lap and legs.

"I don't remember your suitcases being as light as they are now," George commented as he pulled away from the curb.

"We gave most of our clothes away in Guatemala because others needed them more than we did." Lance turned to Lexie and winked. She grinned and leaned her head against his shoulder.

"They didn't fit, anyway," she whispered so only he heard.

He kissed her then looked up at his mother. "Besides, Dad, we knew Mom, Olivia, and Patty would drag us around the malls to shop since Christmas Day is less than a week away."

"You're right about that." Amy again looked around her seat back. "The fun begins tomorrow afternoon. Olivia and I figured to let you sleep in your first day back, but then you're not allowed to be slackers. Time is too short. Patty, Greg, and the children will join us. Are you rolling your eyes at me, young man?"

"No, Mom. Never." Lance leaned forward and kissed his mother.

"You'll have to do better than a peck on the cheek, son. I expect a full-on bear hug and a lot more kisses when we get out of this van."

"My pleasure."

Lance obliged his mother the moment they got out of the van in the restaurant parking lot.

"Oh, I've missed you so, Lance." Amy pulled his head down and rained kisses on his face. "My boy is back from the dead."

Olivia didn't release Lexie's hand after they climbed out of the van to pass more hugs and kisses all around.

"Come on, I'm starving," Steven said leading the way. "Doesn't look like the line is too long yet."

"No, we're early enough to beat the regular dinner bunch, though Mondays probably aren't too crowded anyway," George said.

"Usually, I'd say you're right, honey, but the public schools are out for the holidays, remember? Everyone seems to like to eat out during the weekdays when the kids are on vacation." Amy craned her neck to see how many people waited in line ahead of them.

"Ah, yes, but I made reservations, so we shouldn't have much of a wait."

The hostess led them to a long table, and they began to seat themselves.

"Feels warm enough here." Lexie smiled at George and began to remove her coat, scarf, and first layer before she sat.

The silence at the table warned her. The secret was out.

"Lexie?" Olivia couldn't look away from Lexie's expanding middle. "You're pregnant again?"

"Yes." Lexie sat down and smiled at her mother and Amy, "Surprise!"

"When?" David looked from Lexie to Lance, and back at Lexie.

"At the end of March, or during the first week of April." Lexie reached for a menu. She saw the surprised looks her mother and Olivia gave each other at her words.

"But Lexie, you look-" Amy blushed and looked down.

Lance laughed. "What, Mom? Lexie looks as if she could deliver sooner than March?"

Amy nodded.

Lexie met Olivia's eyes. "Do you remember one of the relatives at the reunion a couple of years ago saying that identical twins run in this family but often skip to the third or fourth generation?"

Olivia nodded.

"Well, the pattern continues. You, Dad, and the Garretts will be grandparents to a set of twin boys in a couple of months."

Her words garnered the expected squeals, hugs, kisses, and conversation.

"Oh, how can we get everything done in the time remaining?" Olivia opened her purse and took out her pocket calendar and pencil.

Lexie reached for her mother's hand. "I forgot how super-organized you are, Mom, but we have time. Just enjoy the moment."

"I am enjoying the moment. But have you thought about all the things you'll need to get ready before the babies are born? We'll need to plan a baby shower and decide what you want to include on the gift registry. I wonder who we should invite to the shower, and where the party should be held? We'll need to get a room ready for the twins once you and Lance know where you want to live, and then-"

"Mom." Lexie silenced her mother with a head shake. "We don't need all this. One of the things Lance, Stevie, and I learned by living in Latin America is how to live comfortably with much less."

Both her brother and Lance nodded.

Olivia stared at Lexie. "You've changed. A lot. You seem like a different person."

"I am a different person in many ways, Mom, but I'm still your daughter, and I love and appreciate you."

While they waited for their food to come, questions and answers bounced from one side of the table to the other. Lance described the sadness and heartache he experienced while he helped rescuers dig more than fifty bodies from the mud, and he told of his multiple attempts to leave the jungle. Steven spoke of his friendship with Nico, and Lexie shared her love for Oscar and the people who cared for the orphans.

"When you think of your service in Costa Rica and Guatemala, what is the most important lesson you learned, Lexie," Amy asked and waited as Lexie gathered her thoughts and formed them into words.

"I never thought of myself as a timid person, but I now know fear has the tendency to hamstring me, Amy. I almost allowed the emotion to stop me from obeying the Lord on several occasions. Misery walks in fear's footsteps. I've learned trust and fear are polar opposites. When I lived with fear, I didn't trust in God's goodness or faithfulness. When I trusted him through the most painful, difficult times, my fear lessened or disappeared altogether."

"What's next?"

"Your guess is as good as mine. I don't know, but Lance and I intend to follow our destiny."

"Where ever destiny leads?"

Lexie smiled and reached for Lance's hand. "Yes, where ever He may lead."

ABOUT THE AUTHOR

Derinda Babcock taught English Language Learners for almost twenty-five years. During her teaching career, she worked with students of all ages and many different linguistic and cultural backgrounds. The richness of this experience lends flavor to the stories she writes. She enjoys historical research and crafting stories that entertain, encourage, and inspire. She writes from a Christian perspective.

AUTHOR'S NOTE

Though the setting for *Following Destiny* is contemporary, the research process took as much time, or more, as the Oregon Trail and Civil War research I did for *Dodging Destiny* and *In Search of Destiny*. Lexie's journey sent me to many internet sites, maps, newspapers from Cost Rica and Guatemala, documentaries, and YouTube videos. I learned the most, though, from interviewing friends who were born and raised in these countries, and who still visit family there.

The more I recognize and understand the dangers facing those who obey the call of the Lord, the more I am filled with awe and humbleness at their willingness to risk everything for the cause of Jesus Christ. Missionaries and Bible translators suffer every day for His name, and they so need our prayers and support.

If Lexie's story touches you and moves your heart toward those who give so much for the Lord's sake, I ask you to join me in supporting these two organizations:

Wycliffe Bible Translators: https://www.wycliffe.org/

Hogar Amor del Niño / Love the Child (A Christian orphanage in Guatemala): http://www.lovethechild.org/

The need is great.

Thank you for taking the time to read *Following Destiny.* If you enjoyed the story, please consider telling your friends or posting a short review in Amazon or Goodreads. Word of mouth is an author's best friend and is much appreciated.

www.derindababcock.com

www.facebook.com/Derinda-Babcock

www.pinterest.com/derindababcock

www.linkedin.com/derindababcock

www.twitter.com/derindababcock

Quote from Matthew 25:23 New King James Version of the Bible